P9-DWZ-480

WITHDRAWN

THE HEARTLESS

Also By David Putnam

THE HEARTLESS

A BRUNO JOHNSON NOVEL

DAVID PUTNAM

OCEANVIEW PUBLISHING
SARASOTA, FLORIDA

Copyright © 2020 by David Putnam

All rights reserved. No part of this book may be reproduced in any form or by any electronic or mechanical means, including information storage and retrieval systems, without permission in writing from the publisher, except by a reviewer who may quote brief passages in a review.

This book is a work of fiction. Names, characters, businesses, organizations, places, and incidents either are the products of the author's imagination or are used fictitiously. Any resemblance to actual events, businesses, locales, or persons living or dead, is entirely coincidental.

ISBN 978-1-60809-378-6

Published in the United States of America by Oceanview Publishing

Sarasota, Florida

www.oceanviewpub.com

10 9 8 7 6 5 4 3 2 1

PRINTED IN THE UNITED STATES OF AMERICA

To my wife, Mary

THE HEARTLESS

CHAPTER ONE

THE COUTROOM WAS packed—all attention riveted on Deputy District Attorney Nicky Rivers. She tilted her head in my direction, and for a moment, her eyes caught mine, her expression unmoved—but that was enough. I flashed on the memory from the night before in the front seat of my Ford truck. Her parting kiss had been alive with emotion. It had not been our first kiss—not by a long shot—but this one, for me anyway, had been different. This one beckoned me to take our relationship to the next level of commitment.

But here in the courtroom, I knew what she was going to do next, and I'd warned her against it. Not in a courtroom filled with friends and family of the victim.

She picked up a legal pad and approached the witness on the stand. Pam Peterson, the deputy coroner, had already been on the grill for more than an hour under cross-examination by Gloria Bleeker, the defense counsel. Now it was Nicky's turn for redirect. "Ms. Peterson, can you tell the jury again how the victim was killed?"

Peterson looked at Judge Connors first and then back at Nicky Rivers. "As I said before, the victim's throat was cut with a thick serrated blade."

Don't do it, I whispered.

"How deep?" Nicky asked.

"Almost to the point of decapitation."

Judge Connors said, "Counselor?"

Nicky ignored the warning. "Ms. Peterson, do you know if the victim's five-year-old daughter was present during this brutal attack?"

Gloria Bleeker stood. "Objection."

Nicky proceeded against the judge's earlier recommendation and pushed the button of the remote in her hand. A PowerPoint presentation in full color depicting the violent death of the victim came up on the television screen positioned directly in front of the jury.

A loud din rose in the courtroom.

I sat at the bailiff's desk, my finger poised on the panic button, ready to push it. I watched for something to ignite the small riot, something thrown, an object, a punch, a shove. An action that would force me to protect the evil that sat quietly in the defendant's chair. Force me to defend Louis Borkow against the innocent and misguided in the courtroom audience. The panic button would summon additional help that would arrive too late. Lives would be disrupted, people hurt. And for what? Not justice. Not by any stretch.

Judge Connors had instructed me not to push the button in the standing-room-only court except in an extreme circumstance. According to him, "This monkey shit of a circus already has too many reasons for an appeal and we don't need another one. So don't you push that button, Bruno, unless you're absolutely sure."

Louis Borkow sat unperturbed at the defendant's table and used the verbal disruption—the yelling from the audience, the rap, rap, rap of the judge's gavel—to, one at a time, stare down the members of the jury. Twelve of his "peers" who sat in the jurors' box, tasked with giving him the needle for the brutal slaying of his black girlfriend. The jurors would have every right to fear him if there had been one chance in a million he'd ever see the light of day. He would never get out, not with all the evidence stacked against him. The jury was smart enough to know it.

Borkow's jet-black hair made his pale skin seem even whiter, and his intense blue eyes brought out the psycho in him. He was the most dangerous threat in the room, so I watched his every move.

The Honorable Judge Phillip J. Connors, in his black robe, continued to bang his gavel until calm gradually returned and everyone sat down in their bench seats or went back to leaning against the wall. Two uniformed extra-duty deputies, on overtime, stood behind and to each side of Borkow. Not so much to restrain him but to keep the crowd from tearing his skinny ass apart. Keep the crowd from dragging him out in front of Compton Court and throwing a rope over the lowest branch of a pepper tree.

With order restored, Judge Connors said, "If it happens again, I'll clear the courtroom, and this proceeding will be closed to the public. Now"—he looked to Deputy District Attorney Nicky Rivers and pointed his gavel at her—"let's move on, shall we, Counselor? I think you've made your point with those crime scene photos. Don't you?"

I took my finger away from the panic button and stood. I'd been sitting all morning. I let my thumbs hang on the top of my Sam Browne gun belt, my uniform shirt a little too tight at the buttons. Two years earlier I'd left the violent crimes team and transferred to court services to fill a bailiff position. The desk job had added an extra ten pounds and damn near drove me stir crazy. For the umpteenth time I silently swore I'd start running again on my next days off.

Deputy DA Nicky Rivers looked down at her yellow-lined notepad as if deciding what to do next, what witness to call, what evidence to present. She didn't need to check anything; she only wanted the pause so everyone had time to refocus on her. Which wasn't difficult. Her custom-made suits were modest enough for an attorney, but when combined with elegant silk blouses and strappy heels, her onstage persona was unparalleled. Those brown eyes, sparkling with vitality, and those luscious lips and that cute little nose perfected her magnetism.

She brought her yellow Black Warrior number-two pencil up to her mouth to tap her front tooth, a nervous tic she worked hard to overcome. This she had told me in a whispered confidence over dinner one night.

In every trial, she played the role of lion tamer, her chair and whip guiding the jury, the audience, and even the judge, toward the conclusion she wanted, a master at manipulation, a crackerjack attorney with no equal. I may have been a little biased.

I would have felt sorry for Borkow having Nicky as an opponent if he hadn't deserved everything coming his way.

"Ms. Peterson," Nicky said, "can you please continue with what you were saying before the interruption? Apparently, the court has decided we no longer need the photos of the crime scene."

Nicky clicked off the audiovisual equipment and didn't look at the judge. But I did. He scowled and shook his head. He wouldn't let it slide, and later, in his office away from the jury, he'd warn her one last time before he sanctioned her on the record.

Pam leaned into the mic. "I'm not sure what the question was . . . ah, that's right. Ah, no, I have no way of knowing if the decedent's five-year-old daughter was present when the defendant, Louis Borkow"—she pointed at him again—"decapitated her with the thick-bladed, serrated knife we found at the scene."

Gloria Bleeker jumped to her feet. "Objection, Your Honor! Now that's the second time the jury's heard hearsay testimony, which is nothing more than morbid supposition, myth, and rumors. It violates my client's right to a fair trial."

Judge Connors banged his gavel as the din in the audience again started to rise. "Council approach."

The phone on my desk rang. Bleeker and Rivers moved to the judge's bench as he leaned over to whisper to them as if they were two errant children. I didn't have to be up there to know what Connors was telling them. I picked up the phone, hit the button on the phone's console, and said in a whisper, "Deputy Johnson, Superior Courtroom Three."

"Popi!"

Olivia. My daughter.

Only Olivia hadn't called me Popi in years. Every time she called me "Bruno" it grated on my nerves and at the same time made me a little sadder over a childhood lost.

"Popi." She sobbed. "Don't be mad. Please don't be mad at me."

"Sweetie, what's the matter? What's happened?" My tone turned loud and no longer followed courtroom decorum.

"I'm with Derek." She suddenly lowered her voice. "And . . . and they have guns."

My back went straight and my hand gripped the phone too tight. Derek Sams, every parent's nightmare. "Olivia, honey, I won't be mad; who has a gun? Where are you? Tell me where you are."

The courtroom went quiet and I felt everyone turn to look at me, even the judge and the attorneys.

"Just tell me where you are. I'll come and get you." She was supposed to be in school. I'd just gotten her back two weeks ago after she'd run away. Fourteen years old and she'd been out on the street on her own for three days and two nights before I tracked her down. I should've taken Derek by the neck then and throttled his seventeen-year-old ass.

"Popi, I don't know where we are. I snuck into the other room. I'm in the closet on the floor with the door closed. I'm so scared."

"It's okay. It's okay, baby. Listen to me—what did you see? What was around you when you pulled up to the house?"

Everyone in the courtroom held their breath, still looking at me. Everyone except Louis Borkow, who smirked, clearly enjoying my distress. He ate up the violence about to rain down on someone dear to me. When I had the chance, I'd pull him aside and have a heart to heart with him while his face was mashed up against the wall.

Her voice suddenly shifted to a smaller whisper. "I'm in a house in Compton. I think it's blue and white with a big tree and . . ."

"What street? Do you remember the street? What's the house close to? A market, a church?"

"They got a gun to Derek's head. They're going to shoot him. You have to come. Hurry. Please hurry."

"Olivia, stop. Listen, take a breath, baby, and relax. You're gonna be okay, I promise. That's good. That's good, honey. Breathe. Now think. What street are you on?"

She hesitated a moment as she thought about it. "Pearl, yeah, I think it's Pearl, off Alondra."

"I know where that is. I'm coming for you, baby. You sit tight, I'll be there in less than five minutes. Here, I want you to stay on the phone and talk to a friend of mine, okay? Stay on the phone."

"Okay, Popi."

I held the phone out. Nicky Rivers hurried over and took it from me. I took off running.

"Bruno!" Judge Connors yelled. "Bruno, where the hell do you think you're going? You're not going anywhere. You call it in. You have patrol respond. You're too emotionally involved."

"There's no time for that. I can get there faster. It's not far."

"No, you're not going, not without backup."

"I'm sorry, Your Honor, I'm going."

I stopped and looked back. Connors stood as he stripped off his black robe. In a controlled voice, he said to the two extra duty security deputies, "This court stands in recess. Lock down the defendant, then come back and escort the jury to the jury room." The judge wore a starched white long-sleeve shirt buttoned all the way to the top. He reached under his bench and pulled out a large-frame revolver he kept there for emergencies and shoved it into his waistband. "You're not going without backup. I'll go with you."

CHAPTER TWO

I RAN TO the elevator, the judge close at my heels. I stopped, looked at the lit floor numbers above the elevator doors, and couldn't wait. I went for the stairs. The door banged open. I put my shoulder to the wall, let the handrail slip through my hand, and did a controlled fall down to the next landing. My feet slapped hard and it jolted my teeth.

Judge Connors yelled, "Hey, wait. Wait up. Shouldn't we call this in to the patrol dogs?"

"No, we can get there faster than the deputies. I told you, it's not far."

I slid down two more levels to the bottom and broke out into the blinding daylight, headed for my Ford truck. A few seconds later, the judge exited the same door. "Bruno?"

I was too focused on getting to my daughter and for a second forgot where I'd parked. I hesitated while I got my bearings and my eyes adjusted to the light. The judge caught up, breathing hard. "Let's take my car—it's closer. Come on, it's over here."

"Only if I can drive."

He tossed me the keys and hurried around to the passenger side of the beige four-door Mercedes parked in a slot with his name stenciled on the courthouse wall. Something I'd told him about in the past, that he shouldn't advertise where he parked, not out in the open, not in an unsecured parking lot, and not with the kind of people that came through his courtroom. He put criminals away with heavy years, and angry families had made their displeasure known. He replied to my comment the same each time by putting his hand on the stock of the gun in his shoulder holster: "It's America and I'll damn well park wherever I want and to hell with them. I won't shirk from my God-given freedoms."

Only the judge had never been in a violent confrontation and had no idea what it took to drop the hammer on someone, to experience the instantaneous snap of violence that changes your life forever. He was too in love with the idea of carrying a gun and fighting off avenging interlopers to consider the aftermath. And I was taking him along as a partner in a critical situation.

I backed out as he yanked his foot in and closed his door. "Hey? Hey?" He put one hand on the door handle and one on the ceiling as I jerked the steering wheel this way and that, negotiating the parking lot, the tires screeching. "Bruno, you're a little het up over this. When we get there, I want you to let me do the talking. Tell me what's happened. Olivia's in a gang house and someone in there has a gun?"

He'd gleaned that much from my side of the phone conversation.

The way he described Olivia's plight brought home the seriousness of the situation my mind had automatically tried to sidestep and downplay.

I barreled out of the parking lot onto Willowbrook Avenue, turned south, and almost sideswiped a blue Honda Civic. The driver, a black high-school-aged male, laid on his horn. I stole a look at Judge Connors. He had overly tan skin from playing too much tennis, a shock of gray hair gone white, and sad brown eyes. I said, "My sergeant is gonna have my ass as it is for leaving the court without department approval. You shouldn't be anywhere near this sort of thing."

He grinned. "That's exactly what I'm talking about. You're too emotional, too vested in this. You're not thinking straight. You think I give two shits about what your sergeant thinks? Let me handle this. Okay?"

Back in the day, Connors had been a sheriff's deputy, who worked the jail, and then as a bailiff while he attended night school to get his law degree. He had never worked the street or had the opportunity to throw down on someone with a gun. When he passed the bar, he quit the sheriff's department and went to work for the district attorney's office. As a DA he excelled and moved his way up until he tried all the high-profile homicide cases. He was a living legend among cops and known as a hanging judge among the criminals. The governor appointed him to the bench ten years ago.

I gunned the Mercedes' big engine and made a wide sweeping turn to eastbound Alondra. "I know the place we're going—it belongs to the Blood gang, the Mob James Piru. No offense, Judge, but you've been out of the game for a while, and I'd feel a lot better about this if you sort of hung back a little."

Not that he'd ever truly been in the game.

"Fat chance. Don't you worry about me, son."

"Here we go. We're coming up on Pearl." I slid the pristine Mercedes to the curb on Alondra, five or six houses from Pearl Street, slammed it into park, and got out. I pulled my uniform shirt out of my pants and unbuttoned it, my fingers not moving fast enough.

"What are you doing? We need that uniform in case this thing goes wrong."

"We won't get in if they see a uniform walk up to the house. A tee shirt might get a little closer before they make us." I didn't tell him I didn't want to misrepresent myself or the department in a situation where I expected my anger to get out of control. "You have something to put over that gun in your belt?" I tossed him the keys. He went to the trunk, opened it, took out a blue windbreaker, and shrugged into it. I unsnapped my Sam Browne and took it off. I pulled the gun and tossed the gun belt on the seat. I slammed the door and headed down the street in my green uniform pants and white tee shirt, holding the gun down by my leg.

The neighborhood seemed quiet enough. Most all the houses needed new stucco, and some grass seed. All of them without exception sported wrought-iron bars on the windows and doors. And gang graffiti. Compton PD had lost the battle and the hoods owned it.

I turned the corner onto Pearl with Judge Connors two steps behind. I put the gun in the waistband at the small of my back. Three houses down sat the house Olivia described, blue with white trim.

CHAPTER THREE

A SMALL BLACK kid, maybe ten years old, not old enough yet to make his bones in the gang, saw me coming down the street. All these little guys were called poo-butts—a classification within the gang until they made their bones. This one whistled, then yelled, "Five-O walkin'." Another kid, older, standing at the open front door to the house, stepped in and slammed the wrought-iron security door. The clang elevated my sense of helplessness. I hurried up to the door and pounded on the warm steel, not standing to the side as procedure dictated, but standing right in front.

From the shaded darkness inside came a confident voice. "We don't want nothin' you're sellin', Mr. Poleeseman, so step off."

"Open the damn door. Now."

"Or what? If you had a warrant, you'd already have broke it down. Go on, get yourself a warrant, Deputy."

I grabbed onto the wrought iron out of frustration and tried to pull the steel door off. The young man inside started to laugh until the door bulged a little.

"What's wit' you? What's you want?"

"My daughter. My daughter's in there and if you've hurt her—"

"Your daughter ain't in here, Deputy."

I backed up and looked around for something, a big rock, anything to help force my way into the house. That's when I noticed the judge had disappeared. He'd gone around back all on his own, a dangerous proposition. No time though. I went back and shook the door and yelled. "Olivia? I'm here, baby. I'll be in there in just a minute."

From inside the voice said, "Olive? Dat's her daddy out there?"

Another voice said, "Oh, shit, you know who that is out dere? That's Bruno Johnson. Man, we're in deep shit, now. I'm outta here."

"I don't care if it's the whole damn SWAT team, dey ain't comin' through that door. I built it myself."

I heard the back door bang open as the gangster fled. Then from inside a familiar voice said, "Open that door and let the deputy in. Do it right now." Judge Connors had gone in the back when the gangster had opened the door.

"How'd you get in here?" a gang member asked.

I went up to the security screen, and in between the wrought iron, I put my hands close to shade my eyes and peered in.

Connors stood in the living room with his huge .44 Magnum pointed at the leader. "You go for that gun, Sonny Jim, and I'll—"

The gun in his hand went off. The retort sounded like a bomb in the enclosed space. The gang leader dropped to the floor as if someone pulled his plug.

Sirens from all over the city came on. Back at the courthouse Nicky Rivers, on the phone with Olivia, had been listening and called it in.

The security door ratcheted and pushed open to the smiling face of Judge Connors. "Come on in, we're having a party."

I pulled my gun and rushed in. I jumped over the downed gang member on the floor and ran for the back of the house. "Olivia? Olivia?"

I rushed down the hallway. The bedroom door opened. Out popped my daughter. I grabbed her up and hugged her. I set her down and ran my hands over her arms and back and head. "Are you all right? Are you hurt? Did they hurt you?"

"I'm fine, Popi. I'm fine." Her face was swollen from crying and wet with tears. A small metallic voice helped to peel me down off the ceiling and out of my panic. Olivia handed me the phone. I took it. "Nicky? We're code four here. We're okay. Thanks. I mean it, thanks a lot."

"Is everything really okay? I heard a gunshot. I called Compton PD. They're looking for the house. What's the address? I'll give it to them."

"What?" Then I remembered the judge and that he might've shot someone. "I have to go." I hung up. With my arm around Olivia, I escorted her back out into the living room. Judge Connors stood in the center of the room with his gun pointed at three black gang members now sitting on the couch, including the one from the floor that I'd leaped over, the one that I'd thought had been shot.

The one sandwiched in the middle on the couch was Derek Sams, the cause of all this heartache. His left eye was welded shut, swollen with purple and his mouth a mess of split lips and broken teeth.

Olivia yelled, "Derek!" She tried to break away from me. I caught her and held on, pulled her in tight.

"You okay, Your Honor?" I asked.

Olivia struggled to get free. "Let me go. Let me go. Derek's hurt."

"I have to tell you, Bruno—" the judge waved his gun like a half-crazed killer—"that was the most fun I've had in years." His eyes were still wild with excitement. I went over to him with Olivia snug under one arm, and put my other hand on his gun to lower it. "It's all over now, Your Honor. Put that away."

"I don't think so, not until the blue suits get in here."

I looked him in the eyes. He looked invigorated, like a twenty-five-year-old, when he had to be in his early- to mid-sixties.

"Did you hit anyone with your shot?"

"What? Hell no. That was a warning shot." He pointed with his gun to the ceiling. "Went clean through, you can see daylight. Isn't that something?" He lowered his tone and leaned closer. "I think that big bad gang member over there messed himself."

Olivia banged on my arm trying to get away. I held on tighter. "Bruno, let me go. Let go of me or I'll scream."

So much for "Popi." I was back to being Bruno.

CHAPTER FOUR

TWO HOURS LATER, after Compton PD took the report and finished all the interviews, I drove my Ford Ranger north out of Compton into Lynwood, then headed on through to Southgate and our apartment. Olivia sat twisted on the passenger seat next to me, looking back through the open sliding window at her boyfriend Derek Sams, whom I made ride in the open truck bed. I wanted some alone time to talk to my daughter about what had happened and to make sure she realized the severity of the situation. That's what I told myself, anyway. In reality, I just couldn't stand the little shit weasel.

I never spoke ill of children or young people; they had it hard enough without adults disparaging them. But it took every ounce of self-control to keep from throttling him for putting Olivia in such a dangerous environment. And maybe I still would. To do anything in front of Olivia would only push her further away. But I didn't know what else to do. I'd tried everything to get through to her.

Olivia shoved my shoulder and scowled. "Making him ride back there like that, you're treating him like a piece of garbage. He's hurt. He's hurt real bad, Bruno. We should be taking him to the doctor right now and not driving him home."

I took my eyes off the road and looked at her. "I don't think you understand—I cut him a huge break. He should've gone to jail. He went to that house on Pearl to cop some dope. Being at a dope house is a misdemeanor. He endangered your life. Don't you get that?"

"No, he didn't. I told you, he went there because he owed them some money. He didn't have it, and he wanted to reason with them. He's really great. I mean, the way he can talk to people. You just never took the time to get to know him, that's all. And that's not fair. If he'd stayed in school, he'd have been the captain of the debate team, I know he would have. Please, Bruno, just once sit down and talk to him. Really talk to him."

She didn't get it. Derek owed those gangsters on Pearl. They'd fronted him some dope, and he'd spent the money before he could pay it back. That's why they beat him.

"He's no good for you, O. Look what just happened. He should never have—"

"Bruno, stop. I love him. Can't you understand that? You need to accept it. Once you do, you'll see that you'll never be able to change it. This is the way it's going to be. Forever. We're going to be together forever and ever. So get used to it."

She talked as if she were older, like a young adult. As if she truly knew how this world worked. When she really had no clue. She didn't know how one poor choice could lead to another and another until it wrecked your entire life. Where had my little girl gotten off to? It seemed just yesterday we'd sat at the kitchen table making macaroni paintings of houses and dogs and cats on blue construction paper.

Why couldn't she see this for the problems Derek Sams had already caused? It was so obvious. The frustration of it made me want to punch something. Like the punk in the back of my truck.

I said, "He's seventeen and you're only fourteen."

"Oh, my God." Her eyes went wide. She turned around, crossed her arms, and looked straight ahead.

"All right, now what've I done?" I should've stayed angry and come down on her with severe sanctions for skipping school to hang out with Derek Sams even after I'd told her in no uncertain terms to stay away from him. But I couldn't. Standing outside the house on Pearl, helpless, unable to get in, I'd experienced a wake-up call. I had just lived through the worst possible scenario where she was only feet away in dire peril, and I couldn't get to her through the steel door. I could've lost her. I couldn't imagine a world without my darling Olivia, a world colorless, sterile, and devoid of all joy.

I nudged her with an elbow. "Come on, O, tell me what I did."

She turned, scowled again, and with too much vehemence, said, "I was going to wait and see how long it actually took before you figured it out. I can't believe this. I really can't."

"Tell me." I nudged her again.

"I turned fifteen two weeks ago."

"What?" My mind spun to catch up. Of course, she was right. I'd screwed up big-time. This murder trial with Louis Borkow had been a huge distraction. "Ah, man, I'm sorry, O, really I am. I've just been so—"

"Busy. I know."

I'd left the violent crimes team, a job I dearly loved, and taken the job in court services for a consistent schedule. Olivia needed more supervision. I couldn't give it to her if I was chasing murder suspects and bank robbers all over Southern California. I needed to pay closer attention. Spend some quality time with my daughter before it was too late. Apparently, that sacrifice hadn't worked either, not after what happened today. Too little, too late.

Fifteen years ago, Olivia's mother knocked on my apartment door and handed Olivia to me. I hadn't even known Olivia's mother was pregnant. She'd shoved our daughter into my arms and said, "Here, she's yours. I can't take it anymore, not right now." She turned and walked out of our life never to be seen again.

Holding Olivia in my arms that day, I'd promised myself I would not be that man who neglected his home life, his family. Yet that's exactly what had happened. Time was the culprit. With the snap of the fingers, time had snuck up on me and snatched away fifteen years. It seemed as if I had floundered and grabbed at it trying to hold on, digging my heels in trying to slow it down.

CHAPTER FIVE

I DIDN'T KNOW what to say. How had she turned this whole thing around on me so fast? I knew I should be stern and hold a hard line, but that didn't seem to be working either. My inability to supervise my own child left me wandering out in the weeds, at a complete loss. Did my dad have it this hard? I'd never paid attention to how he parented. A natural, he'd made it seem so easy. If I ever stepped out of line, all Dad had to do was narrow his eyes and lower his eyebrows. I'd jump back to where I was supposed to be. I'd put my head down and work harder trying to please him.

"He's not a piece of garbage, Bruno."

I checked the rearview. Derek Sams' tinted-red Afro caught the sunlight and made it redder as it buffeted in the warm breeze. He had a spray of freckles across his light complexion that gave the illusion of naïveté; a vulnerability that I assumed wasn't really there. He did have a presence though, a sort of charisma. I'd give him that much. His good eye, the one not swollen over, watched the world go by, his expression neutral. His face had been brutalized from the same gang members he refused to prosecute for the felony assault against his person. They'd really put the boot to him before we got there. I understood his reluctance to file charges: he had to live in the neighborhood, and ratting would make that impossible.

But I could still see through that innocent veneer. I grew up in the ghetto and had worked patrol at Lynwood station. I'd seen plenty of his kind and could predict his preordained outcome— lying dead in a gutter, his life's blood having drained out from multiple gunshot wounds. Another life in the ghetto wasted.

I just needed some way to wrest Olivia from his grasp before it was too late. Unmask the kid and show her the truth. But a little voice in my head kept getting louder, telling me, more often than not, that short of shipping her to a private school out of state, it was probably already too late. I'd missed the window to intervene, and she was already too far gone.

No, no, no, that just couldn't be. The thought of it made a lump rise in my throat too large to swallow.

Another alternative, an option I'd not thought of until that moment, caused bile to rise up from my stomach, acidy, burning a hole in my soul for even thinking about that kind of ugliness. I could easily call in a favor from someone on the street who lived and operated in that world and have Derek Sams permanently erased, have his flame physically snuffed out. That would solve everything. How many fathers in my same situation dreamt of a similar outcome? I shivered and shook it off. Of course, I would never do that.

I checked the rearview again, eyed Derek. A memory flashed of a time years ago when I rode in a two-man black-and-white patrol car with a white deputy I couldn't stand, Good Johnson. At the time we had been driving westbound on Imperial Highway in front of The Nickerson Gardens Housing Projects, the sun slowly sinking low on the horizon painting everything orange and yellow. The long shadows threatened a darkness where evil came out to wander the streets while the good folks hid behind locked doors.

In front of us was a broken-down, rusted-out truck loaded with a pile of green trash bags. A young kid about Derek's age sat on the pile, contented, the wind on his face, his eyes mere slits as he smiled, enjoying the day. In the cop car, Good Johnson grinned as he elbowed me and said, "Hey, look, someone's gone and thrown away a perfectly good Negro." He laughed the laugh of a crazed fool and slapped his leg. I wanted to punch his ugly smug face.

Back in the truck with Olivia, I pulled over to the curb just before Alameda. "Tell him to get in the front with us."

She put her hand on my arm. "Thank you, Popi, really, thank you."

She certainly knew how to yank my chain. She bailed out her door. Her voice went a little squeaky telling him that it was okay to come up front. I turned a bit jealous over her elated expression, the excited look in her eyes, and the tone in her voice. I wanted to sock Derek even more.

Derek got in with a strong whiff of cologne. Olivia's smile quickly turned to a pouty face as she gently touched his injuries and cooed over him. "Ah, Bruno, we need to get him to a hospital. Please drive us to the hospital. Hurry. Please hurry."

"He's fine. He is. Go on, ask him what he thinks about going to a hospital; he'll tell ya, he's fine."

"Your dad's right. This is all about nothin'. I been hurt worse fallin' off my bike."

He was so adept at telling lies, I almost believed it. He wouldn't let down his machismo in front of his girlfriend no matter how badly he was hurt. The foolish code of the gang member.

I took my eyes from the road to look at him. He glared back. He didn't like me either. After a few more minutes, I turned north on Alameda, drove a mile or two, and pulled over to the curb at 101st Street. I wouldn't risk driving so close to the Jordan Downs Projects where Derek lived, not with Olivia in the truck. They both got out and stood on the sidewalk at the front of the truck hugging and whispering, Olivia saying her goodbyes. I waited for her in agony as the long seconds ticked by.

How in the world had she turned fifteen? Somehow, in my mind, fourteen still made her my little girl . . . but fifteen? That changed things in a big way and it really shouldn't have, but it did.

Fifteen made her a young woman.

A young woman who continued to make immature decisions in a dangerous world.

Outside the truck, Derek talked and Olivia listened. She nodded, her eyes not leaving his, as if what he said came from the mouth of a minor god. I knew it wasn't fair, but I needed to drive a wedge between them or Olivia would be destined for the kind of short and unhappy life the ghetto meted out on a daily basis.

CHAPTER SIX

INMATE LOUIS BORKOW sat in the barber's chair in the barber's shop on 3300 of the Men's Central Jail where he was housed, holding court in front of four other inmates.

During his trial he had worn an expensive suit and tie, in a feeble attempt to camouflage from the jury what he kept hidden underneath. Now he wore his clean and pressed jail blues with "Inmate" stenciled in white on the back. The caper he'd intricately planned, and that would go off in one hour, required that he shave his head to change his appearance. But his vanity wouldn't allow it. He loved his hair too much. Always had. Silly really, risking so much for hair.

Choco, a skinny Mex kid, classified in the jail by the hard-core inmates as a "soft," stood behind the chair braiding Borkow's hair into tight, narrow cornrows. Borkow's three other compadres, Stanky Frank, Little Genie, and Willy Tomkins, all black men currently embroiled in their own murder trials, would blend in just fine once out on the street. They didn't need to alter their appearance one iota. Not really fair under the circumstances.

None of the other three would beat their case either. They all knew it. And truth be told, Borkow didn't care if they did blend in or not. He didn't care if they got gunned down ten feet out of the cage, as long as they created a large enough distraction for Borkow to slither away unharmed. They'd have fulfilled their purpose. He only needed to pretend friendship and camaraderie for another hour or so. Thank the good Lord for small favors. He didn't enjoy working with a bunch of ignorant buffoons.

With all the news coverage of his trial, everyone would know him on sight and be looking for a Louis Borkow with big hair. Not a white guy that looked and acted like a white black man.

Earlier that same day, he'd needed to get back from court in order to make the plan work. If he missed the afternoon visiting at the jail, all would be lost. He'd end up on death row. So that same afternoon he had plotted and set in motion a diversion in the courtroom. One that made him immensely proud: one all the inmates in all the prisons and jails would be talking about for decades to come.

Borkow used a homeboy out on the street who owed him a favor. He asked the homeboy to menace the bailiff Bruno Johnson's daughter. Borkow chuckled at the simplicity of it. The caper had gone off beautifully, better than he hoped.

He had hired the best artist in 3300 to sketch temporary ink-pen tattoos on his arms and neck. Big-breasted black girls, and double-barreled shotguns, a street sign with "Piru," and two masks, one smiling and one sad, that depicted the classic street slogan *Laugh now, cry later.* The thing with Borkow, though, was that he didn't believe in the cry part. He believed in himself and nothing more. As far as he was concerned, if you couldn't laugh at any situation, brutal or otherwise, well, it was time to move on and see what came next.

He didn't fear death; he just wanted more time to enjoy the good things in life: money, power, women. Mostly women, women's *feet*, but he wouldn't openly admit that weakness.

And, of course, the look in a person's eyes when they realized their life was about to be snuffed out. That pure panic and piss-in-your-pants fright that suddenly shifts to a sort of calm, and resolve, an acceptance of the fate about to be handed to them at the point of a knife.

The common misperception Joe Citizen had about the jail was that the inmates were all locked up in cells. What a bunch of FOVs—Full On Victims. That's what Borkow called them, the ones who came in, the fish, who thought there would be rules and safe havens to hide from the wolves, when neither existed.

Inmates could move around all day, just not at night after lights out. With any number of excuses, an inmate could obtain a pass from the module deputy for a visit—a legal visit, the infirmary, the chapel, or the commissary—and once outside their module, they could cruise the entire jail, selling drugs, buying drugs, committing rape, robbery, and murder in a confined, overpopulated cage. It wasn't much different than a small city of twelve thousand. Well, the most corrupt and violent city in these United States of America, that is.

It was just as hard for the cops to hang a new charge on the miscreant's new crime. Harder. Inside the Gray Bar Hotel, there weren't any witnesses or even victims for that matter. No one ever saw a thing. "*I was on my bunk doing hobby craft, Deputy.*"

Borkow watched the big clock on the wall as Choco, with his small delicate fingers, tugged and pulled on his hair, weaving it as tight as he could. He'd never seen time move slower as it crept along edging closer every second to 6:00 p.m.—zero hour. The others in the crew grew more nervous. Some actually displayed physical jitters.

"Calm the fuck down," Borkow said. "The deputies are going to read you boys for what this is and that'll be that. We screw this up, they'll put us all in red suits and dump our happy asses in High Power where we'll never get another chance. So take a breath and think about something nice and warm and wet. Think about all of that pussy you're going to have in about an hour from now."

Willy Tomkins, a black guy with dark oily skin that made his face shine, said, "This goes down wrong, we doon have ta worry 'bout no High Power cells. Dey gonna shoot us dead. I mean, dey won't stop shootin' 'til dey guns go empty."

"Like I said, you keep thinking that way, that's exactly what's going to happen. Think about something nice. Think about being free, going to see your family without bars in between you. Think about those chicken and waffles at *Roscoe's*, the hot link sandwiches and chili fries at *Stops*."

He didn't tell them the first place the cops would look was at family and friends' houses and old haunts. Let them find out on their own the hard way. Add to the chaos. Muddy the water.

The floor deputy—or Rover, whom Borkow had befriended—stuck his head in the barber's shop. "Louis, all your visits are here; go on and get your passes from the Booth Bitch."

"Thank you, Deputy," Borkow said, and shot him his biggest smile.

The deputy came in a step farther. "Hey, nice do."

"Yeah. Thought I'd try a new look. Got to do something in here to slice through this boredom, you know what I mean?"

"You have tattoos before? I don't remember seeing them."

"Had 'em for years."

"All right, catch you boys later, I'm on my way to help supervise chow down on 2000."

"Bring me back some prime rib from the officers' mess, would ya?"

"Sure, you're right." The deputy went out and closed the door.

That left only the Booth Bitch, the module deputy who was locked inside his own cage with the phone and control panel to work the gates that let the inmates in and out of their cells in the 3300-cell block.

Borkow nodded to Frank Robbins, known as Stanky Frank due to his questionable hygiene. He was the biggest and dumbest one on his crew. Frank nodded and kept on nodding as he moved around and got behind Choco. Once there, Frank moved quickly to wrap his thick arm around Choco's neck. Nothing more than a squeak got past Choco's crooked teeth. Frank applied pressure. Choco's eyes bulged and his tongue slowly moved out of his mouth, the same as if Frank were squeezing a tube of pastel pink toothpaste.

Borkow didn't need Choco blowing the whistle on them too soon. Once you were in the slam for murder, what difference did one more make? Who knew, Choco might've grown a set of balls and traded the escape conspiracy for a *time served* sentence.

It should've taken two minutes to choke him to death, but Frank's arm was strong, and Choco's neck snapped loud and with enough violence to sense the minute vibration in the air. Frank carried him, light as a feather, over to the mop closet, stuffed him in, and forced the door shut.

"Okay," Borkow said. "Now all you swinging dicks know what to do. Leave in two-minute intervals and meet up in Visiting. Don't screw this up. In less than an hour, we'll all be outside the walls.

"I'll go first."

CHAPTER SEVEN

I DRIED MY hands on the dish towel and hung it up. I'd completed the domestic chore with my mind totally focused on Olivia—how to handle the situation—a problem without an obvious or logical solution.

When I came out of the kitchen, she was gone. She and her best friend, Jessica Lowe, had been sitting on the couch doing their homework. Whenever I would move out of hearing range, they whispered and giggled. Not all that long ago, they talked out in the open about clothes and about books they were reading and loved.

They both attended Destiny Girls Academy on South Broadway. The annual tuition cost the same as a new car. Dad helped out a lot, and I loved him for it, but I felt guilty over not being able to pay for my own family. I'd pay him back as soon as I got caught up.

Even though we sent her to an out-of-the-area private school, I had still royally screwed up, fell asleep at the wheel, and had somehow let a kid like Derek Sams weasel in.

As I stepped from the small kitchen, I froze when an ugly thought hit me. Olivia and Jessica had slipped away without making a noise. My heart skipped several beats.

Not again. She didn't run away again, did she? Was she that mad at me for forcing Derek to sit in the back of the truck, mad enough to sneak out of the house?

Her books lay open on the coffee table next to a notepad. I headed for her room and hesitated, looked over at the open notebook, afraid to snoop. But she was the one who'd left her notebook right there where anyone walking by could take a peek. She'd been working on History and English.

Before Derek had come on the scene, she'd been an A student, and since then her grades had slipped. I checked the hallway to see if she stood there watching. All clear. I sat on the couch and turned the pages.

The notes pertained to *Catcher in the Rye*, a book I remembered vividly from high school. In the margins she scribbled her name under Derek's, both of their names inside little hearts shot through with arrows. Those small hearts numbered in the hundreds and further confirmed her unjust and manic craze over the boy.

I straightened up and realized for the first time the emotional and mental turmoil she had to be dealing with. I'd been in love like that once before—with her mother, who wouldn't have me no matter what I said or did to change her mind. At the time, the woman's lack of understanding hadn't seemed logical to me either. The problem seemed easy enough to fix but wasn't. Now I stood on the outside looking in on that very same problem but in reverse. How could Olivia love someone like that little shitass Derek Sams? What could I do to make her see what she was doing? Somehow, I needed to help her understand my point of view. I moved down the short hall to her room and knocked on the closed door.

No answer. I knocked again.

"Yes, who is it? I didn't order a pizza, and tonight, that's the only reason I'd open my door."

"O, can we talk?"

"Not tonight, Bruno, I'm beat. It's been a bad day. It's starting to really catch up to me. I can't believe what happened. It scared me, Bruno, it really did."

"I know it did, baby, I know it did. Come on, just let me in so we can talk about it? It'll be better if we could talk about it."

"No, thank you. Maybe tomorrow. Okay, Bruno? Tomorrow."

I put my forehead against the door. I wanted so badly to be the one to console her, to be her father. But she was fifteen and deserved her privacy, so I wouldn't go in without her consent. My voice croaked a little. "I asked you not to call me that."

"That's your name, isn't it?"

My fists clenched all on their own as I closed my eyes tight. "O, you can call me whatever you like. I'm going in late tomorrow, so we are going to talk in the morning, you understand?"

No answer. "Listen, I want you to promise that you won't see Derek until you and I have a chance to have a sit-down, a serious powwow, okay?"

No answer. "O, you answer me or I'm coming in." I wiggled the doorknob.

"Okay, okay, I promise."

"I love you, O."

"Ditto—"

I held my breath and listened hard, hoping she'd end it with "Popi." I heard something but couldn't be sure. Maybe I just wanted it too badly.

I gave up, went into my room, and changed clothes. I dressed in a pair of beat-up denims and my khaki-colored truck driver shirt with the name "Karl" in an embroidered patch over the right breast and "Grace Trucking" over the other. The old garb I used to wear while working the violent crimes team. I put on an ankle holster that held a big model 66 Smith and Wesson .357 Magnum. I stuck a matching gun in the front waistband of my pants under my shirt. Next, I took out a dirk, a double-edged knife, and clipped it to the inside boot on the left side. My flat badge wallet went in my back pocket and a *415*

Gonzales sap in the opposite back pocket. I opened my dresser drawer to neatly folded handkerchiefs. All of them were different colors that represented the black gangs in the area: purple, red, and blue, mostly. I took out two blue ones and tied one over my head the way a gangster would. I stuck the other in my back pocket so it hung down in plain view.

I made a show of closing my bedroom door with enough noise that Olivia had to hear it. I went to my bedroom window and eased it open. I climbed out and pulled the window down until it latched. I moved with quiet agility out to my truck, opened the door, and slid in. I'd disabled the dome light long ago. When you tracked murderers, you didn't want to make yourself a target. I put my back to the passenger-side door and eased down until my eyes barely showed above the opposite window ledge, and then I waited.

And waited some more.

After a year in court services, the bone-crushing tedium of surveillance returned, a part of the old job I did not miss.

Down the street a car turned the corner, slowed, and turned off its headlights. I sat up just a little to see.

If it was Derek, I'd ... I'd ... I didn't know what I was going to do.

The car crept forward and pulled to the curb into the one open spot on the crowded street. The streetlight silhouetted the only person in the car, the driver. Many a suspect I'd chased down and put away had threatened me and my family with great bodily harm. I was never one to buy into paranoia and was confident in my ability to handle anything that came our way. Even so, I had paid close attention to all the cars on our street, watched the comings and goings at all hours to get a feel for the norm. This car, at this hour, didn't belong.

CHAPTER EIGHT

THE DRIVER GOT out and stood by the open car door. The dome light was disabled like mine so I couldn't discern who this person was creeping outside my apartment building. The driver eased the door closed without making a sound and walked up to the sidewalk staring at our apartment. I put my hand on my gun and struggled up for a better angle.

The driver moved down the sidewalk and into the halo cast by the streetlight.

"Ah, shit," I whispered. I got out on the passenger side and stood in the shadows. "Nicky?" I said, without yelling it.

Nicky Rivers, the deputy district attorney prosecuting the Borkow murder, the woman I'd put on the phone with Olivia just before I ran out of the court, the woman I'd kissed on the front seat of my truck the night before, had come to see me without calling first. Or maybe she had and I wasn't in the house to answer. I should get one of those new cell phones, but they were too expensive and too big to carry around. They called them "brick phones," because they were the size of a brick.

I'd meant to call *her*, to thank her again for helping out, but had been too distracted by the other problem that consumed my entire being: Olivia.

Nicky looked around for who had called her.

"Nicky?"

This time she zeroed in on the sound. She checked both ways, and crossed the empty street. "Bruno?"

I took her wrist and tugged her into the shadows of a huge bougainvillea bush. The move accidently pulled her in close, her warm chest touching mine. I didn't know why she'd driven out to my apartment at that late hour. But maybe I did. We'd been just friends, workmates, enjoying each other's conversation, the quips, the flirting. The light kissing more as friends and not yet lovers. I'd been out of the dating game too long. I wasn't sure how to read the signs. Did she want to take our relationship to the next level? A conundrum I'd pondered for the last two years. She made the boring job in the courtroom a lot easier to take. That particular kiss the night before confused everything. I didn't want to ruin what we had. I enjoyed her company too much. Was that why she'd come out to my apartment? Did she feel the same way and was here to ease back from the ledge we'd both stepped out on—to keep me from taking that next step embarrassing us both? The idea of her breaking it off between us scared the hell out of me.

She went up on tiptoes to whisper, "What are we doing out—"

Her lips were close to mine. I kissed her. She returned the kiss but not like last night's. She hesitated.

I pulled back.

She looked at me as if confused.

"I'm sorry," I whispered. "I don't know why I did that, I'm sorry. I . . ." I let the last words trail off. They sounded too much like a high school kid buried too deep in his first puppy love.

We'd gone out to lunch many times in the past and had a couple of dinners—maybe three or four. After the dinners, we'd talked for hours. We'd been in a happy friendship groove until last night. That kiss last night had changed everything. Was it supposed to happen that way?

Now, in the shadow of the bougainvillea bush, I needed to be strong and say something first. Workplace romances never worked out. I'd had experience in this arena with Sonya, Olivia's mother. I had to tell Nicky we couldn't continue, we couldn't take it any further. Only the words wouldn't come.

Finally, I started. "I . . ."

"I know," she said. "You felt it, too . . . I mean last night . . . we . . ."

"Yes. I felt it but . . ."

"Oh, you're probably right. I'm only separated; we need to wait until I'm divorced. I think that's the smart thing. I mean that's—"

"What?" Stunned, I pushed her back a little. *Separated? Divorce?*

"What's the matter?" She took a step back. "Oh, you mean you didn't want to go on with . . . with this?"

"No, no, it's not that. I didn't know you were married." The topic had not come up during our lunches or dinners or in the long talks. Or the previous night when we made out in my truck. She never wore a ring. She'd never said anything about a husband.

"Okay, wait. Listen." She didn't break eye contact, her brown eyes, big and lush, absolutely beautiful. She took hold of my hand. "I am separated from my husband. I moved out six months ago, and until last night, I wasn't sure about anything. You helped me make my decision. I'm going to go ahead with the divorce."

"Ah, geez, I . . ."

No way did I want to be any part of breaking up a relationship.

"No. No, you big lug, I'm not . . . I mean, I don't mean to infer anything about you and me so don't go running for the hills, like a typical man, okay? You just made me realize how unhappy I am in my current situation and that I need to move on, that's all. Just take it easy, Bruno."

I nodded, the wordless response making me the world's biggest dolt. My mind spun. I needed to say something. "Who are you married to?"

"What? Who? Oh, Lieutenant John Lau. You know him?"

The blood ran from my brain. I eased back until my legs touched the branches of the bush. My voice came out in a whisper. "Not the Lieutenant John Lau from SEB? You're his wife? You're Nicky Lau? I thought that Nicky Lau was . . ." What I wanted to say was that I thought his wife would be Asian. A stupid assumption I shouldn't have made. I only knew Lau from a brief encounter at a sheriff's picnic at the Shark Park in Pomona. Wicks had introduced us. John Lau was a stout man who looked like he lived in the gym. He wore his denim jeans ironed with a sharp crease. He had predator eyes like Wicks. My first impression was that he was not someone you wanted to mess with, the perfect commander for SEB, Special Enforcement Bureau, the department's SWAT team.

"Rivers is my maiden name and I've always gone by Nicky because I don't like Veronica. That lout of a husband of mine thinks 'Nicky' is too gimmicky for a wife's name. Especially for someone like him who wanted to ascend to the higher ranks within the sheriff's department. That's all he thinks about is making rank."

What a fool. I should've put it together sooner. I never thought about it when I'd first met her. Never for a moment did I think, in my wildest dreams, she'd want to have lunch, let alone that our lives would sync so well together. And that kiss last night . . .

"I know," she said, "it's kind of a bad situation. That's why it's better if we . . . you know, kind of wait until I can at least get the papers filed. Okay? You okay with that, Bruno? We don't take this to the next level until I get the papers filed?"

The words continued to bump into each other and wouldn't cooperate. The *next level*? Is that what I really wanted? And worse, I'd dated a lieutenant's wife, I'd kissed a lieutenant's wife, a major taboo in the unwritten rules in a cop's world. What would Dad say when I told him what I'd done?

CHAPTER NINE

MY EYES ADJUSTED to the darkness. I could see her better in the ambient light cast from the streetlights. My heart pinged a little harder and reminded me I was a fool for thinking I could make the two of us work as a couple. We moved in the same world, but at the same time, a universe apart. As a deputy district attorney, she worked in the educated or intellectual section of the justice system. I populated the knuckle-dragging street-cop part that brought in the bloodied absconders to answer for their crimes.

She said, "I was going to call." She put her hands on my chest and closed her eyes. "Wait. After you kissed me last night . . . after we kissed, that's all I thought about. I wanted to call you. I wanted to be sure you understood about my situation that—"

I put my finger up to her lips. "Sssh. It's okay."

She opened her eyes and moved back in close. I hugged her.

It really *wasn't* okay, but I needed time to think this through. I did like her a great deal—no, I more than liked her. And even though it would be easy to fall in love with her—or maybe that ship had already sailed. I was confused and needed time to think.

She went up on tiptoes and kissed me lightly on the lips, afraid, the same as I was, of a deeper kiss.

She said, "I don't want you to take this the wrong way. I fought over coming here, I really did. I just needed to know. You do feel the same way? You haven't said it yet."

"I'm glad you came."

"You just dodged the question. Did I just make a colossal fool of myself?"

"No. It's not that. I just . . . I'd like some time to think, that's all."

"So then you feel the same way I do, and you just want some time to think about it? Or you don't feel the same way, and you need time to think of a way to tell me?"

I pulled her in close and kissed her like the night before—a very long kiss.

I whispered in her ear, "No, I'm pretty sure I feel the same way you do."

She pushed away, relief plain in her expression. "Okay, then I still think we need to cool it until it's official until I file the separation papers. Even then . . . I mean, if we decide to continue on, we need to keep it on the down-low for a while. This gets out . . . well, you know the kind of problems it could cause."

"I know. And I agree."

She put her head against my chest. I held her there. Her hand came up and felt the gun in my waistband between us that had been poking her in the abdomen. She pulled away little. "Hey." She reached up and tugged at the blue bandana tied around my head, then at the embroidered, "Karl," patch on my shirt. "What's going on here, Bruno? Why are you out here hiding in the bushes dressed like some kind of street thug?"

I didn't answer. I didn't want to lie to her.

She looked back across the street to check the vantage point, then looked back at me. "Oh, no, Bruno. You're going to follow Olivia, aren't you?"

Her revelation was one of the drawbacks of being in a relation-ship with an intelligent woman whose job it was to think like a criminal in order to prosecute them.

She said, "This is not the way to deal with this problem."

She had no business telling me how to father my child. I took in a deep breath before I said something I would regret. "Then tell me what I should do, because I'm at a total loss. I've tried everything. She won't listen to reason. I've talked to her again and again. I can't get through to her."

"That's because she's in love."

"That's what *she* said."

"Well then, you're not listening when you are talking to her."

"You don't understand, he's no good for her."

"How many times have fathers said that over the ages?"

"I know, I just never thought it would be me. Tell me what I should do. At this point, I'll do anything."

"You're not going to want to hear it."

"Tell me."

"You're going to have to ride it out. The more you push, the more she's going to move closer to him. You're going to have to let her find out in her own way, in her own time. If it's not meant to be, she'll figure it out. She's a smart girl, especially if she's anything like her father."

Following Derek into a dope house didn't bode well for that statement.

A car came down the street; the arc of the headlights blocked by the cab of the Ford Ranger kept us in shadow. Even so, I moved around so I stood in front of Nicky.

"You have had *the talk* with her, right?"

"What are you talking about now, what *talk*?"

Nicky didn't answer.

"Oh. Ah, that. Not nowadays. Kids know all about it before they . . . wait. What?"

I just realized what Nicky meant. It locked in along with my ignorance over Olivia's age. How had I been avoiding the issue of her growing up? I turned around and walked over to the truck. I put both hands on the hood and let my head sag. I'd been a bigger fool than I thought. Nicky followed and put her hand on my back and rubbed. She didn't lean in and call me a fool, though I deserved it. I whispered, "She's only fourtee—I mean—fifteen. What the hell." I sighed. "I need to get her on birth control, don't I?"

"Bruno, I can have a talk with her if you like. I can even drive her to the clinic."

I always knew the threat was out there waiting to engulf my child in all of that mess and turmoil. I had put it aside, thinking she was far too young. But she wasn't too young and hadn't been for a very long time now. The frustration of it all amped up tenfold.

"No, this is for me to do. I'll do it." I gritted my teeth. I only hoped it wasn't already too late. Good thing Derek Sams wasn't standing in front of me right at that moment.

"You're in the middle of a murder trial. The judge isn't going to like his star bailiff—whom he greatly depends on, by the way—not showing up to trial."

"I'll deal with that. Thank you, though." The judge would understand and let me off one day.

She put her hand on my arm and pulled it away from the truck. She moved in front of me and again laid her head against my chest. "I'll work on those papers tomorrow, get them filed, and get him served, okay?"

She didn't realize she was heaping more guilt onto the already too-tall pile. No way did I want to be the one breaking up their marriage. But at the same time, that heart ping I had for Nicky worked hard at overcoming that foolish emotion. She was already separated. Under normal circumstances that would've been enough. Not this time, though. Her husband was a cop. Once the word got out to the rank and file—and it would eventually—no one would want to work with me. She knew the rule; that's one of the reasons why she wanted to keep our relationship on the down-low after she filed. I needed some time when she wasn't close enough to kiss, wasn't close enough for me to feel the heat radiate off her body, so I could think clearly about this problem. I knew what I had to do—I had to walk away from us—that's what logic dictated. Only I didn't think I could.

I kissed her forehead. "Come on, it's getting late. I'll walk you to your car."

"So you're going to go inside and forget about following your daughter?"

"Yes, of course. You've helped me see things more clearly now. Thank you for that."

"Good." She took my hand and I walked her down the street to her car. At her car door, she moved in close. I kissed her. She patted my chest. "Listen, one word of advice. Your daughter is a teenaged girl."

"Ah, man."

"No, just listen. Just because she serves you up a fat piece of guilt pie doesn't mean you have to take a bite." She looked up into my eyes. "You understand?"

I nodded. "I understand, but it's hard. She's my daughter."

"I know, but you have to be strong."

"Thanks, this has helped a lot."

"Goodnight, Bruno. See you tomorrow in court."

"See you tomorrow."

Nicky opened the car door and got in. I closed it for her and moved up to the curb and watched her drive away.

I went back to the overgrown bougainvillea, stood in the shadows, and waited.

CHAPTER TEN

LESS THAN AN hour until his visit, Borkow climbed onto his bunk and put his hands up behind his head trying to imagine what it would be like outside the concrete walls, smelling the fresh air of freedom. Soon. He'd never come back. He just needed a couple of minutes to compose himself, and, as he had many times before, he contemplated how he had ended up in such a horrible state.

It wasn't his fault he was stuck in jail pending a death sentence. No, it was Stacy's fault—Tasty Stacy's. After all, he'd given her fair warning, told her far in advance what set him off—what he was most touchy about. He loved Stacy, to an extreme. One night he'd let it slip and told her. Moved up close to her ear and whispered to her his biggest weakness, handed her his deepest and darkest secret. That's what lovers did—they kept each other's secrets.

A new emotion for him, this thing called love. In that moment of weakness, right after she'd finished rubbing her lovely, naked feet up and down his erect phallus, as his body stopped convulsing, that's when he'd gone and done it. That's when he told her. What a fool thing to do. He exposed the most vulnerable chink in his armor and let the words slip. His eyes still crossed in ecstasy, he didn't know why. He'd just eased up and whispered in her ear. Explained to her as a precaution, really. Yes, that's what it was, a precaution. He told her she should never, under any circumstances, accidental or otherwise, utter that horrid little name. That was when he'd whispered it to her—the ugly moniker—*Shoe Freak*. Even then, it caught in his throat like a sideways stick. Sure, he liked women's shoes, but no way did that make him a *freak*.

Stacy resided in an expensive condo in Marina Del Rey and supported herself with the alimony from her second marriage, along with "a little dab of money" from a trust fund.

But one day, she told Borkow to "get the hell out and never come back." Without just cause, she slapped him hard across his face, using her long, manicured nails like a claw, drawing blood. The slap was not a problem. He understood the female psyche better than any man alive. He knew it better than most women. He ran four successful massage parlors, after all.

So he knew if he left without a peep and waited an appropriate amount of time, he could weasel his way back into her good graces, back into those one-of-a-kind lovely feet. He'd bring her an insanely expensive pair of bejeweled *Manolo Blahniks*. That was enough to melt any woman's heart.

At the time of the incident, he'd smiled at her as she continued her rabid insistence to "grab your shit and get the hell out." The demand rolled off his back slick as water off a goose. Sort of.

But then, at the end—at the very end—of that last repeated demand, when he was about to leave, that's when she did it. At the end of that last unfair and untimely demand to leave the premises, she'd added with a sneer, "*You Shoe Freak.*"

This time—like the other two times, when he returned from a fugue state—he was standing over Stacy, a blood-slick Spyco knife in his hand. Bloody up to his elbows. Stacy's five-year-old daughter, Gwen, standing in the hallway, screaming her lungs out.

Borkow tried to tell his defense attorney, a thick-bodied woman named Gloria Bleeker, that he qualified for "Guilty by reason of temporary insanity." But the ignoramus told him he was too sane.

He'd tried to persuade Bleeker that he loved Stacy—no way would he hurt her—that he could convince any psych that he loved Stacy and under any other circumstances would never harm her. But Bleeker would have none of it.

After tonight, though, after he was out of this shit hole they called Men's Central Jail, he'd have to seriously consider paying Ms. Gloria Bleeker a visit, discuss his case with her in person without ten deputies there to back her play. She'd taken far too much from him, and he intended on getting a little payback.

CHAPTER ELEVEN

LESS THAN AN hour later Borkow sat on the stool in Visiting. Across from him sat Lizzette, one of his girls. She looked nervous, but he was confident that she would play her part in the little one-act play about to open to a limited audience in Men's Central Jail Visiting. Ta-da.

The jail visiting area consisted of a long wall with individual windows of reinforced glass in steel frames, the kind of glass with the thin metal wires running through it. There were thirty windows in that section of Visiting each with a phone attached with a metal cable. The visiting configuration looked more like a wide hall with a zoo-like wall running down the middle separating the animals from the weak and vulnerable. Each window had a round stainless-steel seat welded to a round pipe that went through the wall to the other side where there was a similar stainless-steel seat for the inmates to sit on. If the inmate was fat enough when he sat down, the person on the other side would feel the pipe move.

The visitors came through the main lobby and registered with the deputy stationed at a desk who then made the request back in the blocks for the inmate to come to Visiting. On the inmate side, two deputies walked up and down behind the thirty positions to ensure domestic tranquility. Like any other place where people gathered, there was always the possibility of violence created from ill-advised domestic contact.

This jail, due to budget constraints, had yet to put up surveillance cameras. The thought being there were always deputies in the lobby and on the prowl on the inmate side. What could happen?

For the plan to work there were a lot of moving parts, and if any one of them failed, all the inmates involved would be put in red jail uniforms instead of blues, labeled an escape risk, and then could only move waist chained with an escort. All thought of future escape in the toilet.

Lizzette was part Asian and part black, with wonderful green eyes and lush lips. If her feet weren't some of the ugliest Borkow had ever seen, with gnarled toes and an almost nonexistent arch, he might've even loved her.

Now, as she sat on the other side of the visiting window on the civilian side, sweat beaded on her forehead. She kept her hands under the short stainless-steel counter so no one would see them shake.

The surrounding people, friends, and family and children of the other inmates, had no idea of the chaos about to befall them or how their night would be disrupted and forever remembered in nightmares. The civilian side was crowded with two, three, and even four people stationed at each window. All the noise from that side vibrated the reinforced glass windows allowing a kind of hum to get through.

Willy Tomkins—right on time—strolled into Visiting on the inmate side and suddenly stopped right behind Borkow. The stool next to Borkow where Tomkins was supposed to sit was occupied by some no-neck gang puke. That little deviation from the plan bewildered Tomkins, and he looked at Borkow and shrugged.

How did fools like Tomkins survive out in the real world? Borkow grabbed a handful of Tomkins' blues, pulled him down to his level, and whispered in Tomkins' ear, "Quietly, and without a fuss, tell the Mex asshole to piss off."

Tomkins shrugged away and whispered, "Alright. Alright." He straightened his blues, went over, and leaned down. He whispered in the Mex's ear and pointed over to Borkow. The Mex didn't hesitate, his expression filled with fear. He got up and fled, leaving his female visitor to wonder, "What the hell?" Tomkins took his seat and picked up the phone, smiling at the Mex's now confused hina.

Stanky Frank came in next and took his position on a stool, two down, just to the other side of Tomkins. Borkow had chosen him for his strength to lift the window from its frame without dropping it. A clatter that would surely raise the alarm and cut into the precious few seconds needed to get through the window, across the front lobby floor, and out to the street—seconds they didn't own and control.

Next, Twyla, a slim twig of a girl with a blond wig and sunglasses, came into Visiting on the civilian side of the reinforced glass-framed barrier, carrying a big purse that hung off her shoulder. She sat at an empty window waiting for Genie, the last in their little cohort.

Tonight, all of his women wore provocative dresses that showed plenty of leg and overly exposed, bolstered cleavage.

The smartest of his crew, Sammy Eugene Ray—Little Genie—brushed by him, cool, as if this day resembled all other days. Without his help, Genie would forever live in the hallowed halls of the Gray Bar Hotel for the killing of four opposing gang members who had tried to move in on his dope territory. Eighteen months earlier, he'd pled guilty to avoid death row, and got for his trouble four consecutive life sentences without the possibility of parole. Genie looked harmless—shorter than most murderers with his perfect mocha skin and an unassuming air. But the secret weapon in his criminal endeavors—the one he wielded like a knight with a killing sword—his movie star charisma, backed up with a five-hundred-watt smile. Flashy white teeth and sparkling eyes had the women swooning—and women were the key to any successful criminal enterprise.

For the last month, Genie had had his best girlfriend, Scarlett, come in for visits—an absolutely gorgeous young woman, who didn't wear bras underneath sleek dresses that hugged every curve like a car on a Grand Prix track. Scarlett was a key component to the entire operation. On every previous visit, she'd sat on the civilian side of the glass, feigning interest in Genie—all the while turning her big brown eyes on Deputy Masterson, a man known for his fervent interest in women. Deputy Masterson was one of the two deputies on the inmate side of the glass. He always watched out for Genie's visitors and positioned himself behind Genie so he could peep Scarlett. Sometime during each visit, Scarlett would lean in with her arms up for cover on the sides. She'd dip down the front of her dress, letting those lovely breasts out to rest on the stainless-steel shelf in the partially sectioned-off visiting window. The cold stainless steel made them pucker and give sort of a smile.

Borkow had been present on a number of these occasions and witnessed the mesmerizing effect the *lovely ladies* had on Deputy Masterson. From the look in Deputy Masterson's eyes, this part of the plan would go off without a hitch.

Tonight, instead of Scarlett, Twyla arrived to visit Genie. Deputy Masterson looked disappointed, even angry—Scarlett was conspicuous in her absence.

Now everything was in place and ready to go.

In walked Scarlett on top of a sensational pair of *Christian Louboutin* pumps that made even Borkow's mouth water. She stood against the wall on the freedom side of the glass right behind Twyla and caught Deputy Masterson's attention. Borkow watched out of the corner of his eye as Masterson's expression shifted to a huge smile, the leer heavy in his eyes. Scarlett held up the flat of her hand and pointed with an index finger. She silently mouthed the words, "Come. Meet me out here."

Masterson's tongue shot out and wet his dry lips. His entire being hummed with anxiety, his body wanting to chase his desire, the logical thinking part of his brain holding him back, one foot on the accelerator and one on the brake. He held up his wrist and pointed at his watch. He said, too loud, but not loud enough to penetrate the reinforced glass, "I get off at eleven."

Scarlett stuck out her bottom lip in a huge pout. She held up her hands and shrugged. She started to turn to leave when Masterson about jumped out of his skin. "Wait. Wait." He fled his post without proper relief, going around the rows of visiting aisles, and headed the long way around to get to the lobby through the bowels of the administrative part of the jail. His partner deputy was at lunch.

Borkow swiveled on his stainless-steel stool. He said into the phone to Lizzette on the other side of the glass, "Okay, do it now."

CHAPTER TWELVE

BORKOW WATCHED LIZZETTE and Twyla go into the big purse and come out with two battery-powered drills outfitted with a socket tip.

The glass windows of Visiting had been designed five decades ago before the advent of battery-powered drills. Who would've believed that no one before that moment had spotted this glaring defect in the jail security and taken advantage of it?

The girls wore large oven mittens that covered the drill housing to muffle the sound. Everything had been planned down to the smallest detail. In the previous weeks, and at his direction, they had built a similar structure in a broken-down garage in Compton. They practiced again and again until their hands acted all on their own, like the women who riveted the planes in the factories day after day during World War II.

On the jail side, Frank and Genie walked up and down the row ordering everyone to, "Shut your traps and sit your asses down." Borkow pointed to the visitors on the freedom side and gave them the same order. No one moved on either side. No one breathed.

Borkow had questioned his decision to bring Frank along on the escape, the big lumbering oaf with the IQ of an igit. But now Frank had more than earned his position. Everyone on both sides of the glass knew what was happening and still they did nothing to raise the alarm.

Off to the right at the end of the visiting hall, through the doorway into the lobby, two more scantily clad girls started a fight, a real scrap with screaming and scratching, kicking and biting; a diversion to keep the lobby deputies busy.

Lizzette and Twyla, on the freedom side of the reinforced glass, put the drill sockets to the first bolt heads and started backing them out. In Borkow's plan he had allowed for two minutes—that's all he figured his distractions would last. Two minutes. A hundred and twenty seconds for the girls to do their jobs.

Sweat ran down the sides of the girls' faces, the muscles in their arms taut and writhing under the strain as they pressed their weight against the drills.

One by one, the loosened bolts clinked down on the stainless-steel shelf at the base of the window.

Borkow had promised himself he'd remain calm; he stayed seated and pretended this was like any other day. As the critical moment approached, he stood, staring at Lizzette as she focused on the job.

The thick glass sagged open at the top, letting the air on the incarcerated side mix in with the air on the freedom side. When it sagged, the civilians on the other side let out a collective groan. Dangerous men were about to be set free among them.

Borkow scowled and pointed, moving his finger down the line at all of them. They cringed and shut up.

Twyla suddenly looked scared. "Oh my God, Louis, this one's stripping. There's too much paint around it."

He'd been afraid of this, but there hadn't been time to wire-brush the bolts beforehand, not without leaving a major clue for the deputies. "You dumb broad, lean into it. Put all your weight behind it or so help me I'll—" He let the threat die; it wasn't helping matters.

She did as he asked. She got up higher on the stool, shoved one foot hard against the stainless-steel shelf as a brace, and put her hip against the drill. Her concentration narrowed even further. Her gritted her teeth were visible between narrowed lips.

Lizzette bumped her a little, weaseled back in, and went at the last bolt assigned to her.

"Come on. Come on," he said over the sagging window. He resisted the urge to reach through and slap Twyla upside her head.

Lizzette stood back and straightened up. "Got mine."

"Don't dawdle, girl," he half-yelled at Lizzette. "You know what to do now. Get to it." She went back in the bag and pulled out Borkow's change of clothes, hat, and sunglasses.

He turned his attention back to Twyla. "Twyla, you better not screw this up, you hear me?"

The unfastened part of the glass sagged outward even more onto the freedom side.

He turned to the big man, Frank. "Get your ass over here, now. Take the pressure off that last bolt and keep it from falling. Get over here and grab hold, you big tub of lard."

Frank elbowed Borkow out of the way. "Don't you call me that. You hear? Don't do it." He reached and took hold of the tall, narrow piece of reinforced glass, which must've weighed at least a hundred and fifty pounds.

Smoke rose on the other side under Twyla's drill socket. "Louis, it's totally stripped. It's not going to work. Jesus, it's not going to work." She took a deep breath and wiped the sweat from her eyes. "Goddamnit, I'm so sorry, Louis."

No more than sixty seconds had elapsed since the operation began, since the start of the drills and the start of the fight out in the lobby. The people in the lobby still cheered to further incite the combatants.

"Frank," Borkow said. "It's special glass that can't break. It won't cut you. Push it out. Push it, damn you."

Frank pushed. The glass folded and crunched under the force. It bulged and swung out hanging off to one side by the remaining bolt. It barely obstructed the opening, but it did just enough to keep Frank with his hog body from ever getting through.

"Me first," Borkow said, giving into his natural animal instinct. He tried without success to push Frank out of the way.

"Kiss my black ass, white boy."

"No. No. Don't."

Frank shoved Borkow out of the way and swung his large leg up. He stuck his foot through the now-open Visiting window frame.

Borkow gasped. "No. No. No."

Frank straddled the slot, his leading leg and arm stuck through to the freedom side. He ducked his head and tried to get the rest of his body through.

But his fat belly caught.

He clogged the narrow opening. Borkow put his shoulder into Frank's shoulder and pushed. At the same time, the two women on the other side took hold of his hand and arm and pulled.

Nothing. No movement at all. A good ten inches of Frank's gut overlapped the window frame and wouldn't compress enough to let him pass. Ten inches of gut would condemn them all to a lifetime of living in a 10 x 5 foot concrete cell that smelled of sour body odor and ass.

"Lizzette," Borkow said, angry now. "Get the knife and gut this fat fuck." Desperate times called for desperate measures.

Frank's head whipped around. His eyes went wild and bright with fear. Trapped, he couldn't defend himself against some crazy, skinny girl with a blade.

Someone came up behind Borkow and put a hand on his shoulder. Genie said, "Don't, it'll ruin everything. It'll start a panic. Everyone out there will run."

Genie pointed to the throng of other inmates backed into the corner. "Come on, all of you, all together, push."

Borkow said, "All right. All right. Come on. Come on."

Frank suddenly realized the physics involved and what it would mean to his body. His eyes went wide, showing white in his pure panic. "No, don't. Don't."

Too late. Nobody wanted to cross Genie. The group shoved as one. Lots of shoulders, lots of heavy meat behind the added muscle. Frank bellowed. Lizzette, already standing on the shelf, the knife in one hand ready to gut Frank, put her other hand over his mouth, the knife up to his throat. Still a muffled bellow slipped past.

Frank popped out on the other side, his belly badly scraped and bleeding; some of the skin had avulsed, exposing a thick layer of yellow fat. Borkow jumped through. Willy Tomkins came next. Then Genie, who looked back at all the others on the jail side. "Come on. Let's go, everyone."

Borkow quickly pulled off his jail blues. His two women helped out. He recovered at least some of his sanity and held up his hand. "No, don't. That wasn't the plan. A crowd of blues running out the lobby will blow it for all of us."

"Now we need the chaos," Genie said, "as cover."

"No we don't—not that much cover. We need the extra seconds more."

Genie stared at Borkow for a moment. Borkow knew Genie no longer needed Borkow's planning. He could see what Genie was thinking. It wasn't hard to figure out. Genie was finally out and standing in fresh air for the first time in eighteen months. Eighteen long months, an eternity he never again wanted to experience.

Genie made his choice. He held up his hand. "No. No one else comes through. You understand? No one." He pulled his blue jail shirt over his head, exposing his white tee shirt, and casually walked down the aisle. All the visiting civilians moved back against the wall and let him pass. He stopped next to a Hispanic male. "Gimme your shirt, homeboy." The man complied. He pulled it over his head and handed it to him. Genie slipped it on and walked through into the lobby where the deputies were just now breaking up the two women fighting. They'd tried to suppress smiles and let the scrap go longer than needed for the sport of it. The women's faces were scratched, clumps of hair were missing, lips and noses bloodied, and the most important part, their blouses were torn. The bras were pulled down, exposing bare breasts.

Borkow, still in the visiting area, looking out into the lobby, started to follow Genie.

Frank, lying on the floor groaning, holding his wounded belly with one hand, reached out and grabbed a hold of Borkow's ankle as he went by. "Help me."

Borkow glared at Lizzette. She leaned over and clubbed Frank in the head with the battery-powered drill. Frank grunted and let go. "I'll remember this, you white piece of trash." He struggled up onto his hands and knees. Lizzette went to hit him again. Borkow put his hand on the drill. "That's enough. We have to go."

He took in a deep breath, let it out, and strolled into the lobby. He forced himself to be calm, lifted his sunglasses, and winked at one of the girls who'd staged the fight. A newbie jail deputy held her by the arm, his interest focused on her chest. Borkow let his sunglasses down and exited out the front door with Genie and the others right behind him. Then they scattered.

Fifteen to twenty seconds later, the loud jail claxon sounded the alarm for the escape. A car waited at the curb. Borkow got in and was about to close the door when Frank burst out the two double doors bellowing like a bull. "Waiiit for meeee!"

The getaway driver turned and looked over his shoulder at Borkow. Borkow closed his car door and quietly said, "Go."

CHAPTER THIRTEEN

I STOOD IN the dark shadows of the bougainvillea, waiting. Less than an hour after Nicky Rivers drove away, the front door to our apartment eased open with all the lights still off inside. Olivia's dark figure crept out. My heart sank. In that moment I realized that in the past, I'd been grossly negligent by trusting her too much. Sad as it may have been, I shouldn't have waited so long to stake out my own apartment. What an ignorant fool and bad father.

She eased the door closed, pulled the hood to her sweatshirt up over her head, and moved down the street at a quick pace. Alone and on foot in a dangerous world. How many times had she done this?

I waited and watched. If I crowded her, and her plan was to meet Derek on foot, they might see me. If he met her with a car, I'd lose them for sure. I moved from the shadows of the tall bougainvillea and stepped up on the bumper of my truck to get a better view. I rose from a crouch to peer over the top of the cab.

Half a block down, she got into a beat-up wreck, a VW Rabbit parked at the curb. The car's headlights came on and pulled away. I got in my truck, started up, and followed without my lights. I'd done this sort of work many times in the past, following girlfriends of violent criminals. No way would the likes of Derek Sams tumble to the tail.

My imagination ran wild. Where was he taking her? A motel? That was crazy; he was too young to get a motel. But there were some on Atlantic and Long Beach Boulevard that would overlook his age for the right amount of money. The idea of a motel was ridiculous; after hours, kids their age went to the high school under the bleachers or used the dugouts. Only the schools locked them up now and had school police patrolling them.

Where the hell was he taking her?

He drove out to Atlantic Avenue, turned south to Century Boulevard, and then west. He turned into Lucy's, of all places, a Mexican fast-food restaurant where I often took Olivia. Well, I used to anyway, when things were better between us. How had I let time slip past me like a sneak thief in the night? I should've been more vigilant. I thought Lucy's was a special place between us, and now Derek taking her there fueled my already-heated anger. I pulled over and parked far enough away that they wouldn't be able to make out the truck.

Of course, Derek didn't have any money, so he couldn't buy any food. Olivia bought them both some taquitos with guacamole and two sodas with her allowance, money that I gave her every week.

Olivia sat on the outside patio picnic bench like a normal person with her legs under the table. The punk sat on the table with his feet on the bench. They talked animatedly while eating and drinking, using their hands for emphasis, trying to convince the other of their position. What I wouldn't give to hear that conversation. It seemed that Olivia was trying to explain something to Derek who, for some reason, couldn't fathom the words lobbed his way. Olivia seemed frustrated over his ignorance. Or maybe that, too, was wishful thinking.

He slid off the table and sat next to her. He put his arm around her and kissed her on the cheek.

My fists clenched all on their own as Nicky's words about letting her find her own way echoed in my hollowed-out head. The advice didn't seem logical, not when storming over to Lucy's, picking the punk up, and beating him near to death felt so normal, so right under the circumstances. Like a predator after his target, I watched and waited for my turn, my opportunity.

After thirty minutes, they got in the beat-up VW Rabbit and drove back to our apartment. They sat in the dark car with the ambient streetlight making them perfect silhouettes. Their heads came together in a kiss that went on and on.

And on.

Sweet Jesus.

I needed to have that special talk with Olivia, and right away. I'd also take Nicky up on her offer to accompany Olivia to the clinic. I cringed at even the thought of having that conversation.

The kiss continued, as did my anger, which rose by the second. No, I couldn't do it. I couldn't allow this. No way could I just stand aside and let her make her own decision as Nicky suggested. Not one so important. Olivia was too young. She didn't understand anything about the real world, the dangers, how quickly one bad decision could ruin a life. She didn't realize Derek wasn't the only boy or that there were hundreds of thousands of other, *good,* young boys who were easy enough to fall in love with. Why did she have to pick this one? If she'd just let this one go and give some of the others a chance. *Please, O, just let this one go.*

My mind played back the multitude of broken young girls I'd run across while working patrol, girls the street ate up and spit out.

No, I'd do it. I'd take it out of her hands and fix it so she let go of this one. That was the only viable play, and I'd made up my mind to make it happen to the best of my ability. No matter what it took.

The kiss continued. I wanted to know what his hands were doing. But I knew. They were all over my daughter. With that horribly lurid thought, my back stiffened like it always did just before an action, just before I engaged in a violent confrontation with blood and bone.

Only how long had that kiss actually lasted? Had time slowed due to my heated involvement in the situation? Or had it really only been sixty seconds or so, instead of the long, long minutes I'd imagined?

Finally, he unhanded my daughter. They stared at one another for a time, then she got out and hurried away. The louse didn't even walk her to the door. I wanted to pound that little fool into the dirt.

CHAPTER FOURTEEN

THE BATTERED VW Rabbit started up, made a U-turn, and took off. I waited until Olivia made it safely inside and closed the door to the empty and dark apartment. I started up and followed Derek, my hands gripping the steering wheel too tightly.

He headed for the Westside where all projects sat on the extreme south end of Los Angeles. The city had built Nickerson Gardens, Imperial Courts, and Jordan Downs as far away from the heart of LA as possible. The city would not have built them had the federal funding not been so lucrative.

Derek moved around in the area comfortable as a hyena on the African savannah. He lived right off 101st Street not too far from Alameda, on the outside edge of the Downs. To enter the Downs during the day wasn't as dangerous as in the evening. Every day as the sun died in the sky, the good folks went in and locked their doors. All the apartments are constructed of cinder block walls and concrete floors and steel outer doors. When one family moves out, the management goes in with high-pressure hoses, not unlike a zoo enclosure, and washes everything down. They do their level best to hose out all the hopelessness and despair impregnated in the pores of concrete and brick. For the really bad ones, they bring in the steam cleaners. They sprinkle a gallon of Pine-Sol around, replace the broken glass in windows, and reissue the apartment to the next customer hoping for a fresh start.

Derek turned on 101st and didn't make the right turn into the Downs like he should've if he were headed home. Instead, he kept going straight over to Central Avenue. He pulled in and parked in front of Big G's Pager Store. It was an obvious front for narcotic activity, as most of them were. He got out, started for the store's painted-over glass door, and veered to a pay phone on the wall out front. He picked up the receiver, dialed a number, and hung up. He waited. He'd just paged someone to that phone.

Two minutes passed. The phone rang. He smiled and picked it up. He laughed and slapped his leg and acted the fool without being spatially aware of his surroundings. Anyone could walk up and stick a shiv in his back. He wouldn't know it until his lifeless body slid to the dirty sidewalk, his dead eyes looking at nothing. That image of his demise gave a bit of solace, yet at the same time I had to swallow down the sadness of a life lost.

If I didn't fix this problem and save Olivia, I feared I'd never smile or laugh again.

I got out, still unsure of any plan of action, knowing only that I had to do something, that I had to put my hands around his throat and squeeze.

Maybe just a little.

That's all it would take. Whisper in his ear to leave town and never come back, or else next time . . .

If he were smart, he'd get the message before things went too far. But Derek Sams wasn't smart.

Cars whizzed by on the busy street. Central was a main drag that ran through the heart of Los Angeles. As I crossed, I wished for fewer cars and less light. I stepped over the curb and up on the sidewalk. Derek suddenly lost his grin as he froze with his back to me.

I stopped. His eyes had not seen me to register that I stood so close. Something else tore his world out from under his feet. Derek said into the phone, "O, this again, really? I thought we made it past this. Listen to me, we been over this and over this. I'm tellin' ya true, I promise. I tolt ya, I borrowed that money from those dope fiends. I did. I won't lie to ya. I know it was a big mistake and I promise I won't do it again. I know. I know. I said I was sorry. No, I didn't take any rock on credit. I don't care what your daddy, the cop, says—that's not what happened. What? I . . . I borrowed the money to . . . to buy you a present. What? No, I'm not going to tell you what it is, that would ruin the surprise." He listened and nodded. And nodded again. The smile returned to his voice. "Ya, I love you, too, O."

He even used the nickname I had for her, a nickname that sounded disgusting coming from his lips.

His back stiffened. His eyes suddenly focused on the big shadow he caught in the reflection in the window glass.

Me.

He slowly turned. His hand snaked under his oversized football jersey, trying to yank something clear.

With one hand, I reached out and slammed down the receiver, cutting off the call to my daughter. She didn't need to hear what was about to happen.

With the other, I grabbed Derek's wrist and leaned in. "What you got there, under your shirt, poo-butt? You planning on throwing down on me? Is that the play? Not too smart."

He let go. With his one good eye and battered mouth, he shot me a vehement sneer, making my job that much easier. I pulled his hand out and found a Raven Arms .25, a little popgun, a cheap Saturday Night Special made of pot metal. I peeled it out of his hand and leaned in close to his ear. "Boy, did you have this on you while you were out with my daughter tonight? Did you jeopardize my daughter's safety by carrying a gun?"

He tried to jerk away. I slammed him up against the huge glass window of Big G's Pager Store. The entire window shook.

With my hand around his throat, my mouth close to his ear, I spoke in a harsh whisper. "You punkass, I ought to pinch your head off and shit down your neck." His good eye bulged. His battered lips formed a little circle as he tried to push out entreaties to spare his pathetic life.

Down to the right, the door to Big G's opened. Out stepped three senior Grape Street Crips all wearing oversized blue Dodger jerseys. "Hey!" the leader yelled. "What the hell?"

CHAPTER FIFTEEN

I LOOKED AT them and then back at Derek Sams. That's when I noticed that in my blind rage, with one hand I had unintentionally lifted him by his neck until his feet dangled free above the ground. I eased him back till his feet touched before I inadvertently strangled the devil pup. I kept a hold of his scruff and jerked a couple of times to let him know I wasn't done with him.

The fattest of the three gangsters, the leader and mouthpiece, said, "Let him go. He's with us. If you're messin' with him, you're messin' with us. Understand?"

I held on and turned to face them the rest of the way, surprised at the declaration that Derek had joined the Crips, and at the same time not surprised at all.

I let go of the back of his neck. "Don't sweat it, I'm his dad." Derek opened his mouth to refute the accusation. I C-clamped his throat with my left hand choking off his words. His good eye bulged a little.

The leader looked me up and down. "I know you from somewhere, don't I? Where you from?"

I was wearing the blue bandana around my head, indicating that I belonged to some other Crip set. Asking where I was from was like asking what set I claimed.

I swept the bandana off my head. The gang member next to the leader startled and jumped back. "Dat's Bruno Johnson."

The leader smirked. "That ain't no Bruno Johnson. He's dead. And look, his shirt says 'Karl.'"

Shortly after I'd left the street to work in the court, an unsubstantiated rumor went around that I'd met my untimely demise at the hand of a punk named Rodney Simpkins, a big-time gangster that I had tangled with in the past. I'd let the rumor flourish. I wore the tan and green uniform in court, which somehow, to the criminals, changed my appearance just enough to be unrecognizable. It standardized me and made me just another pig in their eyes, a robot of the system, like all the other uniforms.

"No. No. Don't make dat mistake. Dat right there is Bruno The Bad Boy Johnson. Ax poo-butt if it ain't. Go on, ax him."

The leader nodded to Derek. "Ease up on my boy—let's see what he has to say."

I let go of Derek. He slumped over coughing and choking.

I took the opportunity to break down the Raven .25. I tossed the parts out into the street and stuck the barrel in my pocket to discard somewhere else.

Derek recovered enough to point at me and nod. He choked and sputtered. "It's him. He's Bruno Johnson. Do something. Don't let him treat me like this."

The leader straightened up a little. He let his hand slowly wander up to his waistband, where it disappeared under his jersey. "What are you doin' with our poo-butt? You do that to his face?"

I again took hold of Derek by the throat and eased him in front of me. "Let me see your hands, all of you."

The gangster that recognized me turned and took off full tilt down the street. The other one instinctively moved away from his leader, a street tactic. It was harder to hit targets when they weren't so bunched up. He moved his hand behind to his back waistband.

The leader shook his head and looked down the street in the direction his fellow gang member had fled. "Mmm-mmm. Later on, me and dat boy's gonna have words."

I said, "If you two so much as twitch, I'll drop you both. You understand? And I won't lose a minute's sleep over it."

The leader looked back at me. He kept his hand on his gun under his shirt and said, "You didn't answer the question. What you want with my boy?"

"He's been messin' around with my daughter. Now he's got to pay for it."

The second gangster muttered, "Dumbass."

The leader smiled, showing off several front teeth capped with gold. One had the letter "G." "Boy, I hear dat. Fuckin' around wit' Bruno The Bad Boy Johnson's daughter, whatta fool. What are you gonna do wit' him?"

"What do you think I'm gonna do with him?"

The leader slowly brought his hand out from under his jersey. "I think you gonna make him pay the price. Dat's what I think."

"You got a problem with that?"

"No. No. We don't need no fool who's stupid enough to go 'round stickin' his little—"

"Don't. Don't even say it."

"I hear ya, big man. Be on your way wit' ya. Havin' Bruno Johnson out front of my sto' ain't good for bidness."

I let go of Derek's throat and again grabbed him by the scruff. I backed up on the sidewalk, bringing him along.

Derek didn't like that he'd been so easily thrown to the curb by his gang. "Hey. Hey. Don't let him do this. Help. Help me."

I whispered, "Shut up or I'll tell them where I found you today, over in Piru territory at a rock house run by the Bloods." Derek stiffened. He knew they would snatch him right out of my hands and do him dirty for collaborating with the enemy. He decided to shut up.

The leader shook his head, opened the door to his pager store, and with the other one following along, disappeared inside.

I continued to back up until we passed the edge of the strip center and entered the shadows cast by the building in the open field. I spun him around and shoved so hard he almost fell face-first. I caught up to him as he recovered from his stumble and shoved him again. I fought the rising rage, grit my teeth, and clenched my fists. I wanted to pull the blackjack from my back pocket and teach him how the cow ate the cabbage, a term Dad often used. The thought of Dad backed me down a little. If I carried through with what I intended, a long drive out to the Mojave Desert and a lonely drive back, how could I ever look Dad in the eye?

We made it to my truck. I pushed him up against the front wheel well and handcuffed his hands behind his back. He said nothing. I turned him around. The sodium vapor streetlight on his red hair gave it a yellowish tint and made it surreal, clown-like. The swollen side of his face looked right out of a low-budget horror movie. His green eye glared at me. "Whatta ya gonna do to me?"

"What do you think I should do to you? What do you think you deserve? You came to my house tonight. You took my little girl for a ride. You had a gun." I grabbed the front of his shirt. "You little punk, you had a gun. You put her in danger and for what? Put yourself in my place. What would you do if you were me?"

An LAPD cruiser came down the street.

Derek smirked. "Now what's you going to do, old man? You're about to go to jail your own self."

The passenger cop put the spotlight on us. Blinding, turning everything white. I put one hand up to shield my eyes; the other I put on Derek's chest and pinned him against the truck. After a moment, I took my arm down and slowly reached around to my back pocket. I pulled out my wallet flat badge. Derek squirmed and tried to see around me as the patrol car rolled up and stopped. I flipped them my badge. The sheriff's star glinted in the spotlight. "Sheriff's Violent Crimes Team, code four."

"Help," Derek yelled. "He's going to kill me. He's kidnapping me. You have to help me."

The patrol car moved forward, coming a little closer to the passenger's open window. I smiled at the officer and said nothing, just shrugged and shook my head.

The patrolman smiled and asked, "You want us to transport him for you?"

"Hey? Hey?"

I grabbed a hand full of Derek's jersey, shook him a little, and said to the patrolman, "No, thanks, I got it. You have enough problems with that pager store across the street where I just nabbed this guy."

"You took him out of Big G's? By yourself?"

I said nothing.

Derek struggled and tried to break away. "No. No. Wait. He's going to kill me. Really. You have to believe me."

I smiled again and shrugged. "Seems everyone I arrest nowadays says the same thing."

"I know what you mean, buddy. Good luck, and hey, keep your head down."

"Thanks. You boys take it easy."

The passenger gave a salute as they drove by.

Derek sighed. His shoulders slumped. "Ah, man, that ain't right."

CHAPTER SIXTEEN

I DROVE IN and out of streets in a mindless state, trying to decide what to do. It seemed so obvious when I stood out in front of Big G's Pager Store with Derek's throat in my hand, the throb of his heartbeat, the warmth of his skin. None of that mattered. Not while enrapt in rage. I wanted to crush and destroy him for what he was doing to Olivia. Nothing else mattered.

Derek sat as far over in the seat as he could with his back to the door, as though he were trapped in a cage with a hungry animal. In the strobe of the passing streetlights, the truck's interior lit up. Tears glistened on his cheeks and his eyes remained locked on my face, on my eyes. They searched for an answer to whether or not, this night, he'd take his last breath.

The swelling in his battered eye had gone down some. I hated myself for thinking it, but now he looked less like a monster and more like a scared seventeen-year-old kid who'd made too many mistakes. Everyone made mistakes. What chance did a kid have growing up in the ghetto? My brother, Noble, had the same breaks I did. Now he was doing life in prison for murder. He'd never get out, never experience life outside fences topped with razor wire and a cramped concrete cell.

When my mind finally came back to the road, I found I'd driven deep into Long Beach, down by the commercial part of the harbor. I pulled over on a dark side street with no curbs or gutters and few streetlights. The houses sat dark and foreboding.

I shut the truck off. The quiet took over. The windshield turned wet and blurred from the near-invisible mist coming in off the ocean.

"Is this the place?" Derek asked, his voice a croak.

"What?"

"This the place where you're going to do it? You going to do me in? You going to float me out into the ocean? Are you going to leave me for the fish to eat? I don't want to be eaten by the fish. Please don't." His body shook as he sobbed.

"It's what you deserve." I felt bad as soon as the words slipped past my lips. They came from a residual anger that lingered and wouldn't die.

The sight of a child sobbing over what I'd said hurt.

I couldn't do it and realized from the start I never could have. What did that say about me being able to defend and protect my precious child?

I swallowed down the hard lump in my throat. "Then convince me. Tell me why I shouldn't. I've done everything I could to keep you away. I've warned you too many times in the sternest possible manner. You just throw it back in my face, flaunt your arrogance and wannabe gangsta life. Tell me why I should give you one more chance. Convince me if you can."

He just stared. Finally, he found his words. "Because O is the most beautiful woman in the world. She's—"

"Don't call her that."

He opened his mouth to say something else, shut it, then said, "You don't want to hear anything I have to say. You just want me to beg. I won't do it. I won't."

"She's not a woman yet. She's still just a young girl. Too young to be experiencing the things that . . . the things that . . ." I couldn't say it, not in front of him. He'd suddenly shifted from a vulnerable teenager back to street punk, which set my rage back on a low simmer. I didn't like myself for it. My hand shot out and grabbed his oversized Raiders jersey and yanked him over. I pulled him right up to my face. "I can do it. I know I can. If it means saving my daughter from the likes of you, I can do it." I stopped short of saying, *And I don't care what kind of black mark it would leave on my soul as long as my daughter is safe.*

The devil's advocate in my mind whispered in my ear.

Then what? What if you do take this punk off the board? What makes you think there won't be another? And another?

"No. No. Wait. Okay, okay. I'll beg. If that's what you want. I'll beg. I promise . . . I promise I'll never see her again. Just don't hurt me. Please don't hurt me."

"How am I supposed to know you're telling the truth this time?"

"You don't. But I give you my word as a man. I swear. I never did that before. When we talked before."

"You mean each time I warned you to stay away?"

He nodded.

I held him close for another beat, then shoved him off. He wasn't a man, not even close, so how could he give his word? He was just another misguided wannabe gang member trying to find his way in a complicated world. That was the other side of my brain talking, the side that said Derek Sams was broken and could never be fixed, that the world would be a better place without him. "Where are you from?"

"What? Like what hood?"

"No, dummy. Where were you born? Do you live with your folks? Tell me the truth."

"No, I live with my auntie."

"Where are your folks?"

"My mama was a crack whore. She died in San Bernardino when I was just a kid. We buried her there. My daddy doesn't want anything to do with me."

Saying that about his mama had to be difficult. I grew up without a mother and when asked about her, I never wanted to talk about it. "Where's your dad right now?"

"Barstow. He works for the railroad."

I started up the truck.

"Where we going?"

I didn't answer him, just drove. What the hell was I going to tell Olivia?

The morning rush-hour traffic hadn't started yet. I made it downtown in less than an hour. I parked, came around to his side, opened the door, and took the cuffs off.

"What are we doing here?"

"You really want a second chance?"

"Yes, I do."

"Then prove it to me. This is the last time we're going to talk about this. The next time you won't even see me coming. Your world will just all of a sudden go black. You understand what I'm saying?"

He rubbed his wrists that had red indentations from the cuffs. He nodded, the fear plain in his eyes. "Why are we at the bus station?"

"You're no longer welcome in Los Angeles. You need to go back to your daddy in Barstow. There's nothing for you here. Nothing that you're going to like if you stay." I grabbed him by his shirt and yanked him along. I escorted him to the ticket window and bought him a one-way ticket to Barstow. Then I escorted him over to a bench where we'd wait the hour and a half until his departure time.

Neither of us spoke. He relaxed and lay down on the bench but didn't close his eyes all the way, still too wary.

Guilt over what I'd done started to creep in and smother me. I kidnapped a seventeen-year-old off the street and threatened him with an ugly death. I'd worked hard all my life to protect children, and with the first difficult situation that I didn't know how to handle, I defaulted right to what I knew, what I'd lived with for most of my career with the sheriff's department. I defaulted to violence in its ugliest and purest form.

"Hey," I said. "You hungry?"

"I could eat."

"Stay here. I mean it." I got up and went over to the vending machines watching him out of the corner of my eye. I bought him an egg salad sandwich, some chips, and a soda. My bad self hoped he'd get food poisoning from the vending machine sandwich on his long bus ride to Barstow.

He sat up and ate ravenously. He misunderstood my magnanimity and talked and talked the entire hour and a half. The more he talked, the more he turned into a real person, a vulnerable kid. In the end, when I put him on the bus and watched it drive away, I was content with my choice not to do him harm. Though, some of the passengers looked at the injuries he'd received at the hands of the gang members and then looked back at me with contempt. I could live with that—at least he was still breathing.

I walked back to my truck alone as night handed off to the predawn, painting the horizon in bruised purples and dark blues. This was going to be a new day, a good day.

Yet, that bad-self of mine whispered again: *You're a fool. You should've driven him yourself to Barstow and handed him off to his dad. Made his dad accountable.*

CHAPTER SEVENTEEN

As soon as I got in the truck and started home, the adrenaline bled off; along with it came bone-racking fatigue. I knew all the shortcuts and drove like a fiend, canted forward in the seat, my face right up in the windshield, to keep from falling asleep. Each time I dozed, my chin banged the top of the steering wheel and woke me. I was getting too old for all-nighters. In a few hours, I'd pay for it working the court. I didn't know how I'd stay awake for another day of Borkow's trial. I'd have to stand through the whole sordid affair.

I eased the front door open, stepped lightly into the apartment. I quietly closed it, the click too loud in the perfect silence. I stood there, listened, comforted, finally sequestered away from the street and the hyperawareness needed to stay alive.

I didn't have to check. I sensed that Olivia was in her room. Over time, cops develop certain survival instincts lacking in Joe Citizen. One is that as soon as they cross over the threshold, they can sense whether a house is empty.

I took a deep breath. That's when the fatigue really hit hard. Unseen weights pulled at my body, making me want to ease down to the floor, curl up, and go to sleep. Forget everything for a few short hours.

I needed to stay awake. I needed to have that talk with Olivia. Nothing else mattered. I walked around in circles in the apartment living room, trying to stay awake while deciding what to do. What to say, how to even start a conversation that dealt with such sensitive topics?

She'd be awake soon. In what? I checked the clock on the wall. Two and a half hours. That meant I could sleep for a glorious hundred and fifty minutes. That sounded even better.

But what if I didn't wake in time? That would be a total disaster. I could set the alarm, but on a few occasions, I'd slept through the annoying buzzer. And Olivia, she'd do whatever it took to get out of the house to avoid the father-daughter talk I'd promised her the night before. The promise I'd elicited from her just before she violated my wishes and snuck out to see Derek. No, I definitely had to be awake to talk to her.

I stopped circling and did the only logical thing my cotton-laden mind could conjure up. I eased down to the floor, put my back to the front door, and waited.

The last remnants of recent memory played back on the big screen behind my droopy eyes, the words Derek Sams spoke as we sat together on the bus bench, the story describing his tumultuous childhood. No child should ever have to live through something like that.

I didn't want his words to haunt me, but no matter how hard I tried, they did.

And as it turned out, they would forevermore.

*　　*　　*

I woke with a start and didn't recognize what had happened, where I'd been, or where I'd ended up. What the hell?

I was still sitting on the floor by the front door. The natural morning light made the apartment appear different, somehow safer, neutral ground. My mouth was beyond dry. I should've drunk a full glass of water before sitting down to sleep. It would have also served as a wake-up call.

Suddenly, I had the overwhelming desire to pee and realized my hand had fallen off my knee and now rested in a bowl of warm oatmeal on the floor. That's what had awakened me. Along with the bowl there was a small plate with two pieces of toast, lightly browned, just the way I preferred it, with melted butter. My errant hand had overturned and spilled the oatmeal. I smiled. Olivia must've made me breakfast before she hurried off to school.

Before she went off to school?

I tried to jump up, but my body wouldn't comply, not at first. My back ached and my knees hurt.

I noticed a stick in my other hand with a sign at the top. I turned it around. I chuckled. Olivia had written *Save a Dolphin, Don't eat Tuna.* She had been kind enough to make me breakfast then tag me with a sign as if I were on some kind of sit-in to save the planet. I didn't know where she got her sense of humor, but I dearly loved it.

Then I noticed a string around my neck that hung a small sign chest high. It read: *Hi. I'm Bruno the Clown. Don't Clown me.*

Olivia didn't like it when I dressed in my street garb to chase violent criminals: the truck driver shirts with the name "Karl," and the John Deere ball caps. She said I looked more like a rodeo clown dodging the sharp horns of the bulls instead of a streetwise plainclothes detective who chased violent criminals. She must've wondered why I was dressed that way. I hoped she didn't think that I'd transferred out of the court and back to the street. I would never do that to her. Especially now when she needed me the most.

I wiped the lukewarm milk and oatmeal off my hand onto my jeans. "O? Are you still here?"

Please, baby, still be here. We really needed to talk.

I'd driven home from the bus depot fighting a pitched battle over whether to tell her about what I'd done to her . . . boyfriend. I had a difficult time thinking of him that way, as The Boyfriend. He was more of a reprehensible sneak thief who'd, over time, crept into our lives undetected and stolen my daughter, the most precious thing in my life.

This morning, how could she have gotten out of the apartment with me in front of the door? I struggled to my feet, bones creaking.

A hitch in my back kept me hunched over until I could slowly straighten up. I lifted the string and sign over my head. I leaned back over, hand on one knee, and recovered one piece of toast. I took a big bite, hungrier than I thought. It was still warm so she'd just left. For tactical reasons, I kept the back door barred and double dead-bolted. She had to have gone out her bedroom window again. I hated when she did that, and she knew it.

I ate while walking down the hall to the bathroom, discouraged at my failure. It was scary that she could put a sign in my hand and one around my neck and make breakfast without waking me.

The phone rang and I realized the time. I was going to be late. I let it ring. It never stopped ringing. I jumped in the shower, shaved, dressed, and hurried off to work.

CHAPTER EIGHTEEN

I DIDN'T GET far on my way to Compton Court before the guilt returned over what I'd done the night before—a few hours before. The look in Derek's eyes when he thought I was about to feed him to the fish in Long Beach Harbor, coupled with his rambling words about his childhood while he ate the vending machine egg salad sandwich—the guilt from it caused my stomach to cramp.

I did a quick detour and headed to Dad's house on Nord in The Corner Pocket of Los Angeles. The house I'd grown up in. I parked in front as Dad came out the front door wearing his blue-gray postal pants and shoulder-strap tee shirt. He was also on his way to work. Only *he* was on time. He'd been a postman as far back as I could remember. He never missed a day sick and rarely used all his annual vacation time. He considered his job a service to the public and treated it as such with unmatched loyalty and dedication. He still carried a lot of lean muscle and looked good for his age. He stood a little shorter than me and kept his hair shaved close to his scalp.

I got out of the truck and stood by the passenger door. His smile faded when he read my expression.

"What's going on, Son? Is something wrong with Olivia?"

The words hung up in my throat. I didn't know how to tell him what I'd done. I nodded.

He came close, put his warm hand on my shoulder, and gave it a comforting squeeze.

"What's wrong?" he asked, "What's wrong with Olivia?"

"It's nothing new. We've talked about it."

"Derek, again?"

I nodded.

He shook his head. "I'm afraid to ask. What have those two done now?"

"Yesterday, while I was in court, O called me. Said she was in a rock house in Compton with Derek. She said the gangbangers had guns. She was scared to death."

"Oh, dear Lord. What happened?" His fright subsided quickly. His eyes narrowed in anger.

"I figured out where she was and went and got her. She's okay."

"Thank goodness. I can understand why you're upset. I'm glad you came to me, to talk it through before you did something stupid to Derek."

I broke eye contact and looked away.

"Oh, no, Bruno, what did you do? Is the boy okay?"

"I'm sick over this, Dad. I didn't know what to do. I acted before I thought about it. Now I think I might've done the wrong thing, in the way I handled that boy. I shouldn't have done it. Once O finds out about it, she's never going to talk to me again."

"Bruno, what did you do?"

"Last night Olivia wouldn't talk to me. I told her we'd talk about it in the morning.

"She was real upset over Derek getting socked-up in the rock house. I knew she was going to try and see him. I waited on the street and followed them. They went over to Lucy's off Century, talked for a while, and then he brought her home."

"Okay, and . . ."

"Then I followed Derek."

"Ah, Bruno."

I again looked away from his eyes and down at the dirt in my old front yard, ashamed as I stood before him. "I grabbed Derek out in front of Mr. G's Pager Store over off Central."

Dad muttered, "Hmm, that's not a good place for that boy to be hanging out."

"I know, but it's worse than that. The place in Compton where he took O was Piru. Bloods. Big G's place on Central is run by the Crips. Derek's playing both ends."

I didn't have to say more. Derek wouldn't be long for this world if either side found out. Olivia would be caught in the crossfire.

"I wanted to hurt him, Dad. I mean, I thought I was going to permanently solve the problem, with a little blood and bone." It was a term we used while working the violent crimes team. Dad had heard it before and knew its meaning.

"I'm glad you didn't. You didn't, did you, Son?"

"When I grabbed him, he had a Saturday Night Special, in his pants. He had it there when he was out at Lucy's with O."

"That little son of a—"

He caught himself. He rarely used profanity, said it only served to "let the fool out of a person." Derek's antics had almost succeeded in making my father a fool.

"What happened? What'd you do with him?"

"I put him on a bus to Barstow. He said his dad lives out there."

Dad shook his head. "That's not going to solve your problem."

"I was hoping you wouldn't say something like that."

"Taking him off the street like that was wrong. But I can't say that I blame you."

He thought about it for a long moment, choosing his words. "You didn't come here because of the guilt that's eatin' at you."

"What?"

"You came here because of what you almost did. That's what scared the hell out of you. This isn't something new. We've talked about your temper before. You know right from wrong. You did the right thing here, Bruno. So ease up on yourself. You don't have it in you to hurt a child."

I nodded, still looking at the ground.

"Look at me."

I looked up at him.

"You didn't hurt the boy, that's what counts. Your moral standards stopped you from doing something you would've regretted the rest of your life."

A lump rose in my throat. More shame.

I had not always done the right thing. Once I had strayed from the path. It was something I'd never told him, never told anyone.

Not all that long ago, I'd crossed the line when I captured Leroy Gadd and turned him over to a street gang to administer the proper dose of justice our legal system would have hemmed and hawed over. Leroy Gadd was never seen or heard from again. I lost many nights' sleep over what I'd done. But at the time it was the only option. Leroy Gadd had killed my best friend, Ned, along with two other friends, Ollie Bell and our team sergeant, Sergeant Coffman.

I nodded, unable to talk. I swallowed hard. "What am I going to do about O?"

He shook his head. "There's nothing you can do. You're dealing with an immovable force of nature."

"I don't understand. What are you talking about?"

"Love. It's like an invisible wall that can't be breached or overcome no matter how hard you try. Wars have been fought over it. Olivia will have to work her way through it on her own. She has to open her eyes and see what's going on for herself. All you can do is give her your best counsel and wait. But don't push too hard. She has to be the one to make the choice."

It was exactly the same thing Nicky had said the night before.

"How come everyone can see the answer as plain as day and I can't?"

Was I that ignorant when it came to love? To being a good father?

Dad smiled. "The answer to that is simple. You're afflicted by that very same force. The love of your daughter. It's blinding you to what's really at play here. Now, I have to get to work or I'm going to be late." He patted my shoulder again and started toward his car.

"There has to be something I can do. There has to be."

He turned back, dead serious. "There is one thing."

"What? Tell me. I'll try anything."

"Get her a cute little puppy."

"A puppy? Are you kidding?"

He winked, went to his car, got in, started up, and drove away.

A puppy? How could . . . And then I realized that it wasn't a perfect fix but it was something. If Olivia had something else to love, to direct her affections to, a distraction of sorts, it might be enough of a diversion that she could finally open her eyes and see the danger right in front of her.

I took a deep breath. Some of the weight lifted off. It was going to be a great day. I whispered to no one, "Thanks, Dad."

CHAPTER NINETEEN

I PARKED MY truck in the unsecured employee parking lot and ran for the side door of the Compton Courthouse. I pulled it open to the back stairs that led upward, then froze. Slowly, I turned around. My mind locking on to what I'd seen. In my haste, I'd subconsciously recognized some of the people rushing out the front door of the courthouse, heading to the jury-only parking area. They were from my courtroom. They were jurors for the trial of the murderer Louis Borkow.

My first thought: the judge had been suspended pending judicial review. Suspended on allegations from yesterday's little field trip to the rock house on Pearl. The place where he'd fired a shot through the roof. That meant my sergeant would be waiting on me for the same reason: suspension. With it I'd be restricted to my apartment during business hours while they investigated. If I wanted to go out, I'd have to call Internal Affairs Bureau—IAB—and ask permission. Damn. How would I be able to supervise Olivia?

I ran up the stairs to the third floor, my breath coming hard when I got to the top. I really needed to start running on my next RDOs—regular days off. That was, if I still had a job.

I hurried to my courtroom, stopped, and tried to catch my breath before entering. All the people in the halls waiting for their court

cases stopped to look at me. I took in three long, slow breaths. I held
the last one, and went through the double doors and on through the
next set of double doors and into the courtroom.

Esther, our court clerk, an older Hispanic woman with gray hair,
looked up at me and didn't smile.

She always smiled.

"What's going on, Esther? Bad news?"

She nodded. "You better take it up with the big boss."

"Am I in trouble?"

Now she smiled. "Now what in the world would you have to be
worried about, Mr. Bruno Johnson?"

I nodded toward the back chambers. "Unauthorized field trips,
for one."

She laughed and pointed. "You better get back there. You don't
need to worry. He thinks you're some kind of hero. He said he never
had so much fun."

I followed orders and went through the door behind the judge's
podium to the hallway in back of the court used by inmates and
jurors. I crossed the hall and knocked lightly on the door to the
judge's chambers, the same as I had done a thousand times in the
last two years.

The judge yelled a muffled, "Come."

I entered to find Borkow's defense attorney, Gloria Bleeker, and
Nicky Rivers, both standing, arms crossed, both mad as hell.

I lifted my hands. "Okay, what's going on?"

Nicky walked by me with her back to everyone else. She mouthed
the words, "Call me later." She went out the door in a huff. I'd never
seen her so angry. I hoped it wasn't over our situation.

Gloria Bleeker wore a tan and darker brown pattern skirt that
matched her suit coat. She was thick-bodied with dark brown hair
going gray. She'd been in the trenches a long time and it came out in

her everyday cynical tone. She only stayed in the business because she liked the money.

She wasn't a bad person. I'd helped her out one night long ago, when I was a patrol deputy and pulled her over for drunk driving. I cut her a break and drove her home. Afterward, I asked her to take on a few cases pro bono, all of them kids who needed a break from a skewed justice system. We'd meet periodically for lunch, but we never discussed business.

Gloria shrugged and headed out the same way Nicky had left. She'd cooled a little and didn't seem as upset. "It's a mistrial, buddy boy. Imagine that? Hooray for us, go team."

"A mistrial? Why? What happened?"

Gloria didn't stick around to explain and left it to Judge Connors to pass on the bad news. A mistrial was the best thing that could've happened to Borkow. Time was definitely not on his side when it came to the evidence and witness statements. In fact, he had nothing else to depend on except for the passage of time and the erosion of memories.

With the mistrial, both sides would have to start all over picking a new jury, giving another opening argument, putting on the same witnesses—the whole shebang.

When the door closed behind Gloria, I faced Judge Connors ready to be dressed down for my tardiness. He didn't tolerate anyone being one minute late. I'd never given him reason to talk harshly until that moment. Maybe what Esther had said about yesterday would give me a little cover.

He leaned back in his chair, one foot up on the desk, his black robe unbuttoned and hanging open. "I guess you haven't turned on a radio or TV since last night, huh?"

I shook my head. "No, sorry. I was a little busy."

He picked up the newspaper on his desk and tossed it closer. "Organized escape at your downtown jail. Guess who?"

I reached for the paper. "You have got to be kidding me. Did they catch him yet?" The sheriff didn't tolerate breaches in his security and took them as a personal affront to his integrity. In the past, when someone in his custody went "over the wall" or was accidentally released through a clerical error, he put everything on hold and threw every available resource at the problem until the violator was back in custody. Usually far worse for wear, booked in at the hospital ward, broken and bandaged. The violator had to be recaptured right away or there would be automatic lawsuits against the department for failure to protect in the crimes committed while the person was out on the lam.

"Better read that," Connors said. "Not one, but four got away. All of them in for murder. Can you believe it? Bad Day At Black Rock for the sheriff's department. Just the one, though, ruined my damn trial. I can say it now. I was all ready to give that ol' boy death row, for cutting that mother's head off in front of that poor child. Giving him the needle would've done society a great service."

Connors tended to ramble on during moments or events over which he had little control.

I looked up from the paper, a big ugly story, with the power drills and the semi-clad women fighting in the lobby as a distraction. They made the sheriff's department look like a bunch of circus monkeys chasing around a greased football. There was going to be some real heat over this one. "This is really going to cause some problems."

"You think?"

"Oh, I'm sorry for being late today, Your Honor."

"I guess it doesn't really matter today, now does it? So you lucked out. Are you okay? You look ridden hard and put away wet. Girl problems, I'm guessing?"

"Yes, but not the kind you're referring to. I'm just a little tired."

"Olivia again?"

I nodded and grew angry. Even though I called him my friend, I was uncomfortable with him knowing about my personal problems, my shortfalls when it came to fatherhood.

Someone knocked on the chamber's door. I headed toward it. "I guess I better get into my uniform."

"The trial's trashed, so if you want to take a few days you can. We won't go up on another one, not right away."

I put my hand on his door and half-turned. "Hey, that would be great. Thanks, Your Honor, I think I will." With a couple of extra days off, I could keep a close eye on Olivia at a time when she needed me most.

I opened the door. Lieutenant Robby Wicks from the violent crimes team stood there with a huge smile, one that didn't bode well for me.

CHAPTER TWENTY

YEARS EARLIER, I'D been hand-picked by Lieutenant Robby Wicks for his newly formed violent crimes team. I didn't have any detective experience and transferred right in from a patrol assignment at Lynwood Station in South Central Los Angeles. I took one of the four slots that the most experienced detectives from all over the county wanted and had lobbied for.

I'd only met Robby once, when he had worked an overtime slot as a field sergeant at Lynwood Station. That particular hot summer night I tracked rusty water from a hit-and-run vehicle's ruptured radiator. I did it running in the street following a leak as the water evaporated. The driver had hit and killed a young girl, a child in the crosswalk. Hit her so hard the fabric of her dress imprinted in the chrome of the vehicle. When I finally caught up with the driver, I had to cross the line into the gray area of the law, and at the end of my boot I made the arrest. Robby was there to pull me off the suspect, who ended up hospitalized. Robby wrote what had happened to the suspect in his Use of Force report, *"All the Injuries were sustained in the car accident."*

Robby Wicks had seen something in my unwavering tenacity and call to violence that he liked. That episode had exposed something hidden in me that I did not like and that he had easily recognized.

Together, for many years, we chased the most violent criminals Los Angeles County had to offer. It was as if Los Angeles was Robby Wicks' own private game preserve. Working with Wicks called to mind the famous quote from Hemmingway that I'd seen posted over Blue's desk in the narco office:

There is no hunting like the hunting of man, and those who have hunted armed men long enough and like it, never care for anything else thereafter.

Wicks fell heavily into that category. What I feared most was that I did, too.

When I made my decision to leave the team for a stable schedule in court services, Wicks did everything in his power to talk me out of it. In the end, we parted angry. He couldn't—or wouldn't—understand my position—that my daughter had to come first. He could only see how I was messing with his uncompromised need to hunt. I had been his one and only hunting partner, someone he trusted implicitly to back his play no matter how far he ventured into the gray area of the law.

Now he stood in front of me at Judge Connors' chamber door, smiling like old times. He stuck his hand out. "Bruno, damn good to see you. You going to ask me in, or I gotta stand out here all day?" I hadn't seen him in two years. He acted as if nothing had ever come between us. I took his hand and shook but didn't return his smile. When the wolf knocks at your door, you don't invite him in, you grab your gun. That wasn't fair. I liked the man. I could even say, in a weird sort of way, loved him. I respected no man more, except my father, but for entirely different reasons.

These weren't my chambers to bar his entry. I didn't have that authority. I stepped aside. He entered with a trailing whiff of cologne. He wore his usual brown polyester Western-cut suit. His expensive ostrich-skin cowboy boots had been replaced by highly polished black Wellingtons. He didn't care that his Western garb was outdated. Over the years he'd developed a brand, the way he looked, the way he talked, the way he treated certain people, and stuck to it. He wanted everyone, the good guys and the bad guys, to instantly recognize him when he walked into a situation. He wore his hair short above his ears and long on top combed to the side like a kid in elementary school. He was anything but. He had intense brown eyes that bore into you even during the most innocuous conversations. Out of view and concealed in a hip holster, he carried a Colt .45 Combat Commander, a gun not approved by the department, a gun with the blood of many who'd gone up against him—gone up against us—the blood deeply engrained in the blue steel and stag grips.

He moved right over to the desk, leaned in, and shook Judge Connors' offered hand. "Good morning, Your Honor." He sat in one of the two chairs in front of the desk, something you didn't do in Judge Connors' chambers, not without being asked to first.

Connors stared him down. "Cut the shit, Wicks. What do you want?" I marveled at the clash of two obstinate men who always had to have their way.

I'd kept track of Wicks over the last two years with members from his team who came in to get search warrants or arrest warrants signed by the sympathetic Judge Connors. I was envious of their job, of their continued friendship with my old friend, envious of a job I wished like hell I had never left. They had intimated at first, and eventually came right out and said it, that Robby Wicks would do anything to get me back on the team. He had even asked them to test the water when they saw me, to see if I'd take an offer to return.

Robby never came with them. He wouldn't lower himself to that level of scut work or to swallow his pride and ask me to come back.

In my mind, real or imagined, he wanted to avoid any kind of contact with me as it further impugned his reputation. No one left his team the way I did. You promoted out or you just didn't leave. That's the way he looked at it. Leaving to go to court services gave him a black eye, and he didn't like it. Now he sat in my judge's chambers, smug and arrogant as hell.

I went over and stood at the side of the desk.

Judge Connors said, "Bruno, weren't you going to take some days off?"

The question shook me out of my stunned reverie and cleared the way for logical thinking. I knew why Wicks had come. A blind man could've seen it. I didn't take my eyes off Wicks. "I think my old supervisor has a favor to ask you, Your Honor. And before he does, I'd like to ask that you not grant that favor."

CHAPTER TWENTY-ONE

WICKS CHUCKLED AND raised his hands. "Bruno, Bruno, I have the milk of human kindness running through my veins. Why do you treat me like this?"

"Go on, ask that favor you got in your pocket. Bring it out and take it for a walk. The answer is no. It'll always be no and there's nothing you can say that will change my mind. You're wasting your time here, Lieutenant." He still didn't get it. Olivia needed me more now than ever.

At the same time, I *did* want to go with him. I wanted back into the hunt that I craved every second of every day. I stood there torn, but resolved.

"You got it all wrong, my fine Negro friend. The favor I have is something I'm doing for you." He pointed at me.

He didn't mean anything by calling me a Negro. It was his way of trying to weasel back in with me. In the past, while men hunting the worst of the worst, we were equals. He'd call me names without vehemence or malice. It was more out of camaraderie that, as odd as it sounded, brought us closer together. I did the same. My usual for him was WT, White Trash.

I looked at Connors. "Your Honor, tell him no and tell him to get the hell out of your chambers."

Wicks' mouth dropped open, still smiling. I had to return the smile. I said, "No, this is not going to happen. Forget it."

Connors said, "I'm not the fool you two apparently think I am. Lieutenant Wicks here wants you back TDY, temporary duty, to chase these four violent shitasses who escaped from the jail. Am I right, Lieutenant?" Connors tapped the newspaper on his desk. "I'll grant that request on one condition."

Wicks and I both quit staring at each other and looked at him. I said, "What?" I couldn't believe he'd throw me under the bus that quick when he knew my situation at home. "No," I said. "Not under any conditions." I looked back at Wicks. "Get out."

Wicks didn't lose his smile and patted his coat pocket. "You still haven't asked what kind of favor I'm going to do for you. The favor I got right here in my pocket."

I didn't like his smile; it scared the hell out of me.

Wicks looked at the judge. "What condition?"

"That the sheriff's department reinstate my reserve status and allow me to join Bruno in this exciting endeavor."

Wicks again chuckled, his eyes going back to mine. "I think we can work that out. Get your gear, Bruno, we're rollin' out hot just like the good ol' days."

"No, it's not going to happen. I'm gonna take a few days off, family leave. The judge already approved it."

Wicks stuck his hand in his pocket. He and I had only been talking metaphorically about him having a favor hidden away. I held my breath. He was too smug, too confident. Somehow, he knew he had me over a barrel. He wouldn't be there otherwise. I couldn't figure out what he could possibly have that he was so sure would change my mind.

His hand came out of his pocket.

A cassette tape. An ordinary, innocuous cassette tape.

My mind spun a thousand miles a minute. What could he have on the tape that would be a game changer? In the past he'd been known to do black-bag wiretaps. Wiretaps without the sanction of the law. What had I been into that he could use to blackmail me? Ah shit, he knew about Nicky Rivers, our little thing. He knew who her husband was, the lieutenant at SEB. He had somehow obtained a tape of our clandestine tryst. The tryst that was, as of yet, an unconsummated affair.

Connors leaned over, his hand extended. "What do you have there, Wicks? Give it to me. I have a recorder right here."

Wicks handed it to the judge.

I tried to grab the cassette. "No."

The judge pulled it back quick. He chuckled. "Take it easy, Bruno, my man. We're all friends here. It won't hurt to take a listen. Shall we?"

"Don't do it, Your Honor. Please don't." Sweat broke out on my forehead not only for my situation but for the embarrassment of Nicky as well.

He didn't hesitate and stuck the cassette in the recorder on his desk, the one he used to dictate reports and memos for his secretary. Connors said, "Wicks wouldn't dare bring something to me that would disparage your character. He knows how I feel about you. What he has here has to be something else entirely different, and I want to hear it." He poised his finger over the button. "Wicks, you want to say something to set up what we are about to hear?"

Wicks turned deadly serious. "My team was called in to assist on this escape. Everyone in the department has been put on notice that these mutts will be found and found quickly. We started looking into it late last night. This is a recording from Louis Borkow on a jail phone talking with a co-conspirator out on the street who we have yet to identify."

All phone calls in the jail are recorded as a matter of routine. Judge Connors pushed the play button.

I immediately recognized Borkow's voice. "*I want you to do what we talked about.*"

"*Huh?*"

"*Do I need to spell it out for you?*"

"*Naw, I think I got it. You want me to get Olivia Johnson over ta this house on Pearl.*"

My heart jumped up into my throat. A cold trickle of fear crawled up my back. Then it quickly shifted to anger. My back went stiff. I clenched my fists. I wanted to crush the life out of Borkow and would pay anything for that opportunity.

"*That's right, nothing too difficult,*" Louis continued on the tape recording. "*I want you to put her in jeopardy so she calls her daddy for help. I need it done tomorrow at noon or just before, so I can get out of court and catch the early bus back. Can you do that?*"

"*I can do it, but it's going to cost you. You gotta wipe out what I owe dem boys on Pearl.*"

"*That's not a problem. If you do this right, you can be sure I'll take good care of you, ah . . . soon, if you know what I mean.*"

The second voice had a vague sense of familiarity, but I couldn't place it. The guy must've had his hand over the receiver, muffling the words.

The tape went mute. Judge Connors pushed the stop button.

I said to Wicks, "Give me five minutes, I'll get my gear."

CHAPTER TWENTY-TWO

TWENTY MINUTES LATER, I stopped in the hall to listen. Around the corner and a short distance away out of view, Wicks must've been standing with Judge Connors talking in front of the double doors of the courtroom. Connors said, "You wound Bruno up like some kind of toy soldier. Now you're going to turn him loose? Don't you think that's a little dangerous, not to mention unfair to Bruno?"

"Putting Bruno on the case will only be unfair for that asshole Louis Borkow. Borkow's the one who called the game, not me. Think about it. If he kills someone while he's out, there's going to be hell to pay. The county will be on the hook for huge checks with lots of zeros going to the all the victims' families. Not to mention the black eye it's going to give the department. No, Bruno is absolutely our best chance of grabbing this guy quick. So I have no problem as you say 'winding him up like a toy soldier.' The department knows what's at stake; they'll take care of him."

"To a certain point," Connors said.

"To a certain point, that's right."

"That tape proves Borkow used Bruno as a diversion so he could get out of my courtroom and sent back to the jail early. Don't you feel the least bit concerned that you're doing the same thing? You're using him like some kind of tool. He's your friend."

I stayed around the corner out of view, listening as I eased the body armor over my head and strapped it on. I shrugged into my khaki colored shirt with *Karl* embroidered over the breast and the trucking emblem on the other. How was I going to explain this to Olivia?

I stopped dressing to listen for Wicks' answer and held my breath. I thought I knew what he'd say. When you worked together as long as we had, you could finish each other's sentences. But it had been two years since we had worked together, and people change.

Wicks' tone turned more serious, with a hint of anger. "You know as well as I do Bruno is a wasted asset sitting in there behind a desk. This jailbreak is the best thing that could have happened for him. So don't try and lay this off on me. I wasn't the asshole who used Bruno's daughter as a pawn. I wasn't the asshole who organized the biggest escape in the history of this county."

"No, but you are the asshole who played the tape for him."

"You know, you keep talking your trash, Your Honor, and I'm going to have to change my opinion of you."

"That right?"

"That's right."

I hurried around the corner, arranging my guns under my shirt in my waistband. "Hey," I said to get their attention and to disrupt the escalating conversation. "You guys ready to go?"

They both turned to look at me coming their way.

Presiding Judge James D. Hockney, Judge Connors' boss, approached from the opposite end of the hallway. He came up on Wicks and Connors the same time I did. "What's going on here?" he asked.

Connors said, "I think you heard. I had to declare a mistrial due to the escape."

"Yes, I'm aware. And?"

Connors said, "Lieutenant Wicks has conscripted my bailiff to assist in the manhunt."

"I have no problem with Deputy Johnson being utilized for this purpose," Hockney said. "I just want to be sure you know *your* place. After yesterday's little escapade, you tarnished a near perfect reputation and put this court's integrity in question. In other words, Phil, you gave us a black eye. I came down here to be sure there wouldn't be a second lapse in your judgment."

Wicks said, "It's okay. I called and got clearance with my department. Judge Connors' Reserve Deputy status has been reinstated. He will be acting under the color of authority."

"Phil, you're not going. I won't entertain another word about it." Hockney walked off.

Connors muttered under his breath, "That pompous little pissant. How the hell did he find out?"

Wicks shook his head. "That's too bad, Your Honor. I was really looking forward to having you along. I was going to show you how real police work gets done."

Wicks said it with a neutral expression, but I caught that twinkle in his eye that said otherwise.

"I'm sorry, too, Your Honor." I turned to Wicks. "Come on, let's get going."

We walked off. Behind us Judge Connors said, "Bruno, call me with any updates, would you please?"

I didn't turn around. I just raised my arm in the air to acknowledge his pitiful request.

Wicks said in a half-whisper, "You call him, I'll take a big bite out of your ass, you hear me?"

"Yeah, I figured it would be something like that."

We stepped into the elevator as the doors opened. Two gang members dressed in their gang garb—baggy denim pants, blue bandannas, and white tee shirts—started to get on with us. Wicks squeezed in between them and put up his hand. "Sorry, fellas, this car is occupied. Take the next one."

The bigger one said, "Hey. Hey. What the—"

The smarter one grabbed his friend by the arm and pulled him back out. "Jus' shut yo' hole and get outta their way."

Wicks shot them a grin and pushed the button for the lobby. The doors closed and we started down. "Don't look at me like that, Bruno. What, you wanted a member of the court looking over our shoulders while we chase some of the baddest assholes we've ever gone after?"

"How did the presiding judge happen to come sauntering down the main hall just at the right moment? How come you two were conveniently waiting in the hall? Judge Connors never goes out in that hall. He always uses the back one. And Hockney used the words *black eye,* just like you did not minutes ago."

Wicks shrugged. "I don't know what you're talking about." A smile crept across his face.

I liked Connors a great deal and respected him, but he had no business out on the street. He had fired an unwarranted warning shot into the ceiling of a rock house.

Wicks was right about that part. I couldn't help it; I started laughing. It was good to be back in the saddle with my conniving old partner. The laughter helped to lighten a heavy load.

CHAPTER TWENTY-THREE

Louis Borkow stood in Muscle Max, a defunct gym directly across the wide parking lot from his closed-down Grand Orchid Massage Parlor, the flagship of his massage parlor chain, a place where everyone in law enforcement would be looking for him. This had been Payaso's idea, to hide in plain sight right under their noses. Still, anxiety to be on the move, to run, wouldn't let him sit and pretend everything was okay. He paced back and forth, back and forth, and would soon wear a path in the cheap carpet.

The Orchid was the biggest in square footage and had employed a higher percentage of the most beautiful women in his stable: more of the taller, leggy Russians, and fewer of the shorter, dusky Guatemalans that made up his other smaller operations. He yearned for the time past when he could come and go as he pleased from the Orchid, a mere hundred feet away—now the same as a deadly poison if he set even one foot across the threshold.

He'd made the business office of Muscle Max his personal area so he could periodically peek through the slit in the curtains, look across the parking lot to his flagship.

Harold, Muscle Max's caretaker and Borkow's bodyguard, had taken out the desk and file cabinets and brought in a comfy chair and bed along with one of those little refrigerators. The place reminded Borkow too much of a jail cell as if he'd exchanged his air miles for an upgrade, but he still could not step foot outside.

He moved over to the door to call Harold to tell him he wanted Lizzette in there pronto. He'd already been out of jail for twelve hours or more and his need for sex bordered on dire. He craved relief, ready to do anything for it, and would even settle for Lizzette. Lizzette had a dynamite pair of legs. Only she came with an ugly pair of feet. He wasn't a foot freak—he just liked elegant and delicate-boned feet to come with the rest of the package.

Though he did have a thing for cleanliness. He'd sent Lizzette to sit in the Muscle Max sauna for an hour, then the jacuzzi, then the pool. He couldn't wait for her any longer.

Just as Borkow was about to push the door to the office open to check on the holdup, he overheard Harold in the hall whispering in a confidential huddle with Lizzette. Those two were thick as thieves. Lizzette said to Harold, "No, that's not what happened at all. That silly Stacy simply lost her head over Borkow." A sick joke even for Lizzette. They both giggled like a couple of little girls. Harold had a thing for Lizzette that he carried around in his eyes as he watched her walk and move.

Borkow let Lizzette's words roll off his back, but filed them away for later. He stepped backward, away from the door, and deeper into the office. "Harold," he called out, "where's Lizzette? Go get her and send her in."

The door opened. Harold leaned in, holding onto the knob. "Here she is, boss." Harold had muscles on top of muscles and wore a tee shirt two sizes too small. His shoulders humped with muscle, making it appear that whoever had put him together had forgotten a neck.

Lizzette came in, fluffy white terry cloth towel wrapped around her, one of the nice ones brought over from the Orchid. "I'm here, Louis." She didn't want to be there as evidenced by her glum expression and tone of voice. At one time, she'd been one of his best earners at the Orchid, but never a favorite for his personal servicing.

Borkow backed up a couple of steps, took off his shirt, and let his pants drop to the floor, stepping out of them. The back of his legs bumped the bed. He sat down. "That'll be all, Harold. We are not to be disturbed."

"You got it, boss." He closed the door all but a couple of inches. Borkow wanted to believe it was so Harold could keep close tabs on him for security reasons and not because he was a perv.

Borkow picked up a shoebox from the bed next him, forced a smile, and held it out. Lizzette's eyes lit up. She appreciated a nice pair of women's shoes almost as much as he did. And these shoes were top of the line—a pair of $2,400, bejeweled *Christian Louboutins*, Arletta crystal-embellished high heels.

Her angelic face lit up like a child's at Christmas as she snatched the box out of his hands. She let the towel drop to the floor and stood in front of him, bending at the waist to put on the shoes one at a time. He usually loved this part of his ritual, but not with her bony, knobby feet, so he looked away. She strolled nude back and forth in front of him as he looked down her long legs at the shoes.

"Come here," he said.

The light in her expression died. He raised his hand and motioned for her to come closer. She hesitated and finally complied. Still sitting, he reached up and put his hand on her hip, her flesh hot to the touch. Now *he* lost his smile. She'd not gone in the pool after the sauna and jacuzzi. He preferred cool, almost cold flesh, over hot and sweaty. She knew that and did it on purpose, a minor form of revolt. He slowly stood. She took a step back but didn't flee. She used to be more afraid of him. He'd have to fix that. Later, though.

The door burst open and in rushed Harold. "Boss, there's a car pulling up in front of the Orchid."

CHAPTER TWENTY-FOUR

NAKED, BORKOW HURRIED over to the window. Without touching it, he peeked through the narrow slit in the curtains. A black Monte Carlo with dark-tinted windows pulled up and parked among the forty or fifty other cars scattered about the parking lot of the large horseshoe-shaped strip center. People doing business at the hair salon, the auto parts store, the big box pharmacy, and a realtor office. The driver of the Monte Carlo had chosen a slot lined up with the door of the Grand Orchid. Borkow couldn't see the driver of the Monte Carlo and didn't recognize the car as it just sat there, engine running. Cops? Or one of his many enemies eager to kick him when he was down, take him out while his restricted movements made him a prime target? His lack of freedom irked him. He'd give anything to have it back the way it was before Tasty Stacy stumbled into his life . . . and then stumbled out.

Lizzette stood close to him, her back against the wall next to the window. She'd rewrapped the towel around her. Moist heat radiated from her body. He couldn't get a read from her. Did she care if the cops had actually found him?

He'd spent a year all pent up physically and sexually in a small cage awaiting trial while he put together the intricate plan to escape, a whole year without the benefit of female companionship, a year without beautiful feet clad in beautiful shoes. Oh, he so needed re-lief. He didn't need this kind of shit show, not now.

Borkow watched the shiny black Monte Carlo with wisps of white exhaust coming from the tailpipe.

The engine shut off.

The door opened.

He held his breath, ready to grab his clothes and his gun and flee out the back. How had they found him so quickly? The word had gone out that the Orchid was closed to all customers. It had been that way for the past two weeks in preparation for his return. It could be fat Stanky Frank looking to get even for being left back at the jail the night of the escape. That might've been a mistake. If Frank wanted, he could tear down the whole building with his brute force.

A denim-clad leg came out of the Monte Carlo. A beat-up cowboy boot with a silver-colored chain around it stepped onto the asphalt. A medium-sized man rose from the car, stood, and looked around for a tail, anyone who might have been following him. After a mo-ment, he started walking toward Muscle Max.

Borkow let out his breath in a long sigh, turned, put his open hand on Lizzette's face, and shoved her hard. "Why didn't you tell me Payaso changed cars?" She stumbled back on the tall heels, re-gained her balance, and came at him with her nails bared, her mouth in an ugly snarl. Borkow shoved back again and socked her full in the face. She went to the floor with a yelp.

He used one finger and eased the curtain open just a hair. The pleasant throb of his knuckles reminded him he was still alive.

Payaso left the car parked in front of the Orchid and came across the lot right toward Borkow's curtained window.

Payaso never flaunted his money, and he had a lot of it—money he'd earned working as Borkow's number two. He wore simple clothes without flashy jewelry and never got a second look from Mr. Johnny

Law. Borkow didn't even know his real name. Payaso, in Mex, meant Clown. This guy was anything but. He was an expert in the South American necktie, a reputation Payaso wasn't afraid to trade on.

Lizzette had gotten up and sauntered across the room, moving away from him as if nothing had happened. Borkow watched her. He knew the little viper well enough to be cautious. He saw her pick up her purse, open it, and stick her hand in.

He said, "Harold?"

A shotgun's sawed-off barrel poked through the doorway into the room. Lizzette froze. Her grimace shifted to a half-smile. She eased her hand back out of the purse. Her stupid little attempt at a liaison with Harold trying to soften him up hadn't worked out the way she'd planned it.

"I'm okay, Louis, really I am," she said. "That was my fault. I should've told you about the car, that he'd changed to a Monte Carlo." With the heel of her hand, she dabbed at the blood that trickled from the corner of her mouth and down her chin. She scowled at the open doorway. Harold had denied her loyalty and had done his job.

The shotgun barrel disappeared.

Borkow walked over, picked up her fallen towel, and wrapped it around his waist. He moved over to Lizzette. She stood up straighter as he drew near and raised her chin in defiance. She pretended to be brave, holding her ground no matter what. He loved her for it. He kissed her on the lips. "I'm sorry. Please don't do that again. This will be your final warning."

Payaso came in the room.

Borkow stepped back from Lizzette and flicked his hands in dismissal.

Lizzette's eyes softened. "Louis, honey, can I keep the shoes, please?" She thought she could play on the injury he'd inflicted, when he socked her, thought he'd have a twinge of guilt over it.

He gave her the stare.

One leg at a time, she brought her foot up and slipped off a shoe, dropping four inches in height. She handed them over. A little sob slipped out. She loved the shoes almost as much as he did. He'd happened onto her stash of shoes purely by accident when she had moved out of the Grand Orchid and refused to tell him where she was staying—avoided the question with, "Here and there. Just couch surfing till I can find someplace I like and can afford." So he'd followed her one night and hot-prowled her apartment in Santa Monica while she was in bed with her lover Twyla. He hadn't told Lizzette he'd found her clandestine place and relationship. He'd never do anything to her—not unless she violated one of his rules— like Stacy had.

"Please leave us," Borkow said.

She hurried over, scooped up her clothes, and fled on bare ugly feet. His eyes tracked her as she left. If she looked back and scowled, he wouldn't be able to trust her ever again. He watched, sorry and angry he'd treated her so poorly. It wasn't his fault that he had to hide out. It made him edgy.

She made it to the door. She hesitated. Her shoulders pulled back. Her head rose a little.

No, don't do it.

Lizzette turned her head and glanced back before she disappeared through the doorway to the other side. Borkow muttered in a half whisper, "Ah, son of a bitch."

"Harold?"

"Yeah, boss."

"I want to talk to her before she leaves."

"You got it, boss."

Borkow turned his attention to Payaso.

CHAPTER TWENTY-FIVE

PAYASO STOOD QUIETLY off to the side, watching by the window curtains.

"Well?" Borkow asked.

"It's just as we thought; they are getting organized. They have already started hitting all the places we thought they would."

"Then why haven't they hit the Orchid?"

"They figured it the most unlikely place to find you so they set a trap. They've had two cars down the street watching. It won't be long now."

"I don't know why they haven't hit the Orchid yet. They should've hit it first. I want to get back in there. Once they hit it, they'll be less likely to come back."

From the other room, Harold said, "Boss, we got visitors."

Borkow hurried over to the window and took up his perch with his head again pressed to the wall as he peeked out the slit. Ten cop cars, half of them unmarked, zoomed in and surrounded the Grand Orchid. Overkill—too many cops for just him. A black Suburban with an entire SWAT team standing on sideboards brought up the rear.

The sight of all those cops raised his heartbeat, made it race. Sweat beaded on his forehead, ran into his eyes, and stung.

Standing there naked with just a towel, the heavily armed and violence-hungry cops outside—not more than thirty or forty feet away—brought out his vulnerability. Yet he couldn't move. He could only watch and imagine what it would feel like if *he* were actually standing in the Grand Orchid watching his violent demise approach. They wouldn't bother with the warning yell "stop, police," even if he stood with his hands in the air; they would gun him down like a dog. The sheriff's department lost a big chunk of respectability when he'd made buffoons out of them. No, they would shoot him on sight.

Could Payaso have set all this up on purpose so Borkow could see just how serious the situation had become? The rude, insensitive bastard.

Payaso wanted Borkow to take off for Costa Rica. Hide out there for a few years while Payaso ran the operation and the heat cooled. Of course he did. If he let Payaso take the helm, he'd never get it back. And one day while lying on the beach sipping a sickening sweet piña colada, some sicario would slip up behind him and slit his throat.

Just as the men dressed in all black—the SWAT team—hurried to line up for a coordinated assault, a cowboy and a big black man dressed like a trucker exited the lead car. The two ran through the perimeter with guns drawn. The cowboy never missed a step. He grabbed a broken brick from the planter and hurled it at the double glass doors.

The door on one side exploded in a million tiny cubes of safety glass that rained down like an ice storm. The black man went in first with the cowboy close on his heels. Their actions, bold and unflinching, made Borkow shiver. Who were these guys?

It had been Payaso's idea to buy the fitness center. What better place to hide than in plain sight in the same strip center as his beautiful Grand Orchid? Once the cops hit the Orchid, and saw that it was shut down, all but abandoned, Borkow could go back and forth from the fitness center to the Orchid with relative ease and not have to worry much about Johnny Law. He'd have a little more freedom, something he craved the most.

"Hey," Borkow whispered to Payaso, "I am familiar enough with their procedure to know that those two who went in first are going to be in the grease for not waiting for the SWAT boys."

Payaso watched from the slit at the other side of the window. "I warned you about this."

Borkow looked away from the window and over at Payaso. "Tell me again."

"You messed with that cop's daughter. Now he's going to come at you with everything he's got until he puts you in the ground."

"What? You mean that big buck dressed like a trucker is the same slug working as a bailiff in the court?"

"He's not just a bailiff, and you're way off-base calling him a slug. That's Bruno Johnson."

"Who the hell is *Bruno Johnson*? You say it with reverence like he's, what, someone I need to be afraid of?"

"I would be, if I were you."

Payaso never talked that way about anyone, not even the vicious Chinese Tong, who, two years earlier, had tried to muscle in on Borkow's chain of massage parlors, demanding ten percent from his operation for protection. Payaso went head to head with the Tong's street soldiers in three bloody battles and eventually beat them back.

Borkow looked through the slit just as Johnson and the cowboy came out holstering their guns. SWAT had waited, and now ready to go, hurried forward. The lead SWAT guy said something to the cowboy, who flipped him the bird and kept walking.

Johnson stopped and hesitated. He looked around, taking in the entire strip mall. His eyes stopped on the defunct Muscle Max across the parking lot.

"*Shit.*" Borkow pulled back from the window. "He just looked this way. Did you see that?"

"That's what I was trying to tell you. This mayate has the instincts of a jungle cat. You should never have poked him like that."

Borkow held his breath and focused on Johnson through the slit. He watched until Johnson lost interest in the fitness center and headed for his car where the cowboy waited.

Borkow let out his breath and waved his hand at Payaso. "Couldn't be helped. We needed the diversion or the jailbreak would never have happened. I wouldn't be standing here otherwise. We'll just have to live with the consequences."

"Don't know if we can."

Borkow left his perch and walked toward Payaso. "You telling me you're afraid of . . . what did you call him . . . this, this mayate?"

"Not for me. I'm just afraid I won't be able to keep him off you if he keeps kicking in doors like that. You just saw how he works. He doesn't give a shit about the rules. Those kinds of cops are the most dangerous. He kicks in enough doors, someone's gonna squeal."

"Then take the offensive. Knock him off his game. We know his Achilles heel. Hit him again where it hurts so he has something else to keep him occupied."

"I wouldn't do that if I were you."

"I don't care what you would do or wouldn't do. Get it done. Get that bailiff's daughter. Now, where are we with my wonderful defense attorney, Ms. Gloria Bleeker?"

CHAPTER TWENTY-SIX

BORKOW TOOK HIS sunglasses from his pocket and put them on even though the moonless night hid everything or it at least turned it to dark shadow. He pointed. "Not here, you bonehead. Don't park here—pull up away from the streetlight." Payaso did and killed the engine. Borkow wore a Dodgers ball cap down low over the glasses and a bulky navy-blue windbreaker to further disguise his shape and size. Hell, in Hollywood everyone dressed like that.

He followed close on Payaso's heels. Payaso moved with deliberation, as if he, too, lived in this spectacular upscale apartment complex on North Bronson, just south of Fountain. He came to a side entrance, a heavy security gate that blocked the long walkway from the street. Payaso didn't slow. In one easy motion, he pulled a six-pound, short-handled sledge from his back waistband and gave the dead bolt lock a long sideways swing. He whacked it with a violence that vibrated in Borkow's teeth. The dead bolt lock shot out the other side and clattered on the concrete. The gate swung open a smidge. Payaso kept moving right on through as if nothing at all had happened to slow him down.

Borkow double-timed to catch up to him and whispered, "Remind me after all this is over how easy that lock was to take out. I'm never going to live in a so-called security apartment, that's for damn sure. Security my aching ass."

"Sssh."

"Don't sssh me. Where we going? How much farther is it?"

Payaso stopped at a crossroads in the walkway and looked in each direction, getting his bearings. He had scouted the location only hours before. He continued without a word. Every apartment was inset and sheltered from view by thick shrubs, hedges, and stunted trees. Payaso chose one and moved through to the small entry area by the front door. He put his ear up to the wood and listened. Borkow went to the right and peered through the window between the curtains and into a slice of light coming from inside. He lifted his dark sunglasses. The big-screen TV was playing an old black-and-white movie with Bette Davis. Now that girl knew how to rock a pair of shoes.

Payaso pulled back the sledge to obliterate the doorknob. Borkow grabbed his arm. "Wait. She's on the phone. The person on the other end will hear us and ruin everything. It'll force us to move fast when I don't want to. Step aside. Yeah, that's it. Move farther back there in the shadows. Now just follow my lead."

Borkow straightened his windbreaker, checked that his hat and sunglasses were in place. He rang the doorbell. A long minute passed. He held his breath. The outside light came on. Behind him the bushes whispered as Payaso slipped back deeper into the shadows.

The curtains parted. Borkow didn't look; he just stared at the door and pretended not to see her. The muffled words "Who are you? What do you want?" made it through the door and outside to him. He shrugged as if he hadn't heard, reached out, and again pushed the button for the doorbell.

The locks on the door clicked. What a fool. Borkow had never heard a sweeter sound. The door swung open ten inches or so, far too wide for a cautious person. And Gloria Bleeker had more than enough reason to be cautious.

Gloria Bleeker, dressed in a gray velour gym suit, had a phone receiver with a long cord pinched between her cheek and shoulder as she spoke. "Yes? Can I help you?"

Borkow smiled. He took off his ball cap and sunglasses. Gloria's mouth dropped open and her eyes widened. She said into the phone, "Claire, honey, I'm going to have to call you right back." She hung up.

"Gloria, are you going to ask me in, or you going to make me stand out here all night where someone could see me?"

"What the hell are you doing here, Louis?"

"I've thought it over and I think the smart move is to turn myself in."

She tentatively stuck her head out and looked around for any other interlopers lurking in ambush. "How did you find out where I live?"

Borkow raised his hands. "Gloooria?"

"Oh. Sure, sure. Come on in. It's real smart that you want to turn yourself in. It's the right thing to do, really. Come on in, and I'll make some quick calls to get it set up."

Borkow waved his hand behind him so Payaso wouldn't follow right away. Borkow stepped in and pulled the door almost closed behind him, leaving it open just a crack.

He sunk into deep white fur carpet, like stepping onto the back of an Angora cat. He looked down at his feet. "How the hell you keep this shit from getting dirty?"

"I keep it clean by making everyone take their shoes off. Take 'em off, Louis."

While he kicked off his shoes, he checked the place out. Her furniture looked uncomfortable, cold and without the least bit of taste; all chrome and glass and black leather, antiseptic as an operating room. The light's reflection off all the white gave him the urge to squint. How pedestrian and sterile. He could never spend so much as an hour in a place like this.

"Are you alone?"

Her expression shifted to fear. "What?"

"Take it easy, Gloria. I just want to be sure there isn't someone here who's going to phone the cops before we're ready to . . . to, you know, surrender. That's the word they use, right? Surrender?" It was hard for him to get that word out. It stuck in his throat like a sideways chicken bone. No way in hell would he ever do something that stupid. Surrender, of all things. He'd leave that for the spineless pussies. He'd never go back. Never.

Gloria relaxed. "Yes, I'm alone except for Nelson. He's in the bedroom."

"Nelson?"

"Yes, he's my—"

Payaso burst in.

CHAPTER TWENTY-SEVEN

"Oh my God." Gloria's hand flew up to her mouth. She took in a deep breath to let out a screech. Payaso stifled half of it with a gut punch. She bent over and lost her dinner, which included an unhealthy portion of red wine that spattered over the white fur carpet in a splash of Technicolor.

Borkow shook his head. "Tsk, tsk, I'm betting that'll be impossible to get out. They're going to have to cut and patch it to make it work. I had that same problem one other time, but it was on Berber and it wasn't red wine." He chuckled at his little wordplay. She coughed and gagged and tried to talk. Attorneys were like sharks: if they quit talking, they sink to the bottom and drown.

Payaso shoved her into a chair and secured her hands and ankles to the arms and legs with gray duct tape.

Bleeker sputtered and choked out the words. "No, Louis . . . don't do this. Please don't . . . do this. I've only tried to help you. I have never done anything to hurt your case. I'm on your side, you have to know that by now. Please, don't do this."

Payaso yanked a cloth napkin off the table, wadded it up, and stuck it in her mouth. He put another piece of tape over it so she couldn't spit it out. The napkin made it difficult for her to breathe.

Her nostrils flared wide with each intake of breath. From the time he punched her to taping her mouth, less than a minute had elapsed.

Borkow hooked his thumb back over his shoulder. "She said there's a dude in her room, named Nelson."

Payaso nodded, pulled out his sledge, and headed for the bedroom.

Borkow moved in close to Gloria. Her eyes bulged larger as he drew near. "*Glooria*, you know what I'm here for, don't you. Just tell me where it is and we'll be on our way, lickety-split."

She shook her head from side to side, her face bloating red.

"Really, you're saying you don't know where the money is? I don't believe you, *Gloooria*."

Gloria Bleeker was one of the best, if not *the best*, homicide defense attorneys in the City of Angels, and initially he couldn't entice her to take his case no matter how much money he tried to tempt her with over the phone. She did agree to an attorney visit and met him alone in the attorney room of MCJ. She'd done her homework. She somehow knew all about his business, how much money it made, and more important, how much he had on hand. She demanded one hundred fifty thousand dollars in cash as a retainer and five hundred dollars an hour if his case went to trial. Then, if she did get him off, she wanted a three-hundred-thousand-dollar bonus. Well, of course it was going to trial. She wanted the money in cash so she could avoid the taxes. In her tax bracket, that would mean another thirty to thirty-five percent bump. At first, he said, "Hell no, bitch," and left her alone at the table to ponder just how much money she'd walked away from. The massage business was all cash, so he did have that kind of green saved, but it would seriously draw down his reserves. Draw them down to damn near zero. But that wasn't the problem— it was the principle of the thing. She had him over a barrel and was sticking it to him. He could not allow her to do that.

Someone must have ratted on him about having that much cash on hand—four hundred fifty K. When he got out, he'd find the disloyal weasel and knock the wheels off his little red wagon.

He needed the best attorney or it wouldn't matter how much cash on hand he had or how much he hated to give in to a woman who lorded over him because of his situation. He finally agreed to the one hundred fifty thousand dollars as a retainer against five hundred dollars an hour and to the bonus. If she got him off, he'd grudgingly give her the three-hundred-thousand-dollar bonus. What price freedom, huh?

At their second meeting, bitter over the deal, he signed the agreement. When he got back to his cell and stretched out on his bunk, the idea of losing that much green gave him a pain in his gut that would never leave.

Payaso came out of the bedroom. "Just about all of it is here, little over a hundred grand. The dumb broad had it in shoeboxes on the closet floor. On the floor, can you believe it? It's the first place a break-in artist would look. She's got some pretty nice shoes, loads of 'em. You want that I take them, too?"

Borkow's mouth dropped open. "You have got to be kidding me. Dumb bitch. Now she's going to tell us what she did with the rest of it—the fifty K. You didn't see where she might've hid the other fifty K, did you?"

Payaso shrugged. "No. But that other dude—Nelson—he is a dog, a puppy, *perro pequeno negro*." He put his hands out in front of him indicating a small size.

"Get all the cash. Put it in a trash bag and, yeah, go ahead and grab up all the shoes while you're at it."

"What about the dog?"

Borkow hated dogs. He put his index finger to his throat and slowly drew it across.

Payaso nodded and disappeared back into the bedroom. A few seconds later a puppy yelped—then stopped.

Borkow leaned over Bleeker and whispered in her ear, "You should never have treated me like I was some kinda clown, Gloooria."

CHAPTER TWENTY-EIGHT

WICKS DROVE THE big Dodge. I stared out the windshield. Just after nine at night, and I should have been home with Olivia. Not being there to see that she was all right, to talk to her about Derek, hollowed out my gut and left me empty. To counter the feeling, to shove it aside, all I needed to do was think about the tape recording of Borkow talking to someone on the street, arranging to put Olivia in danger for the sole purpose of drawing me out of the courtroom. I wanted to tear Borkow apart, make him wish he'd never heard the name Johnson. And I would. He didn't have long to wait before I came up on him, took him by the neck, and squeezed.

He had to be the first priority now.

I rolled down the window to let in the warm summer evening. I couldn't shake the cloying scent that had hung heavy inside the Grand Orchid. Too many perfumed candles and incenses had ended their lives in that place. They lit them in an attempt to mask the lack of hope and despair and hide the odor of the sexually deviant. The sickening sweet odor clung in an invisible sheen, thick as a gel, to the walls and floors and curtains. Now it permeated my clothes and skin. It'd linger there for a day or two as nothing more than an ugly afterthought.

As soon as the glass door came down and I stepped inside, I knew we'd find the place empty. Anyone who could plan such an audacious jail escape was not going to be found that easily. We were going to have to dig him out of his hidey-hole, and it would take a lot more than shoe leather to do it. It'd take a similar cunning, a criminal wit.

At the same time, something niggled at the back of my brain. That feeling only came around when I'd missed something, usually something big. I played back everything we'd done since we left the courthouse, all the houses we'd hit, all the people we shook down, but nothing bubbled up. The Grand Orchid, for some reason, bothered me. Maybe it was the odor. Or maybe it was the many individual rooms with the beds and rumpled towels strewn about, the hidden cameras that captured the multitude of sex acts to be sold on an even broader market. Or the idea of all the women that were needed to run an operation that size. The terrible waste of life. And for what?

No, it was something else. I'd missed something important.

"What are you thinking, big man?"

I didn't answer, just watched the houses zip past in a blur of speed. Everything was bathed in orangish-yellow sodium vapor streetlights that fought back the encroaching darkness, the place where evil lurked. Locked gates and wrought iron on windows and doors buttoned the houses up tight. Some of the yards had oscillating sprinklers working hard to keep the dry summer heat from killing the rest of their lawns, the only evidence of life inside waiting out the dawn.

"Bruno, my friend, you're too wrapped up right now. You got the scent of revenge in your nose and you can't smell anything else. You're running too hot. Back it down a couple of notches and refocus. Think about how we're going to find this little puke. You've got to be able to visualize it."

He knew me like a brother and could read me like a spouse. I missed working with him.

He put his hand on my shoulder and shoved. "Hey, anybody in there? Talk to me, my fine Negro friend. Fire up that brilliant man-hunting brain of yours and let's put this guy on a slab."

"Why don't we pick this up in the morning, all right? Just take me home. We'll get him tomorrow after I've had a good night's sleep."

"Hey, come on now, it's too early to call it a day. You got any ideas at all? 'Cause I'm drawing a big zero here and the clock's tickin'. I have to report to the deputy chief in less than an hour and I better have something for him or he's gonna hand me my ass in a hat."

"Yeah, I've got a few ideas, but I need to get home tonight. I need to talk to Olivia. It's important."

"Didn't you call your dad to look after her pending the outcome of this operation?"

"Don't try and come between me and my daughter, Robby. You'll lose." I never called him by his first name. He didn't like it. He even preferred "Asshole" over his first name.

We drove for a couple of minutes more. His jaw muscles worked as he suppressed his anger. "Okay, I'll take you home. Just tell me what you got in mind. I'll work on it through the night, and if we don't get him by morning, I'll pick you up bright and early."

He was playing me. He knew I wanted to be in on the take-down—*that I had to be in on the takedown.* He was trying to push my buttons, and it was working. I needed to push back.

I looked over at him. "Alienating other members of this department isn't going to help find this guy. You were never like that when we used to run together."

He looked at the road, looked at me, then back at the road. "What the hell are you talking about now?"

"We need to work with, and get along with, the other members of this department."

"Agreed, but I don't know what you're talking about."

"We should've waited for SWAT to clear that building. That's what they were there for."

"You goin' soft on me, big man, is that it? Were you afraid to go in there after a weasely piece of shit like Borkow? He's a skinny little pencil-neck, know-nothin' white boy. How tough can he be?"

"You know better than that. Going in before SWAT made them look like a bunch of idiots. You couldn't leave it at that; you had to go and flip off the team lead."

"What? Oh, no, no. You got that all wrong. It's not what you think. I know the guy. I flipped him off because he wasn't supposed to be going in on that raid in the first place. And he knew it."

"What are you talking about?"

"Lieutenants are supposed to stay at the Incident Command Center and direct the op. When the captain's not around, that cowboy takes the lead. His boys love him for it. That was Lau. He and I went through sergeant's school together. He's a real comer and he's going to be the sheriff one day, you wait and see if he's not. You'd be smart to hook your wagon to that rising star."

"Lieutenant Lau?" I asked, my voice more a croak.

Nicky Rivers' husband.

The Nicky Rivers who I had a thing for. The Nicky Rivers who I'd already kissed too many times and twice more passionately than the others.

When the SWAT team had passed by, I hadn't seen his face well enough to identify him. He'd had his goggles on and his balaclava covering his head under a Kevlar helmet. I didn't know how Wicks could identify him well enough to flip him the bird. Maybe it was Lau's voice when he called us assholes, uttered with complete contempt as he went by on our way out of the Grand Orchid.

"You okay, partner?" Wicks asked. "You look like you just ate a bad taco or something."

"Yeah, you're right, my stomach's a little sour."

"I'll drop you off and pick you up in the morning. We'll get an early start, say oh-dark-thirty. Now tell me what you got."

"What?" My mind had shifted from Olivia to Nicky and then to Lieutenant Lau. I had inadvertently got myself into a real mess. But it wasn't too late to extricate myself, and, hopefully, without anyone finding out. If the department at large somehow got wind of my indiscretion, it would compound the problem tenfold.

"Come on, gimme your best ideas about how to take down this puke."

"Alright. Listen, I ... ah. You remember that place over in Torrance, right on the border of Hawthorne? The one we hit when we were looking for T-Dog—you know—Roy McKinney?"

"No, I don't. But keep talking."

"A massage parlor that belongs to Borkow over off Hawthorne Boulevard, where McKinney used to go to get a rub-and-tug. You remember, the Willow Tree."

"Okay, we hit that one already today. Zero. Zip. And?"

"Back then there was a woman working there. I remembered her when we were in there today looking for Borkow."

"Buddy boy, all they got working in massage parlors are women. You're gonna have to gimme a little more."

"You going to smart off or do you want to hear this?"

He chuckled. "Yeah, go ahead."

"When we were looking for T-Dog, we talked to everyone in the place. We pulled them all aside and talked to them individually."

"Okay, I remember that. And?"

His eyes diffused as his mind worked on another problem, probably trying to remember the event I described.

"This one girl wore a real nice pair of pumps."

Wicks snapped his fingers. "That's right, now I know the T-Dog you're talking about. He was an Avalon Gangster Crip, who'd gunned his two nephews over a half pound of coke. We got him on 133rd east of Wilmington. You took down that door hard. Old T-Dog was sleepin' on the couch, and he jumped straight up into the air like a cat with a firecracker up its ass." Wicks laughed. "I remember how big his eyes got, huge. He was so scared he crapped himself."

"That's him."

"He's doin' time now and he's never gonna get out. How's he gonna help find Borkow if he's in the joint?"

"No, you missed what I'm saying here. The girl, she was wearing a pair of shoes worth two or three grand."

Wicks looked over at me and smiled. "I gotcha. You're saying girls in massage parlors don't wear shoes like that. So she has to be one of Borkow's Ho Chi mamas."

"Exactly."

"Yeah." Wicks shook his head. "But if she is one of his special girls, and she does happen to know where Borkow is laying his head, he has to trust her a lot. She isn't going to just flip and talk to us. We're gonna need a twist on her."

"Or?"

"Or what?"

"We can get a wiretap on her place and—"

He snapped his fingers again. "And tickle the wire."

I nodded and smiled.

"That's brilliant. It's going to be a lot of bullshit paperwork, but that's truly a brilliant idea. Especially since we got nothing else. What's the name of this broad?"

"Her name's not an easy one to forget. It's Lizzette."

CHAPTER TWENTY-NINE

WICKS PULLED UP and stopped in front of my apartment complex. He double-parked with the engine at a low rumble. "Talk to your daughter; get all that shit straightened out so you can have a clear head in the morning. We'll get this guy tomorrow."

I opened my door and stuck my leg out. "I wish it were that easy. I mean about talking to O."

"It is, buddy boy. An obstinate woman just needs a good slap on the ass and made to understand that, in no uncertain terms, you're the boss." He moved the flat of his hand in a lurid wave as if slapping a woman's rump. He could be a real pig at times. He realized that he was talking about my daughter.

"Wait, you know I'm not talking about Olivia here, right? I meant women in general."

"Is that right? So I should ask your wife, Barbara, if that's how it really works? See what she thinks of your theory?"

He smiled. "Whoa there, cowboy. Barbara doesn't qualify under the *every other woman* standard. You know that. She'd burn us both down if you were dumb enough to tell her what I just said. And I know you're not that dumb. You're not, right partner?"

I smiled. "That's the only intelligent thing you've said all night."

The door to a car parked at the curb two cars away opened and drew our attention. How could we have missed an occupied vehicle so close?

Out stepped a long, beautiful leg. We silently watched. The leg turned into a sleek woman wearing a pencil skirt and a pair of nice heels.

I recognized her lovely face.

I muttered under my breath, "Ah, shit."

"Hey," Wicks said. "Isn't that Nicky—" His head whipped around. His eyes glared at me. "Tell me it ain't so."

Words fled my brain. I didn't know how to begin to explain, to make him understand.

"This is absolute bullshit, Bruno, and you know it."

"It's not what you think."

"Oh, it's not? It's nine thirty at night, pal." He jabbed his finger toward the windshield. "She's parked in front of your apartment. Go on, tell me again it's not what I think. Get the hell out of my car. To think I was buying that bullshit about you wanting to talk to your daughter."

"Let me explain."

"I said get out."

I did as he asked. I leaned in. "See you in the morning, then?"

He took off with a chirp of the tires. The momentum closed the door. He dodged around Nicky and gunned the car down the street. She watched it for a second, then walked toward me. "Was that Robby Wicks?"

"Yeah, and he's not happy. He's friends with your husband."

She looked uncomfortable. "I know."

"What are you doing here?"

She reached out and took my hand. "I'd tell you that I was worried about you . . . and I am. But really, it's just that I don't have the trial to think about anymore and, well, Bruno, I kinda got lonely."

I stood there stunned, still trying to accept how things had spun out of control so quickly. In the space of two minutes, life had complicated tenfold. A beautiful and smart woman, whom I wanted, stood in front of me and I couldn't have her.

When I didn't reply and immediately return her romantic sentiment, she said, "I'm sorry, I didn't mean to get you in a jam with Wicks. I had no idea he'd be dropping you off. Your truck's not here, and I thought you'd be alone when you did show up." She paused in the uncomfortable silence. "Maybe I should go."

I didn't release her hand, just pulled her in close and hugged her. I put my head down in her hair. She smelled wonderful. I held her tight, not wanting to say the words that needed to be said.

We can't see each other anymore.

She struggled a little and pulled her head back to look into my eyes. The pang in my chest that had been there since the night before when we kissed in the front seat of my truck grew larger.

"I filed the papers today. He'll be served tomorrow at eight thirty at his office. I would've had it done tonight, but he was out on some operation."

"Oh, man," I said.

"What?"

I said nothing and looked down the street where Wicks had driven off.

She followed my gaze and turned back to me. "Oh, no. You're right. If Wicks talks to my husband, he'll think the papers are because of us, that I did it because of us. That's not true, Bruno. I told you that. You know the truth, right?"

The words "my husband" pinged around in my head.

Her concerned expression shifted to an unsure, nervous smile. "What the hell. What's done is done. We can't do anything about it now, right?"

She wanted me to tell her that everything was all right when it wasn't. I needed to walk away—had to walk away. It was the only logical thing to do. But right there, in the moment, logical didn't matter; it didn't seem real. What I wanted most was to kiss her again, to make sure that same feeling was still there.

I did. I pulled her in tight, kissed her. She relaxed in my arms and went with it. Nothing had changed—the same passion was there.

Maybe Dad was right about women and love. You couldn't fight it. You just had to go with it and hope when you tumbled out the other end, you weren't too bruised and broken.

And, in the end, it did have the absolute ability to start a war.

Still in my arms, she swayed a little on her heels and shivered.

We stared at each other.

I tried to think how long it had been since I'd shared anything with a woman. Two years, maybe more.

She leaned in closer, put her arms around my neck, and rested her head on my chest. When she spoke, I could hardly hear her. "Bruno, how long are we going to stand out here?"

She sounded as scared as I was about starting a relationship.

Then I thought about her husband. How, for many years working patrol, I had responded to domestic calls arising out of love triangles, how easily they could turn violent and even deadly.

My head nodded, but my mind said, *No, no, no. Don't. Run away. Run away.* I took her hand, and we walked up to the apartment.

At the door I stopped and fumbled, trying to pull the key from my pocket. "What do you think your husband will do if Wicks tells him?"

With a serious expression she said, "I wouldn't want to be you. He's one tough son of a bitch with a mean-assed temper."

"Really, are you kidding me?"

She shrugged, still solemn. "No sense crying over spilt milk, right?"

CHAPTER THIRTY

I GOT THE keys sorted out. Stuck the right one in the lock and froze. I put my forehead to the door and closed my eyes. What the hell was I doing? Everything in my heart and soul said this was right—that this was what I needed—what I had to have. And yet the rational side of my brain called me a damn fool and ordered me to walk away.

"What's the matter, Bruno? Come on, hurry up." Her voice a husky whisper. How did women turn that voice on and off like that at just the right moments?

"I'm sorry, I can't." I turned around to face her.

"What's the matter?" She moved in close, her warm breath on my chin.

I moved her back a little, afraid I'd lose my resolve. "I . . . I got too much going on, right now. Maybe we can . . . you know, later on, after I get this thing with my daughter straightened out. And it's also not a good time because this case with Borkow is going to keep me running hard for the next couple of weeks until we bring him down."

What was I saying? I fought the urge to bring a knuckle up and bite down hard so the pain could help clear away the needy lust and desire that pulled on me like a tractor beam.

She opened her mouth in shock. I guess she wasn't used to being turned away. She recovered, her eyes narrowed. She shook her head. "No, that's not it."

"What are you talking about?"

"This isn't about your daughter."

I straightened up, trying for indignant and failing. "What? Of course it is."

"No, it's not. This is about that damn *code*, isn't it?"

"The *code*?" I tried to play dumb. But she'd hit it exactly right. She'd read me like a book. I liked her even more for it.

"It's that macho, make-believe code you have for your bullshit boys' club. I know you're not afraid of him. I know you, Bruno Johnson. Like everyone else, I've heard all the stories. You're not afraid of the devil himself. No, it's that damn code, all right. That stupid, ridiculous code that says one brother cop can't go out with another brother cop's woman. Even if they're separated, even if they're divorced." Her voice went up a little. "That's it, isn't it? Shame on you. I thought you were braver than that."

Behind her, a voice broke in. "Uh, excuse me."

I looked over Nicky's shoulder as Nicky turned around. Olivia came up on the walkway, approaching the apartment from the street. She looked distressed.

Out on the street, a car had come up and stopped right out front. I'd missed it. Street survival goes out the window when you kiss a beautiful woman. I bet a lot of cavemen got eaten by dinosaurs from the same phenomenon. In the car, Dad bumped the horn twice and drove off.

What the hell could Dad be thinking with me kissing a woman on the front walkway when I'd told him I had to work? And with Olivia in such a mess? I'd explain it to him in the morning. I was doing a lot of that lately.

Nicky walked away from me, stopped, and took Olivia's hand. "If you ever want to talk?"

Olivia looked at her like she didn't understand. Nicky kept going toward the street. With each step the emptiness inside me grew larger.

Olivia came toward me, her arms out. I took her in a hug. I couldn't watch Nicky leave and pay close attention to my daughter. I'd hurt Nicky and wanted more time to explain it to her. With a little more time, I could make her understand.

"What's the matter, kiddo?"

She said nothing and just held on as if I were a life preserver. I'd easily pay a million bucks to be her life preserver, full-time. What a feeling to be needed in such a way. I held on tight, shifted her around, and unlocked the door. Her hair smelled of cigarette smoke.

I turned the light on inside and closed and locked the door. She broke away and faced me. "Popi, I . . . Popi . . ."

"What is it?"

"I need your help."

She had her mother's green eyes and my skin, only not as dark, more of a light mocha. In another few years she'd move from beautiful to absolutely gorgeous. Then what would I do about all the boys? With her brains and good looks, she could go anywhere and do anything.

"What is it, kid? What can I do?"

"I know you're going to think I'm crazy for asking you of all people, but I know how good you are at your job."

"What's the matter? What's happened?"

"If you do this for me, I'll never ask anything of you ever again."

"Tell me."

"Derek's gone. I can't find him anyplace. Can you find Derek for me, please, Popi?"

Her words hit the same as if someone kicked me in the stomach. I should've known, should've seen it coming. I could only nod. I moved to the kitchen to get some milk to cool my soured stomach. To give me some time to recover, to think of what I'd say. Which truth I would use. An omission was the same as a lie. I'd always told her the truth and insisted that she do the same. To tell her the truth about what I'd done with Derek would wreck our already tenuous relationship. Wreck it for good. I'd made a huge mistake with no way out.

"Popi?"

I took a glass down from the cupboard and went to the refrigerator for the carton of milk. I poured half a glass. I moved over to the table and sat down still at a total loss as to what to do. What to tell her.

Stall.

"Tell me what's happened." I took a drink.

She sat in the chair next to mine and took my hand in hers. "He was supposed to meet me after school today. He never showed up. I called his house and no one answered. And when his auntie finally did answer, she said she hasn't seen him. I'm scared, Popi. He's never done anything like this."

I hated the little bastard even more for putting me in such a bind with my daughter, for putting that kind of hurt in her expression.

I looked into her eyes, now filled with tears.

"Popi, please?"

"He's a seventeen-year-old kid. He's just out on his own somewhere probably trying to . . . you know, find himself. If he doesn't turn up on his own in the next couple days, I'll go find him."

"Really? You will? You promise?"

I nodded.

"Why can't you go find him right now? Please?"

"You have to trust me." Those words came hard. "He'll turn up all on his own, I promise." If she found out, if Derek came back and told her what I'd done, how could she ever trust me again?

She got up and sat in my lap. She put her arm around my neck and hugged me. Her tears mixed with mine, warmed and wet my cheek.

Her outward display of love was something I'd recently missed and yearned for. I wanted to revel in it. Instead I lowered my head in shame like the dirty dog that I had become.

CHAPTER THIRTY-ONE

HOURS LATER AN annoying car horn drew me to the front door with sleep heavy in my eyes. I checked the clock on the wall. Two in the morning. I had tossed and turned and finally fell asleep around midnight. I peeked out the edge of the curtains without disturbing them.

Wicks sat in his black Dodge in the middle of the street. After our confrontation over my violating the unwritten rule, he would've sought out the closest bar. He'd have tried to find the answer at the bottom of a whiskey bottle as to why I'd embarrassed him by stepping out with Lau's wife. He'd be piss-drunk and surly by now, a physical and mental state I did not want to confront.

He laid on the horn again. He wanted me to come outside so he could berate me.

Olivia came from her room rubbing her eyes. "What's with the noise?" She suddenly came awake. "Is it Derek? Is that Derek out there?"

I stopped her when she rushed toward the front window. "No, baby, go on back to bed. It's just my boss, Lieutenant Wicks. Go on back to bed. I'll go out and talk to him."

"You sure it's not Derek?"

"Yes, I'm sure. Go on now." I waited until she'd gone back into her room and closed the door. I unlocked the front door, froze, relocked it, and went for my gun. I'd shucked on a pair of pants and now stuck the gun in my back waistband. Over the years I'd come to subscribe to the main precept in the Robby Wicks School of Violence: *You never needed a handgun until you really needed a handgun.*

The car horn again tatted out an ugly beat. The black Dodge, with its tinted windows, took on the persona of a hungry beast waiting for a chunk of meat to be tossed to it.

Outside, the heat had come down a little and it was probably close to eighty without a breath of wind. I padded out to the sidewalk in bare feet. Cars packed the street so Wicks had double-parked. The tint on the windows wouldn't allow me to see inside. I got closer and held my ground at fifteen feet away. I held up my hands and shrugged. I wasn't going give in and open the passenger door or come around to the driver's-side window. If he wanted to talk, he could get out and come to me, like a normal human—like a friend.

He honked again. What a horse's ass.

I didn't move.

Finally, he leaned over in the seat and struggled to get the window down on the passenger side. "Get in the car, asshole."

"Why?"

"We gotta roll. Get in the car, now."

"I can't leave Olivia by herself."

"There's been a killing. The shit's hit the fan. Get your ass in the car now."

I turned and ran yelling over my shoulder. "I'll call my dad and be right out."

He hit the horn again and held a long blaring bleat. A neighbor opened his door and yelled, "Knock it off or I'll call the police."

Wicks yelled back, "I am the police, asshole."

Inside, I hurried to my room, got dressed and properly armed. I knocked on Olivia's door. "I have to go out. I'm going to call your grandfather to come over."

She spoke through the door. "You don't have to do that. I'm fifteen, Bruno. Quit treating me like a child."

It went against what I thought best, but I'd been using my dad too often lately. And deep down, I really didn't want him to know I was going out so late at night. Shamed that I had returned to shirking family obligations. "Okay, but you stay here, and in the morning go right to school and come right home. You understand?"

She opened her door dressed in the robe I'd bought her last Christmas. She smiled. "Thank you, Popi. You go on now, and make the street safe for white women and children."

She knew that little statement grated on my nerves. Three years ago, she'd heard Wicks use it at one of his backyard barbecues. I pulled him aside at the time, and yet again, told him I didn't want my daughter exposed to that kind of talk . . . that kind of world. He'd waved it off, half-drunk. He controlled his language the rest of the afternoon. I didn't think Olivia had heard it until she used it a few months later when she was angry over me staying out three days straight while running hard on the violent crimes team, chasing a trigger-happy shooter. Overtired and run-down, I'd yelled at her. She'd cringed and started crying. I had never yelled at my daughter before. The unfortunate event was the one that precipitated my transfer to court services.

"You know I don't like to hear that kind of talk. If you're trying to show me you're old enough to stay home on your own, you just earned a mark against it."

She put her hand on mine. I don't know how she did it, but she made her eyes bigger and more vulnerable. "I'm sorry, I was just being funny. I'm tired. I haven't slept much because Derek's gone. Really, go on, I'll be all right."

She had met Derek when I wasn't there to oversee her life. This time I wasn't out chasing the evil that walked the streets but instead working day shift in the courts. I had missed an important window of opportunity to stop the blossoming love at its root. Insidious evil came in many different sizes and packages. Even so, still, my fault.

She said she'd gone to the park to read a book, Ayn Rand, *Atlas Shrugged*, a pretty heavy read for a fifteen-year-old. A basketball from the nearby court bounced over, rolled, and hit her foot where she sat on a picnic bench. The way she told it, she was enthralled in Ayn's words and put her foot on the ball to keep it from moving. Someone came over, took the ball out from under her foot, and stood there until she looked up. She said, "And that was it. I knew we were meant to be together."

As a father, I had the right to suspect that Derek Sams had rolled the ball over on purpose for no other reason than to talk to her.

I kissed her forehead. "Thank you. I'll see you tonight, okay?"

We still hadn't had the in-depth talk about sex and boyfriends . . . or the damning truth about what I'd done with Derek. I knew I shouldn't put it off. It was like taking a tablespoon of bad-tasting medicine that would burn all the way down and never stop burning afterward. I just didn't want to do it and would subconsciously put it off as long as I could.

I got in the Dodge and closed the door. The reek of bourbon filled the air. Wicks gunned the car. The acceleration shoved me back in the seat.

"You're gonna pile this thing up, then what are you going to do?"

He finally took his eyes from the road to look at me. In the strobe of the streetlights the skin of his face sagged more than I remembered. Age had not been kind. Why would it? He lived life as if every minute could be his last. Or at least that's how it seemed.

"What are you saying, that you want to drive?"

"Yeah, that's exactly what I'm saying. I don't have a death wish. I still have a family to think about."

He yanked hard on the wheel and steered the car almost to the curb. He shoved it in park and bailed out. He came around the front in the white blaze of the headlights. I slid over and took the wheel. He got in and slammed his door.

I put it in drive and pulled away. "Where to?"

He shooed me with his hand. "North, just head north up to the 101." He put his hand into his suit coat pocket and took out a silver flask. He opened it, put it to his lips, and tilted it back.

I reached over and snatched it out of his hand.

"What the hell?" He grabbed at it.

I tossed it in the back seat. "If you're watching my back, I need you sober. Well, as sober as possible, anyway."

"Watch your back? Like you're watching Lau's back?"

"We going to do this now?"

"As good a time as any." He poked my shoulder with a finger. "Lau's a friend of mine. Just like you used to be, buddy boy."

"I'm still your friend."

He shook his head. "No. No, you're not. Not after doing that. No."

"What did I do?"

"No, I'm not going to ... No." He turned and looked out the windshield and said nothing. His head swayed a little in his drunken stupor.

We drove on for a couple more miles.

Finally, I said, "You going to tell me what's going on? Where are we going?"

"Just drive, asshole, I'll tell you where to turn. Take Alameda up to the 10 freeway to the 101."

I did as he asked and just drove.

CHAPTER THIRTY-TWO

OFFICIAL POLICE BARRICADES blocked the dark street. A slick-sleeve rookie redirected the idiot drivers who still pulled up expecting to get through. I double-parked alongside a black-and-white LAPD cruiser, and what looked like a plain maroon detective's car. I got out and tried to keep up with Wicks. He quick-walked toward the upscale apartment complex, his gait steady and unimpaired by the alcohol. I didn't know how he did it.

"You going to tell me what we're doing here?"

He said nothing. Kept walking. He took out his flat badge wallet and flashed the crime scene security officer. He told the officer our names. The officer logged in everyone who entered the scene with the date and time. At the door to the apartment, we stopped and put on disposable booties and latex gloves. Inside, lights burned like a noonday sun. I had to squint when I stepped across the threshold. Too much brightness reflected off all the white carpet and chrome.

My eyes adjusted to the light. I brought my arm down. The place smelled of sour throw-up and warm metallic iron juxtaposed with a hint of sweet plumeria.

"Hey," Wicks said. "Watch where you're stepping with those size-sixteen Bozo shoes." He put his hand on my chest to stop me from taking a step that would've tainted the crime scene. I froze and looked down at the mess on the carpet. For a second it looked like blood with bits of human tissue, stark against the white fur carpet. Then I realized the source of the foul odor. Some unfortunate soul had lost his dinner.

I scanned the room and stopped at the chrome-framed pictures on the wall. They depicted two women nicely dressed at various events with high-powered city and state government officials. I took a closer look. I knew her, Gloria Bleeker.

"Ah, shit," I whispered. "This is all about Louis Borkow, isn't it? That dirty son of a—"

Of course it was. Why else would we be there?

Wicks stopped advancing deeper into the room and looked back. "Yeah, it's a real pisser, ain't it? One from the other team got taken off the roster." He moved on to the kitchen. "Come on, she's in here."

I didn't know if he referred to his homophobia or because she was a defense attorney.

I didn't need to see another body. I'd seen enough to last ten lifetimes. On lonely nights, even after two years in court services, they continued to parade across my dreams and with nonverbal communication that asked, *"Why me, why did I have to die? Why are you still alive and I'm not?"* I didn't have that answer for them and never would.

Unlike Wicks, I considered Gloria a friend. I wanted to remember her the way I'd seen her last.

Wicks had brought me along for a reason, to see the heinous work of Louis Borkow. He wanted to keep me angry, keep the blood spoor in my nose, a coach preparing his player for the game with a visual pep talk. What an inconsiderate ass. I didn't want to work with him anymore. He'd changed too much.

Or maybe I had.

My feet continued to move and follow him into the kitchen, where forensic techs shifted around to different positions to take photos and measurements.

I stole one quick glance at Gloria and looked away. In the past I would examine every part of the victim and try to imagine what they were like while a living, breathing human, what they were like before the violence and mayhem snuffed out their life. In this case I already knew.

Poor Gloria.

I didn't want that anger Wicks tried to evoke. I got an eyefull anyway.

Borkow had used something heavy and blunt to cave in Gloria's forehead—right in the center. The depression malformed her face, made her a mere caricature of the Gloria I had once known.

In that quick glance, my mind took a snapshot that would stay with me forever. Her eyelids were tented, revealing only half of her pupils and the whites of her eyes. Her mouth hung open and her purple-pink tongue lolled out. She'd been gagged at one point, and a napkin with a strip of duct tape hung from the side of her cheek. Borkow had wanted her to tell him something important that she'd refused him. He'd used pliers on her as a form of inducement. She sat in the chair half-naked, her breasts exposed and bloodied.

I looked away, shamed at my friend's naked vulnerability. I tried to remember happier times, the lunches we'd had together at outside restaurants on warm summer days. Her smile, that spark in her eyes, the lilt in her voice, all of that gone now, stolen by a true waste of skin, someone who needed to be escorted off this earth in the most violent manner possible. As Wicks would put it, with a little *blood and bone.* I agreed with him at least on that point.

No one was going to beat me to it, not this time. Wicks would have to climb over me to get to Borkow first. Wicks had gotten out of me what he came for.

In a semi-daze, I backed out of the kitchen as Wicks' pager went off. I could still see his back. He pointed to the phone. "You guys already dust this? Is it okay to use?" Someone told him to go ahead.

I moved into the living room and looked at the pictures on the wall, trying hard to replace the image of the Gloria I'd seen in the kitchen strapped to that chair with her waxy pale skin and depressed forehead that dipped in a V down between her eyes.

She hadn't taken down the photos of her and her life partner, Delilah, a blond, blue-eyed beauty. They had been together for fifteen years but separated a couple of years back. At the time, Gloria had been devastated, and I didn't think she'd ever get over it. I understood the loss of love. I'd lost Sonya for an illogical reason. I understood how it had happened but couldn't fathom, no matter how hard I tried, why it couldn't be fixed, with reason and logic in a conversation between two mature adults.

I had tracked Delilah down and tried to talk some sense into her, but she'd have none of it. She'd already moved on to another relationship. I didn't understand how that could happen so fast. If you loved someone, you loved them for an eternity.

Wicks slammed the phone down and turned to face me, his eyes angry. "Well, that about tears it."

"What?"

He didn't answer. His eyes stared off at nothing as he tried to work the problem just handed to him by the other party on the phone. Based on his anger, it was most likely the deputy chief. In his own mind, Wicks was working the options for any possible wiggle room. I'd seen him do it too many times in the past. His solution would usually mean a deviation from protocol, policy, or worse, the law.

A detective came down the hallway carrying a black ball of fur. "Look at this. Someone dropped this pup in the clothes hamper in the bathroom. Poor little guy's scared half to death."

I craved a distraction and took the puppy from the man. The dog climbed my chest and licked my face. Even under the terrible circumstances, I couldn't help it. I smiled. Puppies can do that to you.

Wicks walked by and let his shoulder bump into me on purpose.

I followed. "Hey, you want to tangle. I'm ready. In fact, I'd be happy to oblige you."

Once outside the front door, he stopped and turned.

"What is it? Tell me." I asked.

"You're officially off the case."

"What the hell? How can that be?"

He spun on his heel and took off for his car. I hurried to catch up. The black puppy kept his moist, warm nose right up by my neck as he snuffled and licked.

Wicks said over his shoulder, "You can't have that dog. It doesn't belong to you. You'll have to turn it over to Animal Control."

"What's going on? What's happened? How can they take me off the case?"

He stopped dead and turned. I almost ran into him.

He pulled his suit coat back and put his hands on his hips like he did when he readied for a speech, or to lecture an errant student who'd just made a near-fatal mistake on the street. "You've been reassigned."

"What? To where?" But I knew. Someone had found out about the thing with Nicky. Now I had just caught a midnight transfer back to the jail where I'd spend the rest of my career in a dimly lit cave filled with animals.

"Here's a bit of irony for you. You like irony, don't you, Bruno?"

"Just tell me."

"You've been reassigned to protect someone."

"Come on, what are you talking about? Who?"

"Who do you think? Nicky Lau."

CHAPTER THIRTY-THREE

Wicks took off for the car without further explanation. The puppy struggled and whined as I hurried after him. Wicks tried to put the key in the driver's-side door.

"No, give me those." With one hand, I took the keys and held the puppy in my other arm. Wicks hesitated, glaring at me. For a moment, I thought he might take a swing. He finally moved around to the passenger side. I reached over, unlocked the door for him, and he got in. I started up, juggling the puppy, trying to keep him corralled on my side of the seat. I suddenly caught a hint, a faint cold fear that Wicks, in his anger at me, might grab the puppy and toss him out the window of the moving car. The notion passed, and I was angry that I'd think such a thing.

"You're worried about me drinking and driving? That little shitass dog's going to get us both killed. You wait and see if he doesn't."

"Tell me. What's going on? Why have I been reassigned to watch Nicky?"

He ignored the question and went back to staring out the window. The puppy settled down with his head on my leg and went to sleep on his side with his belly exposed as if he feared nothing and no one. Under the circumstances, his warmth and the rise and fall of his little chest were a welcome comfort.

I headed back the way we came, taking the same streets in reverse. I hit Sunset and took it west. Sunset Boulevard never slept. People prowled both sides of the street: hookers, drug users, and lost souls, all of them looking for something, Johns or an easy mark to clip or for a place in this world they'd never find. Cars slowed down to cruise as they watched the people on the sidewalks, everyone waiting for something to happen—to light off. And LAPD watched over them all. At dawn that wave of misguided humanity would recede and sleep until the sun set and the moon once again rose to start it all over.

"Why have I been reassigned to protect Nicky Rivers?"

Wicks wouldn't look at me. He reached over and gently stroked the dog's soft fur. "This guy's going to be a monster. Look at the size of his paws. I've never seen paws this big on such a little guy. You going to keep him? Does your apartment allow you to have pets? You better let me take him."

I didn't answer. I drove on into the predawn morning again, a little angry for even thinking Wicks would toss a helpless puppy out of a moving vehicle. I got on the 101 headed south. Wicks went back to staring out the window.

He said, "You don't want him, I'll take him."

"I'm keeping him."

"All right, take it easy. What are you going to name him?"

"I haven't gotten that far yet."

"Bruiser. That's a good name for him. He's going to be a huge dog."

"He's my dog, though."

Wicks nodded as if he understood and again went silent.

After a few more miles he spoke, this time without malice. "You and her, you do the ugly yet?"

"What? No, of course not. I told you it's not like that."

He looked over at me, his face in shadow. "Don't give me that holier-than-thou shit. Like I'm supposed to know how far you've gone with her."

"I said *no*. You have my word on that."

"Like that means a lot after what you've done."

"I . . . never mind."

We again drove in silence.

"You really didn't know?" he asked.

"It's my fault. I never put it together. Her name, I mean. I didn't do it on purpose. You know me better than that. There's nothing underhanded or dirty about it. I'm just a fool for not asking, that's all."

"How many women you know named Nicky? Not a helluva lot. I can damn well guarantee that much." He went silent for a moment. "I tried to get the chief to assign you to Connors—he needs protection as well. But the chief said Connors nixed that idea. Connors told the chief, and I quote, 'I hope Borkow, that little son of a bitch, does take a run at me. I'll blow him right out of his designer kicks.'"

"Yeah, Connors would say something like that. Don't get many judges like him anymore."

"Now," Wicks said, "the chief wants me to put the fox in the henhouse."

"That's not fair, Robby. You do know that they're separated, right?"

"Not till day before yesterday, they weren't. Lau said he never saw it coming. Blindsided him like a gut punch."

"What?" My foot involuntarily eased off the gas pedal. The car slowed a bit on the freeway. "That's not what she told me, I swear, Robby. I'm not kidding. After I found out who she was, she told me they were separated. That they'd been separated for months." The memory of her in my arms, of that last kiss, returned. She'd felt so real—like we belonged together. Maybe I'd been too long without feminine comfort, and I misinterpreted those feelings. Or maybe we were just meant to be together and it really was the lasting kind of chemistry that I shouldn't spurn.

"Yeah, right," he said sarcastically. "And don't call me 'Robby.' From now on I'm 'Lieutenant' to you."

I sped up again and muttered, "Oh, man."

"What?"

"She said she's having him served with papers this morning at 0830, at his office."

"Are you kidding me?" He raised his voice, angry again. "You know what? Don't even talk to me, okay?" He shook his head. "Son of a bitch, how could you have screwed this up so bad?"

"I can't be on her protection detail, not after what's happened."

He said nothing.

"Lieutenant, you have to do something about this."

"You put me right in the middle, buddy boy. The chief and that whole brain trust at the top of the food chain think there's a good chance Bleeker was only the beginning, and that Borkow's going after Nicky and the judge next. The idea being that if we ever do catch up to Borkow and take him into custody, everyone will think twice about taking him to court, including the jury. We'd never be able to find a jury to convict him.

"This is a public relations nightmare. The chief wants the violent crimes team pulled from the chase and put on Nicky and the judge. He said we can't afford another murder. I told him I wanted someone else on Nicky. But he insisted on the best. And guess what, buddy boy, he thinks you're best. I don't know where the hell he got that lamebrain idea. So, short of going to the chief and telling him that you've been playing patty-cake with a lieutenant's wife, you got the job. All I got to say is that you better not screw this up any more than you already have or both our heads are going to be on the chopping block. Now leave me alone and drive."

He scooted down in his seat and closed his eyes. In a few minutes he started to snore. Part of his hunter mentality allowed him to turn off everything in his world and grab some sleep wherever it came available. I wished I could do that.

Let him sleep. I needed the solitude. I had plenty to think about.

Especially the way Nicky had lied to me and why she'd felt the need.

CHAPTER THIRTY-FOUR

I PULLED UP and stopped in front of my apartment. I'd need my truck to go over to Nicky's to be mobile if anything did happen. I looked over at the front door of our apartment and hoped like hell Olivia was still in there and that she hadn't gone out looking for Derek.

Without the motion of the car, the puppy roused and raised his head, ready to play. He jumped up and started licking my face, his paws on my chest. The young and the innocent always gave unconditional love without strings attached. I picked him up and nudged him over to Wicks. The puppy did the same for him and licked his face.

"Hey. Hey, what the?"

He moved to knock the puppy away, but I grabbed it before he could. "You okay to drive now?"

"Sure. I was okay before." He wiped the puppy slobber off with the back of his hand. "Now get out."

"What's the status of the wiretap on Lizzette?"

He fumbled with the door handle and stopped. He looked over at me. "That's no longer any of your concern. You're on babysitting duty, remember? After which you can go back to your nice, safe courtroom and hide out for the rest of your career."

He really did know how to push my buttons. "Did you find Lizzette or not?"

"No. I have someone watching her pad in Santa Monica, but the landlady said she hasn't been there in going on three weeks. So that's a dead end. You have any other bright ideas?"

"No, I'm just the babysitter, remember?"

He clenched his jaw, grabbed the door handle, opened the door, and rolled out. I juggled the puppy and got out on my side, leaving the door open and the car running.

He came around the front of the car, his hair mussed and his eyes bloodshot and heavy with sleep. I shouldn't have talked to him like that. We'd had a lot of good times together, and he'd pulled my cookies out of the fire more than once. And I had returned those same favors in kind. I'd been the one in the wrong, stepping out with Nicky, and my ignorance was no excuse.

I stood in the open door of the car.

"Well, you gonna move?"

I held out my hand as a peace offering. "I just want to say I'm sorry."

"Yeah, yeah, tell it to your priest."

I let my hand drop. "Can you please give me Nicky's address?"

He froze. His mouth sagged open. After a second, he recovered and wagged his finger at me. "Nice try. You're telling me you've been laying the pipe to her and you don't know where she lives? No way, I'm not buying it."

"Really, I'm telling you, I don't know."

"Then if that's the case, you're a detective, you figure it out." He nudged me out of the way, got in, and took off. I watched the red taillights until they made the turn at the end of the street. I didn't know how I was going to make him understand, how I'd make him believe that nothing physical had happened between me and Nicky, or that I really hadn't known that she was married to Lau.

I unlocked the door to the apartment and found the kitchen casting light into the darkened living room. Olivia lay curled up on the couch sleeping with an afghan covering her. She used to always wait up for me sleeping on the couch. Sometimes though, when chasing a murderer, I didn't come home for days at a time. I never realized until that moment what it must've been like for her. I'd been an insensitive fool.

I set the puppy down. He jumped up on my legs, wanting to be picked up. I moved around him and headed over to the couch. The puppy followed and caught sight of Olivia. He ran and put his paws up on the cushion and licked her face. She startled and opened her eyes.

"A puppy, really? Is he for me? I've always wanted a puppy." She picked him up and giggled as the dog bounced around and licked her face, excited that she was excited.

I watched in awe at how young the dog made her look, and it warmed my heart. "What are you going to name him?"

She held him away at arm's length, his pudgy little body almost too heavy for her as he tried to wiggle free. "I think . . . because he is so round and furry and black that I'm . . . I'm going to call him Junior Mint. He looks just like one of those Junior Mint candies you used to always buy me at the movies. What do you think?"

"That's a great name for a puppy."

She got up juggling Junior Mint. "Oh, thank you, Popi. I love you." She came over and gave me a kiss on the cheek as I leaned down to accept it. Her gratitude felt bittersweet. I'd not yet told her about Derek. That black cloud continued to follow me around like a giant sandstorm lurking just off the horizon.

"You have to take care of him, you know. Feed him, wash him, take him out when he needs to go out. Take him for walks."

She hugged Junior Mint. "Oh, you don't have to worry about that. I promise I'll take good care of him. What a beautiful dog, and you picked it out just for me. Thank you, Popi, really." She went up on tiptoes and I again leaned down for another kiss on the cheek. I never got tired of those. No way could I tell her how I'd really acquired the cute little beast.

"You still have to go to school. Put some papers down in the laundry room and come home for lunch to check on him. I have to go out. I don't know when I'll be back, but if I'm going to be late, I'll have your grandfather come stay over."

Her expression shifted to concern. "Popi, have you had a chance to look for Derek? He still hasn't called. Now I'm *really* getting worried about him." With a free hand she took hold of mine. "Could you please look for him? It won't take you long. You're very good at what you do."

"When I have some time, I promise I will. Now I have to go. You be good." I kissed the top of her head. The lie I'd just fed her hurt, and the longer I went without telling her the truth, the worse it was going to be when I did.

I turned and went for the door, trying hard not to look like I was fleeing for my life.

CHAPTER THIRTY-FIVE

I STOPPED AT a pay phone on Wilmington, dropped a quarter, and dialed up Judge Connors. Turning my back to the phone booth, I checked the passing traffic, watching for any ghetto fool who might want to walk up on me.

For normal folks it would be too early to call, but Connors would be out on his back porch smoking his first cigarette of the day and drinking a large cup of black coffee to get his engine started. His wife, Jean Anne, an elegant woman who doted heavily on him, wouldn't be up for another two hours. A woman of means, she had dedicated her life to serving the homeless and worked tirelessly at fund-raising, soup kitchens, and even in the construction of Homes for Humanity. In their house hung a framed photo on the wall of Jean Anne dressed in a white satin evening gown wearing a construction worker's utility belt, replete with a long carpenter's hammer.

I'd only met her once, and my immediate and unfair assessment of the two was to question how the relationship worked at all. They seemed to be polar opposites.

He answered on the first ring. "Talk to me."

"Good morning, Your Honor."

"That you, Bruno? Cut the crap and give it to me. You were supposed to call and keep me updated. I'm a little upset that you haven't.

I gotta hear it from the chief what happened to poor old Gloria. My God, what a crying shame. She was a scrappy insouciant hardass who got under my skin at every trial, but I sure liked that broad. She never backed down from a fight. Come by and pick me up—I want to roll with you. Now I really have to have a piece of this guy."

"I've been pulled from the case."

"You what? Like hell you have. Let me make a call to the chief. I'll fix this, Bruno, I promise I will. Your department owes me."

"This *came* from the chief."

"Doesn't matter, I can still fix it."

"Don't throw your dog into this fight, Your Honor. Don't call him. There are other dynamics at work here, a political subtext, and it's, ah . . . something related to a department policy that the chief's not going to budge on."

If the judge called the chief and insisted, this whole mess could blow up and the thing with Nicky and me might come out department-wide.

"Department politics, huh? That kind of crap could gum up a good sidewalk and make it black as tar. I'll make the call and fix this, you wait and see if I don't."

When he wasn't on the bench, he tried real hard to talk the street lingo, and sometimes he missed the mark by several hundred miles.

"They're just reallocating resources, that's all it is, Your Honor. They're putting me on a protection detail for Nicky Rivers."

"Oh. Oh, well I can't argue against that kind of logic. If I had to make that choice of letting you run and gun after these guys or the safety of little Nicky, I'd agree with them. I'm sorry, Bruno, I can't call the chief. That's probably the right choice.

"You know the chief wanted to put someone on me for protection and you know what I told him?"

"Knowing you, I bet you said something like, 'Let him come, I'll blow him right out of his shoes.'"

He chuckled with the early morning rasp of a smoker. "Damn straight I would. You know where I'm at right now?"

"Yep, you're out on your back porch havin' that first cigarette and drinking that black stuff you call coffee."

"But today I added something different to the routine. That's right, today I'm cradling an Ithaca Deer Slayer twelve-gauge shotgun with an eighteen-inch barrel, and it's loaded with deer slugs."

"You're better off with double-ought buck; number-four buck would even be better. You'd have a wider target acquisition."

"So you're not going to scold me for sitting here in the dark with a 12-gauge? You're not going to agree with your brass that I should have my own protection detail?"

"No, sir. I hope that dumbass Borkow does come sniffin' around and you do blow his ass right out of his designer kicks. It'd save everyone a lot of heartache."

"God damn, I miss talking with you, Bruno. Why'd you call?"

"I don't have Nicky Rivers' new address."

"I can get that for you in a jiffy. I'll just call Esther for it. Give me something harder."

"Are you serious?"

"You know damn well I'm serious. After what he did to Gloria, I'm up for anything. You just name it."

Mentioning Gloria had sparked the ugly memory of what Borkow had done to her not too many hours ago. I again saw the look on her face, her tented eyes, the depressed forehead, and that tongue that lolled out swollen, purple, and pink. Right then I knew I wasn't going to sit idle while others went into harm's way to grab this guy who'd brutally killed a friend.

"You want to catch him fast, put up a ten-thousand-dollar reward for Borkow so we can try and flip some of these people who know him. It's the only thing they understand: money."

"Make it fifty. I'll throw in twenty of my own and I know some of Jean Anne's people I can put the bite on. But, Bruno, I can't have my name anywhere around the money. The presiding judge will have my ass in a sling for sure. I know how to get it done on the down-low and I'll have it for you pronto."

"Thanks, Your Honor. With a reward that big, your involvement will be what ultimately takes this guy down."

There came a long pause. "Thanks for saying that, Bruno. Now hang up and call me back in ten minutes. I'll have that address for you."

*   *   *

After a thirty-minute drive, I pulled up to the quiet apartment complex in Lakewood. The place wasn't chosen for security; it didn't even have a fence around it. In Hollywood, Borkow got past a six-foot wrought-iron fence and a heavy security gate that had a double-key dead bolt, security cameras, and a roving patrol without anyone seeing him to get at Gloria. This place would be a cakewalk for him. No way could Nicky stay a minute longer than it took to pack a small bag and get out.

I knocked on the door of her recently rented apartment at five minutes to five as the anger began to return in how she'd played me for such a fool and lied about being separated from her husband. How she hid the truth that her husband was a cop. She knew the rule better than anyone and what it meant to violate it. I raised my knuckles to knock again when the door swung open. At first, she looked miffed. Surprise took over, then slowly seduction as her expression softened and she smiled, misinterpreting my presence.

I didn't know how women did this thing with their eyes, a sort of illegal tractor beam that should need a license from the Department of Fish and Game for hunting lovelorn males.

She wore a terry cloth robe and her right hand was out of view. "Well, hello, cowboy. What a pleasant surprise." She reached out, took hold of my khaki truck driver shirt, and pulled me inside. I closed the door without thinking about it. I couldn't take my eyes off of her. "You shouldn't open the door like that, it's dangerous."

"Not that dangerous." She lifted her right hand, which held a Walther PPK .380, the James Bond gun, perfect for a woman's grip. Of course, she would be armed and know how to use it; she was married to a SWAT commander. There it was again, still married, and to a fellow deputy on the department.

"It's one thing to have a gun at the right time," I said. "It's an entirely different proposition when you have to look someone in the eye and pull the trigger. If you hesitate making that decision, it will be too late. He'll be all over you and take it right out of your hand. So please, don't ever answer the door without looking."

She moved in close, raised her face just under my chin, and lowered her voice. "I promise. I won't ever do it again." She reached out and slid the gun onto the dining room table and then put that hand up on my shoulder. She waited. I waited and didn't know what to do. I knew what I wanted to do: kiss her.

"Bruno, we're two consenting adults."

"You don't have to tell me." I kissed her. The kiss went on and on.

Eventually, I put my hands on her shoulders and gently eased her away.

Her eyes shifted and her robe fell open as she stepped in close again. I put my hand on her naked hip, let out a long groan, and closed my eyes. *I was going to cave, for sure.* I'd no longer be able to reassure Wicks, if he ever asked me again, "Have you two done the ugly?"

My words came out in a croak. "I didn't come here for this. I'm sorry. This is business."

"What?" She grabbed her robe, yanked it closed, and took a step back, her expression one of concern. "Bruno, what's happened? Did something happen to John? Did someone kill John?"

John? Her concern for her husband—whom she said she didn't love anymore—made me a little jealous, an emotion I had no right to own.

"No, no. But you'd better sit down." I guided her over to the couch that must've come with the furnished one-bedroom apartment. No one in his or her right mind would buy a plaid thing like that, not on purpose. There were no knickknacks of residency, no pictures of family, no souvenirs from trips, nothing that spoke of home or familiarity. It did feel like she'd just moved in and had only been there a day or two and not six months.

"Bruno, what's going on?"

"I'm here because I've been assigned to protect you."

"You what? Why? What's happened?"

I didn't know how to say it. When I hesitated, she said, "Bruno, come on, just tell me straight."

"Louis Borkow killed Gloria Bleeker."

CHAPTER THIRTY-SIX

"OH MY GOD, that poor woman." She hesitated. Her eyes looked past me. "Wait. You said you're here to give me protection? Does that mean Borkow is coming after me?"

"It's just a theory, and I'm here as a precaution. Get dressed. We're moving you."

She took a deep breath. "Give me a minute. You just scared the hell out of me."

Still under the influene of that intimate kiss, I wanted to take her in my arms, console her, let her know she was safe.

When she saw my eyes wander to her lips, she moved to face me, her body just inches away.

"Don't do this," I said. My words came out in a hoarse whisper. They lacked conviction. Death had a way of diminishing inhibitions. Putting formalities aside and getting right to the heart of the matter.

I knew what was coming. She dipped one shoulder and then the other. The robe slipped off. I could feel the seductive heat radiate off her naked body.

I stood on weak knees.

Her eyes didn't leave mine and she said nothing. She didn't need to, she knew she had control.

I reached out and lifted her in my arms. She tucked her head in my neck and her lips grazed my skin.

I knew what I had to do next. At the threshold to her room, I set her down, turned her toward the room, and slapped her hard on the ass. "Get your clothes together. And hurry."

She spun around. "What? Wait."

I gently pushed her into the room and closed the door. Just in time. I couldn't have held out another second. I hurried to the bathroom and splashed cold water on my face. The only thing that had saved me from certain doom were Dad's words whispering in my ear.

I waited in the hall. When she came out of her room, she was tucking a loose-fitting blouse into a tight-fitting pair of denim pants over black cowboy boots. "Where we going?"

"I'm setting you up in an out-of-the-way motel. Then I'm finishing this thing before anyone else gets hurt. Where's your bag?"

She stopped tucking. "No, you're not, Bruno Johnson. You're not dumping me off like I'm some kind of problem you need to hide away."

I couldn't stay with her in a motel and maintain what little integrity I had left. "Then what do you suggest?"

"I'm going with you."

"Oh, no you're not."

"Why not? You don't think I'd be safer with you than dumped off at some fleabag by myself?"

"Quit saying it like that. I'm not just dumping you off. It'll be a nice enough place. Wicks will have my ass if he finds out I took you with me on the street when my job was to keep you out of harm's way."

She folded her arms across her chest and set her jaw. "Well, you're not dumping me off. Either you stay with me or you take me with you. Those are your only two options."

"No."

She started to untuck her blouse. "Then I'm going to change and go into work."

"Why are you doing this? Why do you have to be so obstinate?"

She took a step closer, put her hand on my chest, and lowered her voice. "I can't sit in a motel room waiting to see what's going to happen. Please take me with you. I promise I won't get in the way."

"Oh, man. Okay, but if I do, you duck when I say duck and don't stop to ask why. You'll do exactly as I say. You understand?"

"Yes. Anything you say goes. I promise."

"All right, come on then. I know I'm going to regret this."

She did a little hop to keep up going down the short hall into the living room. "I promise you won't regret this." She picked up the Walther PPK from the kitchen table where she'd left it and started to put it in her back pocket.

I held out my hand. "No guns. You'll not be put in a position where you'll need one. If I have to go knock on a door, you will be sitting in the car waiting."

Her eyes turned hard. She was trying to figure how far she could push the issue. She decided and slapped the gun into my hand. "Fine." She turned and headed for the door. I stuck the gun in my back pocket and followed.

We got in my truck and took off.

"Where we going first?"

"I'm going to try and find a woman that's wrapped up in all this mess."

"That's all you're going to tell me? You're just going to try and find this woman? Come on, Bruno, don't treat me like I don't know what's going on. Who do you think tries your cases and reads all your reports."

I took my eyes off the road to look at her. "Believe me when I tell you that what you see on paper doesn't have the slightest resemblance to what really happens out here on the street."

"Maybe I'll see something from a different perspective that could help."

I downshifted and stopped at a red signal. "All right. A couple of years ago, we were hunting a murder suspect. We tracked him to one of Borkow's massage parlors over at the border of Torrance and Hawthorne, a place called the Willow Tree. There was a woman inside named Lizzette who I think was tight with Borkow. The violent crimes team can't find her. They have her apartment in Santa Monica staked out waiting for her to show."

"Okay, not to throw a wet blanket on this whole idea of yours, but what makes you think you can find this woman when a team of guys can't?"

"Because I'm not going to be looking for her directly. I'm going after a friend of hers named Twyla, another woman who was working at the Willow Tree who was there at the same time."

"I get it. So you're going to move down the chain of associates until you find one of them and then work your way back up hoping someone in the end will give up Borkow?"

"That's right."

"I like it. How do you know where this Twyla lives?"

"I don't. But I ran into her again on another investigation while looking for someone else. Most of these crooks on the street are loosely related with no more than three degrees of separation. When I ran into her, I pretended that I'd never seen her before and filed away the information for a later date."

"Like for today."

"That's right."

"Nice. How much farther?"

"As I recall, she was staying over off Greenleaf and Atlantic in East Compton."

"Good, that's not too far." She went silent for a while and looked out the window to watch the early morning traffic pass through the intersection. I watched her with stolen glimpses. She suddenly lost her smile.

"What's the matter?" I asked.

"I was just thinking about poor Gloria." She still wouldn't look at me and continued to watch the cars filled with people on their way to work. "Are you going to tell me what happened to her?"

"Not if I don't have to. I don't think you want to know."

"Is it that bad?"

The signal changed. I clutched, shifted, and took off without answering her.

CHAPTER THIRTY-SEVEN

DRIVING DOWN GREENLEAF, I realized I'd made a mistake. None of the houses were familiar; no landmarks sparked my memory. I wove in and around the blocks, continually moving north searching for something recognizable.

Nicky caught on to my dilemma. "Bruno, are we lost?"

I didn't answer and made the turn from Atlantic Avenue onto Atlantic Drive. On the left, a large broken-down estate had a deeply set-back front yard that had gone to seed. The one I was looking for. I made one pass and picked a spot down the street to sit and watch. I shut the truck off and scrunched down. Nicky tried to do the same, but the cab of the Ford Ranger wasn't large enough so I put my arm around her and pulled her in tight. Her hair smelled of fresh shampoo and filled a deep yearning. We stayed that way, not speaking, no words necessary.

Two junker cars with thick yellow dirt caked on their windshields sat in front of the target location. From the looks of them, they hadn't been driven in months, maybe years. There was no way to tell if anyone was in the house. No one moved on the street—the type I was looking for wouldn't come out until sunset.

Four or five decades earlier, this part of East Compton, a rural, semi-farm area with huge houses on large lots, had been "the gateway" to Los Angeles. The neighborhood had gone bad. Money fled, and squatters moved in. Shrubs and trees, weeds and tall grass, had long ago taken over houses left to molder into nonexistence. Roofs sagged. Windows were boarded up, and here and there was even a burned-out skeleton.

Nicky said, "Can I ask you something?"

I cringed. "Depends."

She swiveled around to face me. "What's going on with you?"

"Can we please just concentrate on the surveillance?" I didn't want to talk. Words could only mean pain.

She sighed. "Are you going to tell me what I did wrong? I thought we had something good going. I thought you felt the same way. What changed?"

"Bringing personal issues out on the street can distract from the focus of the operation. That's dangerous."

She faced me with brown, angry eyes. "There is something wrong. I'm asking nicely. You owe me that."

"Look, I—"

"It's that damn unwritten rule again, isn't it? The one where cops don't mess around with another cop's woman even if they're separated. That's totally not fair."

I didn't want to discuss an issue that couldn't be logically resolved, especially not with a trained prosecutor. I'd seen her eviscerate people in court. I didn't stand a chance.

"Well, are you going to say something?"

I stared at her.

She slid over, her back to the car door.

"Bruno, say something."

"That unwritten rule is there for a reason. Cops working the street need one thing more than anything else, and that's to be able to trust one another. To have your partner's back is *everything* in law enforcement. Without it, the whole system breaks down. If your partner can't trust you because you're stealing *his* woman or *someone else's* woman, then how can you be trusted to back him in a time of dire need?"

"I understand that but this isn't . . . it isn't like that. It's not."

"Wicks knows."

Her mouth sagged open and then shut. "I figured as much after he saw me in front of your apartment. He's not a fool. I'm sorry it happened. I am. Let me talk to him. I'll make him understand."

"He's a friend of your husband's. Wicks is also my friend."

Was my friend, anyway.

"So Wicks has talked to you about this? Isn't that the pot calling the kettle black? That guy is a hound when it comes to women."

I'd always suspected as much and turned a blind eye when Wicks flirted with women. I loved his wife, Barbara, and didn't want to think of Wicks disrespecting her.

"You keep coming back to my husband. What about me? Don't you care at all about how I feel? About my situation? Don't I have a say in all of this?"

"Of course you do. I do care. But—" I couldn't finish the rest; the words wouldn't come. I didn't have a problem talking to anyone at any time—except when it came to a woman about relationships. My brain just seemed to short-circuit.

"Bruno. Tell me what you're thinking."

"Okay, you said you were separated, living apart, for, what was it, six months? Is that true?"

Tears welled in her eyes. She didn't have to say another word. The truth was plain in her expression. She reached out her hand. I didn't take it. She'd lied to me about the current state of her relationship. But maybe for good reasons, and I should give her a chance.

A shitbox faded blue Toyota Corolla drove past. I caught a glimpse of the driver. Twyla.

She drove into the long driveway and up to the front of the house. She got out of the car. Skinny as a meth freak with bobbed bleached-white hair and legs like sticks coming out of frayed denim shorts anchored by clunky military boots with loose flapping laces. Her purse was like a thief's carpetbag. Large enough to hide a couple guns and still boost full-sized roasts from the grocery. She didn't even look around and headed straight up the driveway completely unaware the house was under surveillance.

I pulled the latch on the door. "Stay in the truck and don't move." Nicky sniffled and swiped at her nose. I didn't wait for her to answer and eased the door closed until it clicked.

I walked around the front and crossed the street. Behind me, the sound of the truck door opening made my back muscles cringe and my shoulders hunch.

The door slammed and her cowboy boots clacked on the asphalt. What the hell?

CHAPTER THIRTY-EIGHT

WE STAYED TO the right side of the driveway brushing along the shrubs, trying not to be seen from the house. The wide front door and windows had long ago been boarded over. No one could see our approach unless they were in the upstairs rooms, looking out the broken windows. I kept moving along the side of the house toward the wood-framed detached garage. I stopped at the corner of the house and put my back to the wall. Nicky came up beside me. I whispered, "You stay right here and don't move. I mean it, Nicky. Don't move." She tried to see around me to the back of the house. She nodded. I pulled a gun from my waistband, eased around the corner and up the three steps of the back stoop.

The back door stood ajar. This was where Twyla had to have gone. I stuck my head inside the doorway. Listened. Nothing. Not a sound. The place smelled of a fragrant air freshener, not what I would have expected based on past experiences of places like these.

I took a step in as my eyes adjusted to the dimness. I was again surprised. My mind had already decided the kind of place I'd find—one filled with trash, rotting garbage, and overflowing toilets that reeked. Instead, someone, probably Twyla, had cleaned and painted and put down throw rugs. Even without electricity and plumbing, she'd tried real hard to make the place a home. It was much different from the last time I'd visited and not the usual habitat of a meth freak or crack head. My guess was that she'd met someone and this was a feeble attempt at making a place like this a home.

I took another step. My weight caused the wooden floor to creak. Deeper inside, I heard someone bolt. I ran blind into the dimness and caught Twyla going up the staircase. I grabbed her by the back of her shorts and pulled her down. She weighed next to nothing. She rounded on me with fists and pummeled my chest and face. I held on with one hand, shoving my gun in my waistband. I grappled with her and pinned her arms. "Stop. Stop it, right now."

She struggled, kicking at my shins with her back to my chest until she ran out of steam and relaxed. She was all bone and thin muscle. She had a burnt chemical reek about her from smoking the glass pipe.

"I'm gonna let you go. I don't want you to run or to hit me anymore, you understand?"

"What do you want? Who are you? Get out. Get out or I'm gonna scream. My boyfriend's upstairs. He's got a gun and he's gonna shoot your black ass."

I held onto her wrist and spun her away. She got a good look at me. "Ah, shit, it's you." She relaxed a little.

I dragged her along back to the kitchen and set her in a chair. "What's going on, Twyla?"

"What are you doin' here, Johnson? Why are you harassing me? I ain't done nothin'."

"You know why I'm here; don't play dumb."

"I don't know nothin' about nothin', so you're wastin' your time."

The floor creaked again in the same place. We both looked toward the back door. Nicky had come in. "I told you to wait outside."

"Has she told you anything about Louis?"

Twyla's head whipped around. "I didn't have nothin' to do with that jail thing. Me and Louis, we're quits, we have been for a while now. You know that. Why do you think I'm livin' in a dump like this? I don't work at the Willows no more. I don't make any money except what I can hustle."

"I'll settle for you telling me where to find Lizzette."

"Lizzette?"

"That's right. Don't pretend like you don't know her."

"I haven't seen her in months."

"She's lying," Nicky said. Nicky leaned with her back up against the kitchen sink, her arms folded across her chest. She looked fierce, in control, like she did when interrogating a hostile witness on the stand.

"Who is this snooty bitch?"

"I'm the deputy district attorney who is going to slam you in CIW for the next ten years if you don't tell Detective Johnson exactly what he wants to know."

Nicky didn't know how to work an informant; it took a certain kind of finesse. You certainly couldn't threaten someone without having something to back it up. And as yet, Twyla hadn't done anything that would warrant serious prison time. She'd only freeze up and say nothing. She knew the game better than Nicky.

I looked at Nicky. "Why don't you wait outside?"

"No, I'm good right here."

"Please?"

She shook her head.

I glared at her. So much for following directions and ducking when I say duck. She was only succeeding in making a duck out of me.

I looked back at Twyla. "Where's that carpetbag you had when you came in?"

"Don't do this, Johnson. You don't need to do this. I'm gettin' out. I'm leavin' town. I'm going up to San Fran. I'm leavin' today."

"That's probably a good idea. Just tell me where to find Lizzette, and I won't bother you anymore."

"Handcuff her, Bruno, let's take her in. We have plenty to put her away."

Nicky had watched too many cop shows and was trying for the good cop–bad cop routine that never worked anymore. Today's crooks were too savvy for it.

"Go on then, take me in. I'll be out in five, six hours at the most, on your trumped-up bullshit, then I'll be gone. Puufft, just like that."

Now Nicky had done it. We wouldn't get anything out of Twyla, not once she dug in her heels. This wasn't working out at all.

"Is that right? Trumped up?" Nicky said. "Bruno, ask her what's outside in the garage. Go on, ask her."

Twyla's eyes went wide. She opened her mouth to refute the allegation and then shut it.

"What is it?" I asked.

Nicky shrugged. "Go have a look for yourself."

I grabbed Twyla by the wrist. She tried to resist. I yanked hard once. She relented and came along. Nicky led the way through the kitchen, down the stoop, and across the cracked concrete walkway to the side door of the detached garage.

I stepped inside. I stood there stunned. I tugged on Twyla's wrist. "Nicky's right. You're going to prison for a long time."

CHAPTER THIRTY-NINE

THE 1973 DODGE Fleetwood, a cab-over RV, rattled and banged with each little bump in the road and gave Borkow a blazing headache along with a mild touch of carsickness. At each turn the mushy suspension canted wildly as if the whole rig might tumble over onto its side. They'd be like a turtle, unable to right themselves, and be vulnerable to all enemies. He sat in the dining area back from the driver's compartment and watched Payaso maneuver through the side streets, regretting now his decision to come along.

The constant rattle-bang, rattle-bang knocked around in his head like a rock in a tin can.

He'd been cooped up too many hours already. He needed to get out of that Muscle Max gym and see the world. Otherwise, what was the sense of being free and on the loose?

The air-conditioning didn't work in the beast, and the inside air had turned stagnant and humid, adding to the overall discomfort. The reek from the bathroom compounded matters.

He didn't like to sweat, a grotesque bodily function he avoided at all costs. His tee shirt stuck to his underarms. Rivulets of sweat ran down his sides to the tops of his pants and chafed at his waist.

Even so, he had to admit, Payaso took good care of him. What self-respecting Johnny Law would pull over a hunk-o-shit like this old broken-down RV to look for his skinny ass? No one would be-lieve "the most wanted man in the seven western states" could be toolin' around in this paint-faded, dented eyesore. It was too far below his new station in life.

That's what the five o'clock news had called him, "The most wanted man in the seven western states," a distinction he had not chased after but was glad to have the title just the same. With it came a large dollop of street cred. Everyone knows you can't get enough of that.

"How much farther?"

"It is better if we go slow, take our time, and stay off the main streets. We stay invisible that way."

"Hey, chili-eater, I didn't ask you that now, did I? I didn't ask why we're taking this route. Why do you always give an answer to a ques-tion I didn't ask? I don't get it." He'd given the same ignorant answer, doling it out for the last hour and a half as if Borkow were some kind of idiot that had to be told multiple times before it sunk in.

Payaso looked up into the rearview and said nothing. His brand of noncommunication irked the shit out of Borkow. When asked, he expected Payaso to answer his question, not some random one of his own liking. How hard was that?

Payaso slowed and jockeyed the wheel into another long sweeping turn down yet another endless side street of ghetto hovels. Depressing. They all looked the same. How could people live in places like this?

Payaso said, "I told you we should've stopped for some enchiladas con mole. You get too sketchy when you don't eat."

"Let me worry about my stomach, okay, amigo? You just get us there pronto."

Over the din of the raggedy RV's rattle and bang, a muffled plea made it out of the bathroom. Borkow got up. He staggered from side to side, fighting to keep his balance, his arms out, hands to the interior walls. He had nothing better to do. He might as well have another go at her. Couldn't hurt. He slid the accordion door to the bathroom open to the reek of body odor and urine, mixed with a faint chemical smell from the toilet. Lizzette sat on the floor all trussed up with gray duct tape. Her face glistened with sweat. Her bottle-blond hair was pasted to the sides of her face and forehead. Her eyes pleaded with him.

"Lizzy, I cut you lose, you promise to be a good girl?"

She nodded vigorously. He leaned over, and reached a jittery hand that shook like a man with a terrible palsy, the *luxury* coach hitting every goddamn little bump in the road. He took hold of the tape on her mouth and yanked it off. She yelped at the pain.

He smiled. "There, I'm sorry, but I really needed you to know the full extent of my displeasure. You understand what I'm saying here?"

She continued to nod and said nothing. Payaso had called him *sketchy*. He didn't feel *sketchy* or otherwise. All the heat, the smells, and the noise irritated his stomach.

He grabbed her bound wrists and helped her to her feet. They both banged from side to side in the small bathroom trying to maintain their balance. He got her out and leaned into her damp and sweaty body, pushing her against the wall while he peeled the tape from her wrists. "There. Now get your feet undone and come sit. Let's talk."

He sat back into the dining couch behind the driver's seat and waited. She slid to the floor leaving a damp smudge on the faux wood panel and worked on the tape like a wild animal in a trap. The skin on her wrists and ankles and mouth turned a little pink from the abuse. Better a little abuse than the alternative.

Payaso looked up in the rearview. Borkow raised his hand and waved. "I know, I know, you don't approve. But she's my main girl. I owe her for getting me out of that hellhole. She gets another chance. You hear that, girl?"

"Yes, Louis. Thank you, Louis. I won't make you mad again, I promise." Her voice came out hoarse from the lack of water.

"That's good. Now come and sit." He patted the seat next to him.

She came over, her feet taking wide sidesteps to keep her balance as she rubbed her wrists.

Louis said, "I'm so sorry about hitting you. I promise it won't happen again."

She hesitated, timid as if he planned to betray her yet again and that this might be a part of a new game of mistrust and torture.

He took hold of her wrist and gently pulled her down. "I said everything is cool. There's nothing for you to worry about."

She nodded and sat.

CHAPTER FORTY

BORKOW INVOLUNTARILY REACHED up and touched his face where her nails, earlier in the day, had raked his cheek. "If you've learned your lesson, what more could I ask? Just so you know, letting you out is not all out of the kindness of my heart. We're on our way to pick up another unfortunate girl. So you have been paroled partially out of necessity, due to overcrowding. But know this: I have no problem piling you girls up in there like cordwood if the need should arise."

"I understand."

He took a cool bottle of Coca-Cola from the cup holder. "Would you like a drink?"

She nodded and grabbed the bottle. A little too fast for his liking, snatching it right out of his hand. She drank like she'd been bound up in a confined space for the last twelve hours with duct tape over her mouth. He put his hand on the bottle. "Not too much. Don't want you getting sick all over my nice digs."

She wiped her mouth with the back of her hand and nodded. She didn't look nearly as beautiful as she used to. The march of time had been an unfriendly bedfellow.

"Now back to the business at hand. Tell me where I can find your girlfriend Twyla? I'm serious this time. No bullshit."

She sat back, her eyes going hard. She still had a bit of steel left in her. That was good. He was glad he hadn't broken her entirely.

"Do you want me to lie to you, Louis? Because if that's what you want, I can lie to you, no problem. If I knew, I promise, I would tell you. But I don't have the first clue where to look for her. Let me out. Let me get cleaned up. I can go around and check some places, ask some people, call in some favors. I know I'll be able to find her if you just give me a chance."

He didn't believe her. Every time she denied knowing anything about Twyla, the image from the night he hot-prowled her apartment in Santa Monica looking for the place where Lizzette had been staying came back vivid as if he still stood in the doorway to the bedroom watching them. That night in the dim light, the near darkness, the naked bodies of Twyla and Lizzette intertwined. From that moment, he knew they loved each other.

So, not to keep close tabs on Twyla, well, that just didn't make any sense at all.

He reached across and took her damp hand. "You would do that for me?"

"Of course I would. Just give me the chance."

He didn't believe her for a second. This new tack of hers was nothing more than a ploy, a diversion until she could get loose and make a run for it.

Twyla was the only one Lizzette would trust to help her make the move to get away from him. He could never break Lizzette. But Twyla was another story. He needed to find her and make an example out of the both of them so the other girls would never even think about trying to run. He'd been away for a year and he had to bring back order or risk losing everything.

"Coming up on the street. This is the turn."

Borkow drooped his head to see past his driver and out the windshield. "This is Southgate? This neighborhood doesn't look half bad. Why, it almost looks like hometown U.S.A. I mean, if you squinted a little and forgot where you were for a minute. Aren't the housing projects the Nickerson and The Downs only about five miles to the west?"

Payaso said nothing. After a moment he pointed. "There. There she is now, coming out of the apartment. We lucked out, *mi amigo*. Perfect timing." He slowed and came to a stop. With all the vehicles parked on both sides, the street was too narrow for any other car to pass. They couldn't stay put too long without being noticed.

Off to the right, a pretty young girl with brown skin came bounding out of an apartment, a smile huge on her face, the classic image of a teenage girl giddy in love. She clapped her hands and ran into the arms of a young, good-looking black kid. Borkow leaned over even more. "Is that who I think it is? I thought you said he left town, that he caught a Greyhound to Barstow?"

Payaso shrugged. "I guess he's back. What do you want to do now? You want me to put the grab on her like we planned?"

Borkow thought through the options. "Naw, it's broad daylight. Why risk causing a scene and burning this vehicle to the cops. It's kind of growing on me now, the noise, the smells, all of it. Besides, if that little shitass is back, we don't need to grab her right now. With his help we can do it anytime. You know what, let's just send a message. That might be enough. What do you think?"

Payaso shrugged. "Not my Monopoly game, jefe."

Borkow wanted to slap the back of his head for his non-answer.

The girl and her boyfriend hurried over to a sun-faded VW Rabbit, got in, and took off.

"Yeah, for right now I think sending a message is the way to handle it. Go on," Borkow said. "Follow them. We got some time."

He reached across the small table, took Lizzette's hand, and squeezed. She tried to smile, but failed.

"She's just a kid, Louis."

"Now, Lizzy, honey, this is none of your business."

CHAPTER FORTY-ONE

PAYASO FELL IN behind the VW Rabbit and followed at a distance that made Borkow nervous about losing them. He couldn't tell Payaso anything; the man went his own way.

Lizzette continued to watch Borkow as if he were some kind of animal. He'd have to work on getting back her trust.

"Hey," he said to her, "come on, ease up on me. I want it to be like it was. You screwed up, I spanked you a little, and it's over. Let's move on, okay? Pretend like it never happened, okay?"

"Really? You're serious?"

He held out his hands wide. "It's me, baby, and you're my best girl. You know that."

She nodded and used both palms to wipe the sweat out of her eyes. "If you're sure, Louis. *I am* real sorry. I do want it back the way it was. You just tell me what you want me to do to show you that you can trust me, and I'll do it."

"Good deal, then that's the way it's going to be. I owe you a great debt for getting me out. That was really something, a feat of unbelievable skill and daring. No one but you could've pulled it off. To prove my sincerity, I'm going to let you have that pair of shoes after all."

She shot him a genuine smile. "You don't have to do that, Louis, really you don't."

"So, you don't want them?" He smiled back, despite the queasiness in his stomach. The rolling hulk of the RV was a lumbering land yacht traveling a sea of uneven concrete.

"I didn't say that. Of course, I'll take them, if you're really offering them."

He picked up her damp hand. "Ah, baby girl, if I didn't know any better, I'd almost think you only loved me for the shoes I give you."

"That's not true and you know it." She smiled again, this time trying for coy and missing the mark. "I also love you for your money."

"Of course you do." He didn't have any true friends, only leeches who hung on him for financial gain.

He shifted in his seat to focus outside the front windshield. The heat and Lizzette's body odor exacerbated his discomfort, taking him to the edge of embarrassing himself. He was about to tell Payaso to pull over when the Rabbit found a place to park on the street with a quick jerk of the wheel and a sudden display of brake lights. Payaso went on by and pulled into the parking lot of Lucy's Mexican takeout. Oddly, though the RV had stopped, the floor seemed to keep moving. Borkow staggered to his feet. "I'm going out to get some air."

"Not a good idea, *mi amigo*. Let me go. I'll get you something cold to drink and a couple of orders of enchilada con mole. They make it good here, even better than *mi tia*, and that's saying something."

Borkow put his hand to his mouth and belched. The thought of eating anything at all, especially something spicy, repulsed him. "No. I said I'm going." He put on his sunglasses and ball cap. At the edge of the couch, from the large carpetbag that used to belong to Lizzette, he reached in and took out his blue windbreaker. He shrugged into it. The heaving floor started to subside; the land yacht had officially dropped anchor.

Lizzette watched him carefully.

He said, "You hungry? You want me to get you something?"

She shook her head. She was going to bolt. Too bad. When he got back, he'd have to fix it so she couldn't—maybe take Payaso's hammer to her foot. Maybe not the foot, but the knee.

She put her hand out and touched his. She whispered, "Please don't leave me here with him. Let me go with you."

"My friend Payaso won't hurt you. Will you, Payaso?"

Payaso, his hands still on the big steering wheel, looked up in the rearview at them and said nothing.

Borkow shrugged. "See, everything is cool." He reached into the bag to feel around for the knife and found it along with another little tool he'd forgotten about. He put them both in the pocket of the windbreaker. "I won't be long. I just need to send that big black bastard of a bailiff a message. Then we'll get back to the gym, pronto. You and I will take a nice sauna and a swim. How's that sound?"

"That sounds great, Louis."

"Excellent, then it's a date."

He went out the side door and down the one step to the black asphalt parking lot. He took a moment to breathe in the hot summer air.

Cars on Long Beach Boulevard zipped by. He watched to see if any of the passengers or drivers did a double take and recognized him from all the recent press coverage. Paranoia—or vanity?

No way anyone could identify him with his disguise. He took in two large breaths, held them for a moment, and let them out. Ah, better already.

He looked inside the windshield as he walked around the RV. Payaso had left the driver's seat and he now sat on the diner couch next to Lizzette. He'd placed his six-pound sledge on the table to menace her. Payaso didn't like Lizzette. She hadn't told him about living in the Santa Monica apartment with Twyla and that they were lovers. Both girls worked for Borkow, and two girls like that were not good for business. Payaso wanted the go-ahead to get ugly with Lizzette over her disloyalty. Borkow wouldn't give it.

Borkow shrugged and moved into the patio area, where a couple dozen people sat at picnic tables eating their chalupas, their chipotle, and churros. He stood in the long line waiting to order at the outside window. He kept both his hands in his windbreaker pockets, his ball cap low over his brow. His fingers clutched the knife in its sheath.

In the parking lot, the RV shimmied a little. Now what the hell was Payaso up to? When he got back, Lizzette better be just the way he'd left her, or else.

Or else what? How could he possibly threaten a man like Payaso? The day would come when he'd have to deal with that problem, Payaso's blatant insubordination. He'd need Payaso a little longer though to take out that big black bastard of a bailiff. The way things were going, Payaso might be the only one capable of doing it.

The wind created by the passing cars and trucks on Long Beach Boulevard fluttered the tattered wheel cover of the spare tire attached to the back of the RV. It drew his attention. The cover touted a smiling, hand-painted mug of a man, one with big black hair, and the words underneath declaring him a member of something called "*The Good Sam Club*." Yes, that's exactly what his new hideout qualified as, a rolling Good Sam Club in need of a couple of new members.

CHAPTER FORTY-TWO

THE LINE AT the outdoor window moved at a snail's pace. Borkow moved up another couple of steps and came even with the picnic table not two feet away from the little chavala western where she sat with her smartass boyfriend. That's what Payaso had called the girl, *a chavala western.*

She clutched both hands of her boyfriend in hers, her adoring eyes eating him up as if he were a hot fudge sundae with extra whipped cream. Ah, young love, who could remember what that was like?

She had the most inviting green eyes. Borkow leaned back a little to inspect her feet. She wore a pair of sandals. Like most women, she'd not emulsified her dark skin well enough. Her feet looked a tinge dusky. But her bone structure on display in those cheap peasant sandals was nothing short of pure art. With art like that you could work on the dusky. He'd even rub the lotion in himself. The thought made a warmth rise to his face. His eyes fell to a silver-colored ring on her big toe that made his heart skip a beat. What a perfect touch of . . . of what? Innocent style? Or maybe *truth*?

"So please, please tell me where you were? How come you didn't call me?" the girl asked.

The smartass kid leaned in and kissed her again for the umpteenth time since Borkow had started watching them. The kid didn't want to tell the girl where he'd been and thought he could sidetrack that undeterred determination with a little lip distraction. Might've worked had the girl not been the daughter of that hardheaded bailiff.

The kid kept looking at the receipt in his hand for the number to their food order to pop up at the take-out window, hoping for that interruption to save him.

"Derek, come on, look at me. I want you to tell me."

He still hesitated and stared at her.

"Why won't you tell me?"

"Okay. I will. If you really want me to, I will. I'll do it. You're not going to like it, though. I'm telling you right now, you're not going to be happy about it. When I do tell you, you're gonna somehow turn it around and blame it on me. I'm going to get all the blame when *I* was the one minding my own business when it happened. I was the one just standing out there on Central at a pay phone talking to you."

Her expression shifted from anger to confusion to fear. The young never hid their emotions well. That's what made them such easy victims. They need to mask it early on—a survival technique—or the street would eat them.

"So, tell me right now if you *really* want me to tell you. I will. I'll tell you."

She hesitated and nodded. "Yes, I do. Please tell me."

He took hold of her hands, looked into her eyes, and squirmed one more time. Before saying anything, he checked around again. Over her shoulder, his gaze stopped on Borkow as he stood in line looking back at them. The kid's eyes tried to peel back Borkow's disguise, as if the kid had caught a whiff of recognition even through the ball cap and sunglasses and bulky windbreaker. Now *this kid* was a survivor.

Borkow didn't look away. He'd never met the kid in person; the kid had taken his payoff via Payaso. Borkow had talked to him on the phone that one time from the jail when he'd ordered up the distraction at the house on Pearl. The boys on Pearl went a little overboard when they socked him up to make it look good. He still carried the bruising and swelling on his face. The dumb little shitass.

Borkow dropped his head a little and lowered his dark sunglasses so only the kid could see and smiled at him.

The kid sat straight up. His mouth dropped open. His eyes went large. He must have seen Borkow on the news reports, *the most wanted man in the seven western states.* His face plastered all over every news broadcast for the last forty-eight hours.

The girl whipped around to see what had caused that kind of re-action in her boyfriend. But Borkow had moved his sunglasses back in place and turned away.

Borkow watched the reflection in the take-out window. The kid grabbed his girl's hand and pulled on her. "Come on. Come on, we have to get out of here. Now!"

"What are you talking about? What about our food? What's going on?"

"Forget the food, come on, we have to go!" He tugged her off the bench so hard she stumbled into the line of customers. Borkow turned, put his hands out, and caught her so she wouldn't fall to the ground and skin her lovely naked knees on the rough asphalt. "Take it easy there, little girl. You could fall and break your nose. You might even skin up those lovely feet. That would be a terrible shame." She looked up at him, scowled as if he were some sort of perv, and immediately shifted her attention back to the kid.

Borkow resented the implication. He gripped the knife in his pocket.

The kid pulled on her arm, his eyes not leaving Borkow. "Come on. *Come on.*"

They hurried away.

Borkow took a deep breath, smiled, and watched them flee to the Rabbit. They got in and chirped the tires as they sped off to a safer haven. Only there wasn't any place safe for those two.

Borkow decided to stay in line. He bought Payaso an enchilada con mole along with some Horchata. He also bought churros for Lizzette. She was sitting back at the table in the RV. Lizzette, *his* very own chavala western, who was also waiting to tell him something important, something she, too, was *dying* to say.

CHAPTER FORTY-THREE

STUNNED, I STOOD in the abandoned garage, but I did have the peace of mind to hold on to Twyla's wrist. Had I let her go, she'd have fled on skinny legs and been difficult to chase down in an open-field pursuit. I tugged her deeper into the dimness to get a closer look.

Just like every deputy on the department, I'd worked MCJ—Men's Central Jail—and had stood my share of watches in Visiting while relatives and friends on the freedom side of the reinforced glass windows visited with the confined—both the sentenced and the presentence inmates.

Before me stood a four-window mock-up that represented a section of Visiting in MCJ. The staged set even had the stainless-steel shelf under the window, and the stainless-steel round seats where the visitors sat. The cost to fabricate a structure that picture-perfect would be enormous. The frames to the windows didn't have any paint. All the bolts' heads were exposed and shiny from overuse. A few even lay scattered on the shelf below the window, a couple on the bare concrete floor.

I yanked on Twyla's arm, spun her around, and sat her on one of the seats. I pointed at the windows as anger rose inside me. She'd been a part of this, a party to Gloria Bleeker's violent death.

"Do you know what this means? Do you know that someone has died? That someone has been brutally murdered by getting her head caved in because of your involvement in this escape?"

Nicky interrupted, "They caved her head in?"

I looked up. I caught her eyes. I was sorry for letting too many words slip. I didn't so much as nod an affirmative response, but she understood just the same.

I turned back to Twyla. "Do you know what that exposes you to as far as time in the can?" I looked back at Nicky, who had gone back to leaning against the doorframe with her arms crossed.

"I can easily get her twenty-five to life. She'll do three-quarters time, eighteen years, minimum before even thinking about parole."

"Eighteen years? Did you hear that, Twyla? You want to go away for two decades?"

She shrugged out of my grasp. "I can't rat on Louis. I won't do it. I'd be dead. Twenty years in the can is better than dead any day of the week." Tears filled her eyes and flowed down her narrow cheeks. "Damn you, Johnson, why'd you have to come here now, this minute? Ten more minutes I would've been gone. You can go ahead and stick a fork in me, I'm done, my life's over."

Nicky said, "We'll give you protection. No one will get to you if you give us Borkow."

Twyla looked up at me and hooked her thumb over toward Nicky. "What world's she livin' in, huh? You know better, Johnson. Go on, tell her. Tell her how that really works. You'll put me up in some sleazebag motel until the trial, feedin' me cold pizza and Chinese. Then once you get what you want outta me, it'll be a big *thanks for showin' up* and good luck with the rest of your life, which isn't going to be too long once I rat."

I sat down on the steel stool one over from her. I wanted to show that I trusted her just a little.

"Come on, let's book her ass, Bruno," Nicky said. "We can move down the line to the next associate. Give someone else the opportunity to help themselves if she won't do it."

I shot Nicky a hard look. She didn't have to be so coldhearted. I liked her a little less for it.

Twyla looked at me with tear-filled eyes. Her chin quivered.

My voice came out in a whisper. "What's it going to be, Twyla?"

"No. I like breathin' too much."

I nodded. "All right, what about Sammy Ray?"

Her back straightened. Something flashed behind her eyes as she thought about it as a real possibility. Then she slumped back. "He's not much better. Everyone on the inside and out is afraid of him, too. I might live a day or two longer if I ratted on him. So no, I don't think so."

I nodded and thought about it for a minute. Nicky started to say something, but I held up my hand. She shut her mouth and continued to stand, leaning against the doorframe, arms across her chest.

"Okay," I said. "What if I do a little changeup in the game?"

Nicky raised her hand. "Hold it, Bruno, maybe we should talk outside before you say something my office isn't ready to back up."

"Hold on," I said. "If she helps us out, you said you were prepared to let her walk on the accessory 'after the fact' charge, right?"

Nicky hesitated. "Sure, along with a three-year probation tail. Someone died, Bruno. I'm not in the business of giving away the store."

"Doesn't matter," Twyla said. "I'm not gonna rat."

"Just hear me out. What if no one hears about you ratting? What if we just happen onto Louis and take him down. No one has to find out that it came from a tip from you. We don't need you to testify on the escape charge; we can find plenty of witnesses for that."

Twyla's eyes lost focus as she thought over this new offer. She started shaking her head before she spoke. "No, Louis isn't human. He'll find out *or* he'll figure it out somehow. No, I won't do it. You don't know him like I do."

"Bruno?" Nicky said.

"Okay, hold on, hold on. What about that same deal for Sammy Ray? Little Genie?"

She nodded. "You're sayin' the same deal with him? That all I have to do is tell you where to find him and I walk?"

"That's right."

"Bruno?"

I held up my hand to silence Nicky before she cheesed the deal that had just started to emerge.

"I'm an officer of the court, Bruno, I—"

Twyla ignored Nicky. "Naw, what would I do then? Where would I go?"

"You were going to go to San Francisco."

She shrugged. "Yeah, but I was gonna hitch all the way. It'd take me forever doing that, if I made it at all. Lotta creeps on the road today. Then once I got there, where would I stay? I gotta start over."

"What about ten grand? What if I can put ten grand in your hand, today?"

Her face lit up. "Ten thousand for Little Genie, not Louis?"

"Bruno?"

"That's right."

She licked her dry lips, her eyes alive with excitement. I had her on the hook. If I could prove we'd keep her safe while taking down Genie, at the same time holding that ten grand in her hand, she might go for Borkow for another ten.

"Bruno," Nicky said, "where the hell are you going to get ten thousand dollars? Our Victim's Advocacy Department has more money than the sheriff's department and no way would *we* cut loose with that kind of money."

I reached out and offered Twyla my hand. "You know me—my word is my bond. I'm offering you ten thousand dollars. Is it a deal?"

"Show me the money, and we've got a deal." She shook my hand.

I said, "I just need to make a quick phone call."

Nicky muttered, "Sweet Jesus, Bruno, you're going to take us all down."

CHAPTER FORTY-FOUR

I HURRIED FROM the phone booth back to the truck parked on Wilmington Avenue, watching the traffic speed by, people in a hurry, everyone with somewhere to go. I got in the driver's side and closed the door. Twyla had to scoot over closer to Nicky. The Ford Ranger didn't leave a lot of room in between.

"Well?" Nicky asked.

"I made the call."

"You're still not going to tell me who you called?"

"No."

Twyla said, "I'm sensing something between you two. I did right from the gate. You have, like, history together, don't you? I mean, like—" she held her arms out as if hugging an invisible lover, closed her eyes, and puckered her lips.

Nicky and I both said, "*No.*"

"Well, maybe you should."

I looked past Twyla. Nicky looked furious.

"Let's step out of the truck and discuss this," I said.

Nicky didn't move. Her jaw muscles knitted as she stared out the windshield. I took the keys from the ignition, got out, and came around and opened her door. She still didn't move.

I put my hand on her arm. "Please?" I gently tugged on her arm and half-pulled her out of the truck, closed the door, and led her around to the back. I let the tailgate down and we sat.

I said, "You and I both know this . . . this thing you're angry about isn't over what's going on with the reward that I just drummed up."

"Oh, is that right? Now you're a couples counselor?"

"Are we a couple?"

"Well, one of us thought we were headed in that direction. But I guess I was wrong."

I got up, stood in front of her, and took both of her hands in mine. I simply looked into her eyes.

After a moment, she spoke, her voice husky. "Okay. Okay. I might have stretched the truth a little about . . . but I did it for the right reasons."

I said nothing.

"You need to get over yourself, Mr. Bruno Johnson. I just said it's not what you think at all."

I nodded.

"Look, John knows it's over. He's known it's been over for five or six months now, just like I told you. Just because I hadn't moved out when I said I did, it doesn't mean I lied to you."

I simply nodded.

"I didn't want to move out . . . because . . . because, well, I guess it came down to me being stubborn. I wanted *him* to move out and he wouldn't—it sounds so damn juvenile."

I said, "You put me in a jam."

"You told Wicks that we'd been separated for six months. That's what happened, wasn't it? And he told you only a couple of days, right? That's what happened back at my apartment. That's why—"

I put one finger on her lips.

She nodded and pulled back a little. "I figured as much. Do you want me to tell you what happened? You want me to tell you all of it?"

"Not my business."

"I want it to be your business. Will you hear me out, please? Just hear me out. I think you owe me that much."

"This isn't the time or the place, especially with the deal we have going down."

"This will only take a second, and it's important."

"All right. But we have a witness in the truck." I pointed to Twyla who seemed to be paying us no attention.

Nicky put her case together in her head just like a good prosecutor would, and she was one of the best. "Okay. Six months ago, before that, John and I grew apart. No one's fault. Our careers left little time for the two of us. I'd been trying heavy-duty murder cases for five years that took every minute of my day and most of my nights. He got promoted and transferred to SEB. That took more of his time.

"We talked it through one night. We both loved and cared for each other and didn't want to give up. Everything seemed good for a while. I thought the train was back on the tracks just in time."

She paused. "It was an accident that I caught onto him. I'd picked up a case downtown at the Criminal Courts Building and ran into an old friend. We had lunch. She knew me by Rivers, didn't know I'd married John Lau. We ran into three of her friends, younger, at lunch. One let it slip she was sleeping with a guy in the sheriff's department named Lau. What were the odds? Lau isn't a very common name, Bruno."

She looked at me for a reaction. I gave her nothing.

"I excused myself, left the restaurant, and took a few days to think about it. I decided I wouldn't give him the chance to deny it, because he would. So I did something I'm not proud of. I followed him in a rental car."

She nodded to herself as if giving approval. I reached over to put an arm around her. "It's okay."

She shook her head and pulled back. "No, you have to hear this. I followed him to The North Woods Inn restaurant. I waited out in the parking lot. Finally, he came out holding her hand. The bastard never held *my* hand."

She shifted her voice to less personal. "They walked across the street to the hotel. The next day I told him to get the hell out. He didn't even ask why. He just told me to kiss his ass, and that I had to leave. It was his house. That was six months ago.

"We've slept in separate rooms since. So, you see, I didn't really lie to you, I just didn't tell you the whole truth. Can you forgive me that small transgression?"

Twyla still sat in the cab of the truck watching us. Only a couple of minutes had passed.

People in cars zipped by on Wilmington, their faces turned to see a black man standing in front of a nicely dressed white woman.

It didn't matter. I kissed her. Kissed her like I did in the bougain-villea bush. For one wonderful moment the kiss made all the silly mess about unwritten rules melt away and turn meaningless.

CHAPTER FORTY-FIVE

JUDGE CONNORS DROVE up behind the Ford Ranger and tapped his horn interrupting our kiss. I pulled Nicky into one last hug and whispered, "Ah, shit."

She peeked over my shoulder. She stiffened. He expression turned proffesional. Back to the problem at hand. "The judge? Really, Bruno, you called the judge and didn't warn me?"

"It's not illegal, is it?"

"Don't try and dodge the issue. And no, it's not illegal, but it's not exactly protocol either having a judge see the informant. That's not the problem here. He saw us."

"If I could've pulled this off any other way, I would have. The judge insisted that he be present so who am I to say different? Conners isn't like other judges."

"He won't be able to preside over the case; he'll have to conflict out."

"I don't think he cares. I think he's just bored with his job and wants a little excitement. He's doing a good thing, helping to take a murderer off the street. And maybe even two."

Nicky put on a fake smile and waved to the judge as he got out of his Mercedes. "You okay, big guy?" she said out of the corner of her smile.

"Fine. I just wish you'd have told me that story back at your apartment when you were still naked."

"Not my fault. That's a male thing. You guys always jump to the wrong conclusions when it comes to women. If you could just slow down long enough to ask, to talk about your skewed emotions, we could avoid messes like this. In fact, we'd probably have world peace."

Talking about emotions was the third rail of relationships and was to be avoided at all costs. I knew that much at least. "You think we could continue this later on?"

"Damn straight we will."

I waved. "Hi, Your Honor."

Connors walked up smiling, wearing tweed pants, a long-sleeve shirt, and loafers. He looked like a lost literature professor from the sixties who had stopped for directions to Haight and Ashbury. He had a nervous tic and continually smoothed down his mustache with two fingers.

He ducked a little and pointed toward the truck cab. "Is that the woman to whom I owe the money?" He patted the bulge of his shirt pocket where the top quarter of some U.S. currency peeked out.

"Yes," I said, glad that he chose to ignore what he'd seen when he pulled up.

"Then I'd like to talk to her."

"Your Honor, that's not a good idea. I appreciate you coming out and the money; it's really going to help, but—"

"My money, my game. And if you're worried about it, don't. I'll indemnify the both of you from any future policy violations. This is all on me." He looked around for a place. "Why don't we step back to my car where there's more room?"

I looked at Nicky. She shrugged.

I waved to Twyla. She got out and followed us to the Mercedes. We got in and closed the doors that vacuum-pressed our ears and muffled the outside sounds down to almost nothing. I sat in the back seat with Twyla. Nicky was in the front with Connors.

"How's this going to work, Bruno?" the judge asked.

"Show her the money, so she knows we have it and that we're not playing any games. Then—"

"Hold on," Twyla said. "I'm callin' bullshit here." She slapped her own hand. "I don't just get to see it; I get the money now or I'm not talkin', pure and simple."

The judge stared her down with his gray eyes. "Young lady, like he said, this is not a game. This is serious business."

"Don't I know it. But I'm the one who has to look out for number one." She hooked her thumb back toward herself. "No one else is going to do it."

"How is your daughter doing?" the judge asked. "Her name's Chloe, right?"

Judge Connors, before he moved up to trying homicides, worked in Family Court, the drudgery of all the courts, a place where nobody won, everyone lost. He also had a memory unsurpassed by anyone I'd ever met, except maybe my father. The freaky kind of memory.

Confidence bled out of Twyla's expression. She nodded and was at a loss for words.

I said, "Give her the money. She's staying with us until this thing is done. Right, Twyla?"

She was staring at the judge. "You're the one who took Chloe from me?"

He nodded. "That's right, but I also gave you visitations and promised to revisit your custody as soon as you got your life straightened out."

Twyla looked down at her hands and picked at her fingernails, already bitten down to the quick. "Chloe's with some very nice foster parents now. She's better off." She looked up, angry. "If we're going to do this, let's get it done. I got places to go, people to see."

The judge pulled the sheaf of hundred-dollar bills from his shirt pocket. The paper bank wrapper read $10,000. He handed it to her.

She started to thumb through the bills, her lips silently moving as she counted.

The judge said, "Well, for crying out loud, what, you don't trust us?"

"It's my life we're talking here. I don't trust anyone when it comes down to me."

We waited until she finished. She rolled the bills up and stuffed them into her front shorts pocket. The wad wouldn't fit all the way and some peeked out.

"Okay," I said. "Where to?"

"Little Genie, he isn't far from his hood. He's hidin' up in the Jungle."

"The *Jungle*?" the judge asked.

I said, "Crenshaw and what?"

"Slauson, just off 10th."

The judge turned back around in the seat, started the Mercedes, put it in gear, and took off into the traffic on Wilmington. "Just tell me where to go. I'm not familiar with that area of Los Angeles."

Twyla muttered, "Most crackers aren't."

I'd leave my truck and come back for it later.

Nicky said, "What are we doing here, Bruno? You are going to call in for backup, right? You can't take this guy down by yourself. In fact, I think for someone like this, protocol dictates that you call and put the SWAT team on standby."

Of course, she was right, but the SWAT team didn't seem like the right fit at that moment. Not with their current commander. "We're just going to peep it, get a feel for the location, and then I'll call in the violent crimes team. That's what they do. That's what they're good at. We'll let Wicks handle it."

"Peep it, that's all, Bruno. I'm serious. Then you're going to call it in."

"That's what I said. Take it easy. I can't call in the violent crimes team until I have something to give them, an address, or at the very least a description of the place."

The judge looked at me in the rearview. For the first time in the two years I worked with him, I couldn't read what he was thinking.

There was no scenario in the world where I would get involved in a violent confrontation taking down an escaped fugitive wanted for murder. Not while driving around in a Mercedes with a judge, a deputy DA, and a sketchy informant. Even to me, it sounded like the start of an absurd joke.

CHAPTER FORTY-SIX

THIRTY MINUTES LATER, the judge turned onto Slauson as the time approached nine in the morning. Go-to-work traffic still clogged the streets with people everywhere, in the convenience stores, the gas stations and coffee shops. All of them blacks, going about their daily routine unaware that there was a murderer of Genie's caliber moving amongst them, on the loose, volatile, and absolutely deadly.

I said to Twyla, "Okay, here we are. We're coming up on 10th. What are we talking about here? Tell us where this place is. Point it out."

She leaned up, trying to see better, her chin a little higher in the air. She pointed. "Make a right. Right here. Yeah, yeah, down this street a little farther down."

"Where, Twyla? Describe it. We're just going to drive by so you can point it out. Give me some notice. I don't want to—"

She slumped down in the seat. "Oh, dear Lord." She put her hand over her face and tried to make herself small.

The judge caught on and slowed to a crawl, then stopped completely.

"Bruno?" Nicky said.

All of those actions happened on the edge of my awareness. I had automatically slipped into hunter mode, my attention focused down range at some furtive movement that caught my eye.

A male black adult, wearing an expensive black leather bomber jacket with the Raiders logo on the back, bebopped out of a wrought-iron gate headed for a Lexus parked on the street. He didn't look like a murderer, or even a gangster hood. He looked like a regular guy going out to his car on his way to work at a small corporate office, the kind of place that stocks a full lunchroom, with bagels and poppy seed muffins and four kinds of coffee.

Nicky followed my line of sight and turned in her seat. She saw the guy in the Raiders jacket. "Bruno, don't you do it. You call it in, you hear me?"

The judge said, "She's right, kid, you need to call this in."

I said to Twyla, "Is that him?"

She slid from the seat down to the floorboard at our feet, curling up into a tight little ball. "Twyla! Is that him?"

She squeaked. "Yes. Yes. Yes. Just keep driving. Keep going. You can't let him see me. He'll kill us all. I'm tellin' you right now, he'll kill us all."

"He's not going to see you, just stay down." My hand automatically went to the door handle. I couldn't let him go mobile; we'd have to find him all over again. I opened the door and popped out. As I did, I said, "Go to a phone and call 911."

The judge said, "Bruno, get back in this car, now."

I eased the door closed until it clicked. I reached under my truck driver shirt and pulled one of the .357s from my waistband. I held it down by my leg and walked casually along the street side of the cars parked on the curb, my focus on Genie.

Working the violent crimes team for all those years, chasing murderous men who had no compunction whatsoever about killing another human, I couldn't help but develop an unwanted taste for death, a big unhealthy dose of it. I hadn't had that taste for more than two years. It returned now like an old friend, hot and metallic, fueling adrenaline that made my pulse pound in the back of my eyes.

With each passing second, I moved closer to my target. Forty feet to go. Almost there. Thirty.

He made it to the Lexus, key in hand, ready to open the driver's door.

In the movies or TV crime shows, the good guy always yells, "Stop, police," or, "Freeze." That stupid move always sparks a foot chase. High drama, for no valid purpose other than drama. That doesn't happen in real life. In this part of the game you always try to get right up on the suspect before he realizes your intent. The goal is to get close enough to chunk him in the head with a blackjack, or as a last resort, club him with your gun.

Genie was smiling, enjoying the day, when his instinct kicked in. Out of the corner of his eye, he'd caught my movement heading right toward him. He lost his smile when his head whipped around to look at me. The shift in expression changed his entire look. Now he projected the face of a cold-blooded murderer that matched what I had expected to come upon. His eyes dropped down to my hand with the gun held by my leg.

Then he did something unexpected—he broke contact with me and looked back to the wrought-iron gate of the apartment complex. He'd come out ahead of his entourage, two thug uglies. His boys there to protect him were now coming out. He yelled to them. "Five-O. Five-O. Goddamn you!"

The two immediately went to guns, pulled them from their waistbands. They yanked them up and fired.

The sound of gunfire ripped open the quiet morning. I ducked and flinched. I fired three quick rounds at the two. Hit one of them.

He spun around but didn't go down. I turned and fired at Genie, whose hands still fumbled with the keys trying to get the car door open. I had to stop him any way I could. One round shattered the rear window, the other two thumped into the back of the trunk. A couple of inches to the left, I would've hit him for sure.

Genie dropped the keys and ran.

I let my gun drop to the ground, no time to reload. I pulled my second .357. The car next to me erupted with bullet holes and broken glass from a fusillade laid down by the other two. I ducked. I popped up and fired all six. I had to stop them quick or I wouldn't have a chance, not against two of them with semiautomatics. I hit the same guy a second time and missed the other. He dropped his magazine and was reloading. The one I'd hit twice wilted to the ground with an audible grunt and went still.

I dumped my empties in the street. The brass tinkled on the asphalt at my feet with the sound of a gentle wind chime. I went for a speed loader in my pocket, my hands solid and sure, but moving far too slow under the circumstances.

I wasn't going to make it.

The guy reloading moved toward me, smiling. He, too, knew I wasn't going to make it in time. He seated the magazine and hit the slide release chambering a round, still moving in closer to look me in the eye when he fired the final rounds into my body from no more than two or three feet away.

I got the speed loader locked in the cylinder, but I was out of time. Everything slowed down.

The other guy raised his gun, the end of the barrel as huge as a train tunnel.

He suddenly flipped backward with the simultaneous retort of a big gun.

I spun around.

The judge stood in the street by the open trunk of his Mercedes, a smoking Ithaca Deer Slayer 12 gauge held to his shoulder. The look of pure shock and fear on his face startled me out of my daze. Real time reengaged.

Behind me, running feet drew my attention. I turned. Genie ran down the middle of the street, opening a broad lead. He was going to get away. After all that had just happened, he was going to get away.

Nicky got out of the Mercedes. She looked scared. I checked out the two thugs. They were both down hard and would not be getting up on their own, if at all.

I yelled to Nicky, "Call 911." I turned and took off down the street after Genie.

CHAPTER FORTY-SEVEN

MY NECK AND shoulder stung. My shirt turned slick with sticky wetness. I'd been hit with pellets from the judge's shotgun. I'd been too close and got the edge of the Ithaca's pattern. I sucked wind trying to pour on the speed and gained nothing on Genie, who was younger and built with more muscle. I stuck the revolver in my waistband and used my arms to pump out a little more effort.

Genie cut across the street and took the first left, heading east. Then he took the first alley, heading north again toward Slauson. Dogs barked at us. We ran past trash cans and derelict cars and fences covered in gang graffiti.

Genie kept looking back. The move slowed him down just a tick. He yelled, "Who are you? Quit chasing me. I swear to God, I'll kill your ass."

I gained on him some more, closed to within ten yards. If he kept looking back and kept wasting his breath to yell threats, then I'd have him.

He hit the end of the alley and turned east again on Slauson, passing businesses. People stopped to watch the pursuit. The high drama. He stumbled and almost fell. I closed on him some more, seconds away from putting my hands on him. He regained his feet and panicked.

He abruptly turned into a big sit-down family restaurant called Mel's. The door slowed him just enough. I leaped and tackled him inside the door. We went down in a jumble of grunts and elbows and knees. My gun popped out and skittered away. His body was coiled like a steel spring, all muscle and motivation, dangerous and unrelenting.

I'd just grabbed onto the tiger's tail.

He turned and slugged me in the head, at the same time kicking viciously at my body. I held on, trying to climb along his waist and torso to get close enough to his head so I could punch him in the face and get a chokehold around his neck to shut him down.

He kicked loose from me, rolled, and tried to scramble to his feet. I got up and drove with my legs. I hit him again, my shoulder down. We flew deeper into the restaurant and crashed into a table of four. People screamed and scattered everywhere. I slipped on biscuits and gravy and scrambled eggs and syrup-covered waffles with whipped cream and strawberries.

"Stop! Police."

The blue uniform of a patrol officer came into view. He'd been eating his breakfast at the lunch counter.

"LA County Sheriff's Department," I yelled. "This guy's wanted for murder."

Genie had regained his feet. I charged and tackled him again. We flew past another table and hit the lunch bar. We flattened an elderly woman sitting there, rolled over her, and fell into the service area behind the lunch bar. The waitstaff ran. I grabbed a six-slice toaster from the counter. It burned my hands, but I clubbed Genie over the head with it. Nothing, no reaction. I hit him again and again. He fended me off with his arms and rabbit-punched me in the face. He hit my nose and made sparks fly behind my eyes.

The cop had come in closer, speaking into his lapel mic, frantic, yelling for code three backup. He pulled his baton, leaned over the lunch counter, and clubbed Genie across the back. "Stop resisting. Stop resisting and put your hands behind your back. Get down on the ground. Get down." The cop climbed over the counter, slipping and sliding, and engaged Genie, striking him as hard as he could with the baton. And still, we couldn't get him into custody. He was the most desperate person I had ever encountered. He had to get away no matter what the cost. This had become his last and only chance at freedom.

When Genie suddenly turned, he had a steak knife in his hand, the kind with a serrated blade to cut through cheap steaks. He stabbed me high in the shoulder. The pain shot down my back all the way to my heels. I pulled the knife out and threw it down.

He turned, raised both his hands, and shoved them into the face of the cop, rushing him, trying to get past him, shoving the cop backward. The cop tried to bat away his hands.

My chest heaved, trying to drag in more oxygen. I ran at Genie and hit him from behind. All three of us flew. We struck the display case by the cash register. Glass shattered. Bran muffins, pecan pies, Rice Crispy treats flew everywhere. In the confusion, I'd lost my grip on Genie.

The cop had a hold of one of his legs as Genie dragged him along headed for the same door that we'd entered. I got up with little strength left and went at him one last time. I leaped just as Genie shook free from the cop. He took one long step on his way to freedom. I hit him, grabbing his leg, and took him down one last time.

I needed something to hit him with, anything to shut him down.

He reared back with his one loose leg and kicked me in the face. The light in the restaurant warbled like heat waves. My hands and arms started to lose their strength. My grip eased.

Genie had won. He was going to get away.

Then I remembered the Walther PPK in my back pocket, the one I'd taken from Nicky back at her apartment. I held on to Genie's leg with one arm as he brought his free leg back to kick me again; this one would shake me loose for sure. There was no way I could let him get away.

I pulled the .380, stuck it to the back of his leg, and pulled the trigger.

The gun popped and jumped in my hand.

Genie's back went stiff then shuddered in a convulsion. He yelped. And, still, he tried to drag himself away with his arms and hands along the carpet. I stuck the gun up against his other leg and pulled the trigger. The gun jumped. More smoke rose in an acrid white cloud.

Then everything went quiet.

CHAPTER FORTY-EIGHT

GENIE STOPPED MOVING forward. He curled up clutching his legs, his face a rictus of pain. He took in a deep breath and let loose a long "Aiiiiiiie," not out of pain but more a howl of regret that his legs could no longer service him in his desperate plight.

I struggled to my feet, the Walther PPK hanging loose from my hand, my chest heaving, not bringing in near enough oxygen. I swayed and almost went down. I bent over, put my hands on my knees, and focused until my heart and lungs caught up. I leaned over and offered my hand to the cop, who was trying to stand. I helped him get to his feet. Blood covered the left side of his face, and on the right his eye was swelling shut. "Thanks," I said. "He would've gotten away without your help."

He nodded, still catching his breath. "You shot him. I can't believe you shot him. He didn't even have a weapon. Jesus, he didn't have a weapon. Man, I really need to see some ID, like right now."

I shoved the gun in my front pocket, took out my flat badge, and handed it to him. Outside, faraway sirens drew closer. I went to the phone that had been on the cash register counter, now overturned on the floor, and picked it up. I pushed down the receiver, let up, got a dial tone, and dialed a number from memory.

Wicks picked up on the first ring. "Wicks."

"It's me." I took in another long breath as he took a moment to pause and decide if he really wanted to talk to me at all.

"Whatta ya need, Bruno? Make it quick."

"I got Little Genie."

"You what? Where are you? What happened? Is he alive? Did you have to shoot him?"

"Just listen, would you?"

"Sure. Sure. Go."

"It went down bad. You're my first call. You understand what I'm saying? Tenth and Slauson, you're going to have to hurry to beat the other detectives."

"I understand. I'll be there in less than twenty. You hold on, pal. You hear me? I'll be there in twenty." He hung up.

I hung up and looked around. The restaurant was decimated. It wouldn't have looked much different if an out-of-control car had driven through the glass wall from the outside. The patrons who had not fled out the front or the back doors stood off to the sides staring in stunned horror. I held up my hand. "It's okay. It's all over."

Two of the people from the table we knocked over lay on the ground moaning, holding their ribs or arms. The elderly woman from the lunch counter lay right where we rolled over her, not moving. Her eyes were closed and her chest rose and fell as she breathed, her cheek in her biscuits and gravy.

I took my cuffs from my belt, bent down, and pulled Genie's arms behind his back and cuffed him. His hands and arms were covered in his own warm blood. I wiped my hands on my jeans.

The cop handed me back my flat badge. I took it and handed him the Walther PPK. I said, "Can you handle this scene? There was an officer-involved shooting about a block down. I really need to get back there."

He shook his head. "No, there's an officer-involved shooting right *here*. You need to stay and explain all this to my sergeant." He looked around in awe. From his expression, he'd never been involved in any-thing so violent. "This is a clusterfuck of the first order. My sergeant's on his way. I don't think he's going to be happy. So no, you're going to stay right here until he comes and says it's okay for you to leave. Which I'm guessing isn't going to be anytime in the next ten or twelve hours."

"Sorry, not going to happen. I need to get back there now."

"You shot this guy in both his legs. He wasn't armed. You can't leave."

"Did you hear me when I said this guy is wanted for murder? He killed three people—those are just the ones we know about. He's death-row eligible. We—that's you and me—we couldn't let him get away under any circumstances. He's a threat to public safety. What I did was what needed to be done and absolutely within the law. Do you have paramedics on the way to treat him?"

"Yes."

"Good. Now, administer first aid to her first." I pointed over to the woman at the lunch counter. "And him second." I pointed to Genie. "Try and stop his bleeding until paramedics arrive. I have to leave. I'll be one block down on 10th, south of Slauson. Tell your sergeant where he can find me. I'm not running away from this, I'm just needed down there."

I walked out crunching broken glass, dodging smashed pastries and overturned plates of food.

Outside, the fresh air smelled wonderful. The bright sunlight made me squint. My whole body throbbed, my face, my hands, my shoulder, and my neck. The more steps I took, the more strength returned.

I thought back over what I could have done differently and found only one thing. I never should've brought Nicky and the judge along. Judge Connors had shot and killed a gun thug. Though justi-fied, not even the great Robby Wicks would be able to sweep that little boner under the rug.

CHAPTER FORTY-NINE

WHEN I FIRST joined the violent crimes team, Wicks had schooled me in how to handle violent situations where, in the split second it took to make a decision—to shoot or not to shoot. Now, even with the right choice, I ended up with the joker from the deck. He'd said, "I'm your first call. You understand? If the shooting stinks at all, I'm your first call."

That's why when I'd called him, I cut right through all the formalities and said it quickly and economically so he'd understand.

I'd called him at his desk at headquarters a good forty minutes away. That's if traffic worked in his favor. Twenty minutes for him to get to the Crenshaw district was a pipe dream. But I had no doubt he would try his damnedest.

Now, after the adrenaline started to bleed off and I turned down 10th, the full impact of what had happened hit me. What a God-awful mess.

Cop cars rolling code-three continued to zip by behind me headed east, going to the mess at Mel's restaurant. Soon they'd be rolling hot down 10th. The street would be clogged with black-and-whites and plain-wrapped detective cars. They'd be there long into the night, with their Klieg lights, forensic techs, the deputy coroner, and homicide detectives from two different agencies, taking notes and measurements, second-guessing every-thing that had happened.

Up ahead, Judge Connors sat on the curb at the rear of his Mercedes, his head in his hands, the shotgun on the ground next to him. I'd done this to him. It was my fault. I'd put him in a position where he thought he needed to take action.

He'd taken a life, a difficult thing to do under any circumstances.

He'd never again be the same. He'd have the nightmares, and the shakes, to deal with in the upcoming weeks and even months. I knew, because I'd been there too often.

Nicky stood close with her hand resting on his shoulder, quietly reassuring him. There wasn't any sign of Twyla; she was either hiding in the car or she'd fled. I couldn't blame her.

Off to the right, in the grassy area between the sidewalk and the apartment, lay both gun thugs, absolutely still—the eerie kind of still that only comes with the recent dead.

When I was halfway to them, Nicky looked up and saw me coming, relief plain in her expression. Her emotions shifted to shock. She ran to me. "Oh, my God, Bruno, what happened? Here, sit down, you need to sit down. Where are you hurt? You have blood all over you." She tried to guide me out of the street. Instead I took her into my arms and hugged her tight. I soaked her up. I wouldn't have the opportunity again for hours upon hours to come.

There wasn't any time to dawdle. Things were going to start moving faster now. I pulled away from Nicky, took her hand, and led her over to the judge. Off to the side in the grass, the judge had lost his breakfast. The sour stench wafted on the still, warm morning air. I squatted down next to him. "You okay, Your Honor?"

He didn't look up and said nothing, his face in his hands. He was right on the razor's edge of going into shock.

I put my hand on his knee. "Listen, I owe you a great debt of thanks that I can never repay. You saved my life."

He looked up, his eyes red and swollen. He swallowed hard. "I what?"

"You saved my life. That guy was about to drop the hammer on me."

"I did, didn't I?"

"Yes, you did. And I'll tell you one thing for sure—I'd have you as my partner any day. You can back me up anytime you want. That was one helluva shot. I don't know many cops who would've taken it. That guy was too close to me. Thank you."

His chin came up a little. He broke into a smile. "Damn straight that was a tough shot."

"Yes, it was." My hand involuntarily went up to my neck.

His eyes finally took me in as he shook off the shock that was trying hard to overcome him. The information from his eyes finally got through to his brain. "Bruno, you're hurt. You're bleeding all over the place. Look at your poor face, your shoulder."

"I'm all right."

"You sure?"

"I'm fine."

"Did you get him? Did you get that son of a bitch?"

"Yeah, with the help of another cop, we cornered him up the street in a restaurant. That's where all the cop cars are going. They'll be coming back here soon. We need to get our story straight."

"There's no *story* here," Nicky said, "only the truth." She pointed to the dead on the grass. "That was a good shoot. You don't get shoots that are that squeaky-clean. So, no, we're going to tell it just like it happened, right down the line."

The judge said, "Yeah? You think so?"

"I was standing right next to you, Your Honor; I saw it all. Bruno's right—he'd be dead if you hadn't taken affirmative action to stop the deadly threat he was facing. You literally saved his ass."

The judge struggled to his feet, a much larger smile trying to make it out of his gloomy expression.

I said, "I don't want to be the wet blanket, but there's going to be some shit about the judge being out on an operation when he was told not to. The presiding judge is going to—"

"Oh, no," the judge said. "To hell with him. I'm not worried about him. What can he say? We took down a murderer and two of his gun monkeys. They called the game, we didn't. Right, Bruno? This was their doing." He'd started talking like the old judge again, using antiquated terms like "gun monkeys" and "calling the game," words often used in old crime novels and movies.

"That's right, Your Honor, you have nothing to worry about with the shooting. She's right, it's as clean as they come."

A wave of dizziness swayed me. I pivoted on my heels, and sat on the curb. I lay back and closed my eyes as the sirens turned down 10th headed our way, growing louder and louder, their echo pinging off the houses.

The shooting on 10th was clean, but what happened in Mel's, the shooting of Genie in the back of the legs to stop him . . . well, that could be viewed a number of ways, and most of those weren't in the vein of how the public believed law enforcement should act. There wasn't any doubt the media would crucify me.

CHAPTER FIFTY

THE PARAMEDICS LOADED me into the back of the ambulance on a gurney and closed the doors. I didn't want to go but couldn't argue with them, not with the world spinning so fast and my stomach trying its best to heave-ho. They said the dizziness came with the blood loss and the blows to the head. Once they got "the volume up" I'd feel better and those symptoms would subside. They had cut off my truck driver shirt to find the two gunshot wounds, one in the fleshy part of my neck and the other high on the right upper back. I tried to tell them that those were merely pellets from the shotgun and no big deal. They hadn't hit anything vital or I'd have already been a lot worse off. It was the steak knife wound where Genie had stabbed me that caused the most pain.

Nicky wasn't a relative, so they wouldn't let her ride along even though she flashed her deputy DA badge. She was a material witness to the shooting. I wanted her to stay and give the judge moral support. The judge had somehow pushed aside his regret and remorse and stood in the street telling everyone who came within range what had happened, an instinctual strategy for sloughing off all the pent-up emotions. His rapid speech and storytelling worked as a distraction, rather than dealing with the true issue.

The paramedic in back started an IV. I immediately felt better. The driver pulled away, headed south on 10th. Through the back window, I could see up to the top of the street. Wicks' black Dodge rounded the corner at high speed. His car brakes hissed and smoked white. He stopped at the clot of police vehicles and got out in a rush. He'd made it in about twenty-seven minutes. Had to be a new record.

I closed my eyes and tried to relax. He'd take care of the judge and Nicky. I needed to get to a phone to call Olivia and Dad to tell them I was okay. They didn't need to see it on the news first. And this *would be* on the news.

The paramedic said, "Okay, I'm going to give you something for the pain." Seconds later the flush of the narcotic covered me all over with a warm blanket. I gave myself to it and drifted off. My last thought went to my guns. I'd left one in the street on 10th and one on the floor of Mel's. I'd get them back eventually, but for the moment I was unarmed, a state I had never been in since I was sworn in as a deputy sheriff. I felt vulnerable and defenseless as I slipped into the darkness.

*   *   *

I awoke in the ER with Wicks standing at my bedside, shaking my arm. "Hey there, buddy boy, how are you feeling?"

"I . . . ah . . . what time is it?" I had a blinding headache.

"Going on six o'clock. You've been doggin' it here for close to eight hours. You going to make a career out of this hospital bed? We need to get back out there to take down Borkow."

"Where's my daughter? Did someone tell my daughter? Where's my dad?"

"Your dad just stepped out to get a sandwich. Olivia is at home. Your dad said something about her being mad as hell about something. Once she heard you weren't hurt real bad and would be home tomorrow, she said she'd talk to you later. That's kind of tough. I guess you were right about needing to have a talk with her. You want me to say something to her? Tell her what a great job you did out there? Tell her that you're, you know, hurt real bad and—"

I held up my hand. "Just stop talking, okay?"

I'd only heard him string lots of sentences together like that when someone from his team was hurt.

"I can throw it right back on her, just say the word. When I get done with her, she'll be like putty in your hands, trust me on this."

"I don't want you to throw anything right back on her or anyone else. Get the nurse. I need to get out of here. I need to go talk to my daughter."

I knew what had happened. There was only one thing that could make her that mad, and without a doubt, I deserved every bit of her anger. I just wished I'd had the nerve to tell her myself about what I'd done to Derek before she'd found out on her own.

I swung my legs over the edge of the bed. The dizziness hit but not nearly as severe as before. I could control it.

Wicks held up his hands. "Whoa there, cowboy. The doc said they're keeping you overnight for observation. You took a couple of hard kicks to the head and you lost a lot of blood. So if you're going to get up, take it real slow."

"Just get my clothes, would you, please, mother?"

I wanted to know where Nicky was but couldn't ask him. He went over to the cabinet and took out a brown paper grocery bag. "Your dad brought these for you. They cut off all your clothes. The way you slept, they think you might have a concussion."

I held out my hands and looked at them. They were bandaged. He handed me the bag. I set it on the bed next to me.

Wicks asked, "What happened to your dickbeaters?"

I held them up, the white bandages like catchers' mitts. "It's from a hot toaster."

He chuckled. "Oh man, I saw that part. You picked up that six-slice toaster and went at Little Genie like some kind of caveman. That was one of the greatest things I've ever seen. I mean, what a brutal fight, winner take all."

"Wait, what do you mean you saw it?"

"Buddy boy, you are a movie star. Old Mel, the owner of the restaurant, is paranoid about his people stealing plates of food and money from the till. He's got the whole place wired for video. We got a beautiful VHS tape of the whole thing."

"Oh, man, you've got to be kidding me."

CHAPTER FIFTY-ONE

I SAID, "Is there going to be any shit over it? I mean the way I took him down?"

Wicks shook his head. "Not from our department. He would've gotten away had you not shot him in the legs. No, they said it was unorthodox, but you get high marks for stayin' in the game like you did. It doesn't hurt that this guy really gave the department a black eye escaping through the window of Visiting like that. The brass are just glad he's back in custody. That was really something, I'm tellin' ya. What a knock-down-drag-out ass kickin'. I wish I'd have been there."

"Huh. That's not at all what I expected as a reaction from the department."

"Now that other copper, that blue-belly, his department put him on admin leave pending disciplinary review. I talked to his lieutenant, who said he'd be surprised if the guy doesn't draw thirty days on the bricks. He may even get the ax. He's on probation."

"Ah, man, that isn't fair. I'm the one who chased Genie right into his lap. He did exactly what he was supposed to do. Can you do something to help that guy?"

"Their department is afraid of that VHS tape. I mean scared-to-death kind of afraid. They don't want what happened in that restaurant to get out. They're sure it's going to leak. Three civilians were hurt and the place was absolutely trashed. They don't understand that it was just the cost of doing business."

"How bad were the civilians hurt?"

"Not bad. Bruises, some broken bones, nothing major, but it's going to be a big paycheck for them if that VHS tape ever makes it to a civil trial. No way can they take it before a jury. Risk management is already negotiating an out-of-court settlement in the high six figures for each of them and the restaurant owner.

"Firing that blue-belly is a preemptive move for their department to moderate the liability for when the tape does leak. They're right; it's way too good for it not to. When it does, they can say, 'See, we took care of our own dirty laundry.'"

Wicks picked up the TV remote and turned it on. "Take a look at this. The story's gone national."

The six o'clock news came on. The talking head with a pretty face and blond hair held an ice-cream-cone mic. She stood on the sidewalk in front of Mel's, her lips moving without sound. Wicks left it muted. Good thing, with my headache.

"You don't need to hear anything she's saying, just watch." The cameraman moved in close going right by her and shot tape of the interior through the window of the restaurant and caught all the destructive aftermath. The mashed food, the overturned tables, the broken glass, all the blood on the floor where Genie ended up with both legs gunshot. It did look like the end result of some kind of B-rated horror movie. Somehow it looked worse than when I was standing in the middle of all that mayhem.

Wicks laughed. "Looks like a pro football game went into sudden-death overtime. I'm tellin' you, this one is going to be talked about in the locker room for decades."

The TV feed shifted to interviews of patrons who'd been in the restaurant at the time. They looked angry and spoke with wild hands.

"Turn it off."

Wicks shut it off.

"How is the judge holding up?"

"He's eating it up with a spoon."

"That's just a façade," I said. "It'll hit him tomorrow, you wait and see. When it does, we need to have someone with him."

Wicks turned serious. "The shoot team is going to need a statement from you sooner rather than later. Nicky backs both of you guys right to the wall. With her in your corner, that shooting on 10th won't be any problem."

"They find both of my guns?"

He ignored that question. "Nicky and the judge told the shoot team everything except how you guys got there. How did you track Genie to that location? Why don't you tell me how that happened and I'll pass it on to the team."

In all the action, the hot emotions, the blood and death, the judge and Nicky had the frame of mind to protect Twyla. Good for them. Now Wicks wanted to know in case he could use the same information to track down Borkow. That wasn't going to happen. He didn't care about informants, and at times, needlessly exposed them to discovery.

"It was an anonymous phone tip."

"Bullshit. Come on, Bruno, don't yank on my dick here."

I said nothing and stared at him. "Does it really matter? I thought you said the department was just happy to get Little Genie back in custody?"

Wicks shook his head, his jaw locked in anger. "Did this tipster also tell you how to find Borkow? He's the one we really need to get. And if this so-called tipster knew where to find Genie, he might know where to find the others."

"No, but the sooner I get home, the sooner the informant might call again."

"Yeah, right. I know bullshit when it's being spoon-fed to me. We're gonna revisit this later, you can bet on it."

He took a step closer to the bed. He pulled out a Smith and Wesson 9mm from the small of his back and handed it to me. "There is going to be some shit over that peashooter you used on Little Genie; it wasn't department approved. You might take three to five days on the bricks, but that's not a big deal. You and I have both been there before. I can cover the loss of wages with some overtime. You know the routine."

I took the gun from him. "Thanks."

It was a good thing I did. The door to the room opened. In walked John Lau, Nicky's husband.

CHAPTER FIFTY-TWO

JOHN LAU CAME in wearing his starched and pressed Los Angeles County Sheriff's uniform tailored to hug his fit body, the creases razor sharp. He wore the tan and green well. He had wide shoulders and a narrow waist. His black shoes were spit-shined to a high sheen, and his gun belt creaked when he walked. His expression didn't betray his purpose, but why else would he be at the hospital if it weren't over his wife, Nicky Rivers-Lau? I remembered the look on Nicky's face when she told me she'd staked him out at the North Woods Inn restaurant and caught him holding the hand of another woman while they crossed the street to the hotel. And what she said about being glad she wasn't me when Lau found out about us.

My pulse rate increased and my face flushed hot. I couldn't keep the guilt from sauntering into the room right alongside him. My stomach churned acid. I wanted to crawl into a hole and pull it in after me.

Lau was Wicks' friend. Wicks was my friend. That dropped Wicks right into the middle of my mess. Now Wicks would be forced to make a choice. I'd been the one to force him into it. It'd been my error in judgment.

Lau came over to Wicks, who watched him, one predator to another. "Evening, John," Wicks said. "What the hell are you doing here?" But Wicks knew. He was testing the water to see if there was going to be a problem. Wicks offered his hand and they shook.

Lau looked half-Chinese with his almond-shaped eyes and his black hair left a little longer than SEB usually allowed. I could see why the women went for him, why Nicky might have loved him. He also had to be smart and cunning to be the commander of SEB.

"I came to ask your detective a couple of questions. You don't mind, do you, Robby?"

"Oh, is that right? Questions about what?" Wicks must not have told Lau about how Wicks had caught his detective stepping out with Lau's wife.

Lau held his hands wide. "I'm not sure I like your tone, Robby. What's going on? I thought we were friends."

"Cut the shit, John. How can we help you?"

Lau's face twisted into a smug grin filled with anger and animus. I didn't have time for this bullshit. I needed to get home to Olivia. I needed to sit her down and explain the best way I could what had happened with Derek. Try to make her understand why I did it. I couldn't begin to think how those words would sound. I didn't have an excuse or valid reason. I had screwed up big-time. That was what I would have to tell her and hope she'd forgive me.

Lau nodded toward the Smith and Wesson 9mm sitting on the bed next to me. "What's with the gun? You two expecting trouble? Maybe I should have some of my guys stationed outside your door? After all that's happened, you never know who might be coming for you."

There it was, a veiled threat revealing his true motivation for standing in front of us pretending concern about another matter.

I said, "I had to leave my two guns at the scene. Wicks was kind enough to lend me this one." I picked it up, dropped the magazine, put the magazine back, and checked the slide to be sure one was down the pipe. I did it to play along with Lau's stupid little game.

Wicks smirked. "John, you might not know how investigators take your gun for evidence since you've never been in a violent confrontation. They hold them for ballistic confirmation."

Lau crossed his arms on his chest, a move that accentuated his thick biceps. "I got a call from Homicide. They told me that a gun registered to me was used in a shooting in that clusterfuck over in the Crenshaw district. I just wanted to know how your guy came into possession of my gun and why he thought he needed to use it shooting an unarmed man in both his legs. I don't think that's too much to ask, do you?"

Wicks didn't have all the facts and this item caught him unaware. He looked surprised. "Why don't we let Homicide straighten out all those minor details, shall we, John? Bruno took down a violent offender who'd escaped from the jail. The same guy I think your *elite* division has been looking for hot and heavy and haven't been able to find."

Wicks had taken my side and forsaken his friend. I'd be in his debt. "Now if you don't mind," Wicks said, "my detective needs to finish debriefing me on what happened."

Lau hesitated, staring Wicks down. Another friendship lost over a woman. He headed for the door. He turned. "I'll come back tomorrow. Then I'll expect answers." He left.

I took a shirt out of the paper bag, dropped the front of my hospital gown, and put it on. I slipped on the underwear and the jeans. I didn't feel as vulnerable with pants on. I stuck the gun in my waistband under my shirt.

Wicks said, "Bruno, seriously, the doc said you need to stay here overnight for observation."

The hospital door opened and in walked Dad carrying a bag with a hero sandwich in one hand and a Coca-Cola in the other. He smiled when he saw me.

He didn't know how much I needed that smile.

I leaned over and slipped into my shoes without putting on the socks. "Hi, Dad."

He came over close. "Should you be getting out of bed right now? I thought the doctor said you'd be in the hospital for at least two days, maybe three. He said you're pretty beat up and took a couple hard knocks to the head."

"I'm fine, Dad." I took the Coca-Cola and sandwich from him even though I wasn't hungry. I opened the can and took a chug, more to show him I was okay.

Wicks said, "I have to make a couple of phone calls. I'll be right back."

"Thanks, boss," I said.

He left.

"Please, Bruno, get back into bed. Do it for me."

"What's going on with O? Wicks said she wouldn't come to the hospital."

He put his warm hand on my chest and eased me back to sitting on the edge of the bed. "She's real mad, Son. She came over to my place with her suitcase. She asked if she could stay for a while. I told her she could. Hope that's okay. I didn't want her out wandering the street. I was going to tell you about it, but you got yourself caught up in that big mess over on Slauson. It's all over the news."

"No, I'm glad you did. I need to talk with her. Can you give me a ride over there?"

"Of course I can, but maybe you should give her a little time to cool off and to think about it."

Maybe he knew better, but right or wrong, I had a desperate need to see my daughter. I needed to ask for forgiveness.

He smiled again. It lit up my life. He said, "Did you give that little girl a puppy?"

I smiled back.

He said, "Cutest darn puppy I think I've ever seen. That was the smartest thing you've done in a while. I wonder where you got that idea?" He winked. "Now that she's staying at my place, you're comin' over any time that dog messes the floor."

"I will, Pop, I promise."

CHAPTER FIFTY-THREE

LIZZETTE LAY NAKED on the short stack of California king mattresses, three of them in a pile situated on the floor next to the Jacuzzi and only several feet from the Olympic-sized pool in the Muscle Max gym. She stretched out, feline in her repose, semi-wrapped in the white satin sheets, emitting a cute little snore. She was a little too skinny and had an expensive tattoo on her upper back, the right shoulder, depicting a woman with blond hair and red lipstick. She said it wasn't Twyla, but Borkow knew better. He sat naked, reclined in his La-Z-Boy chair, feet up, with a vodka gimlet in a highball glass. He was watching the TV, sated from his time in the Jacuzzi, then from the heavy aerobics on the bed with Lizzy. He'd taken a dip in the pool right after and his skin still tingled, a sensation created when he moved from the hot water and then right into the cold. Life was good. He could stay there in Muscle Max a good long time if things just stayed like this. Sure, he could.

To the right of the pool on a repurposed bookshelf, Payaso had put on display the thirty pairs of shoes taken from that lawyer broad's lair on Bronson Street in Hollywood. He didn't like to think of her name anymore, not with the way she'd treated him, not since he had not gotten out of her where she'd hid the rest of his money. He took her expensive shoes instead.

He raised the remote and changed the channel to the news. He wanted to hear his tag again, *"The Most Wanted Man in the Seven Western States."* Maybe after taking out Gloria Bleeker, he'd earned something a little heavier, more along the lines of *"The Most Dangerous Man West of the Mississippi."* Yeah, he liked that one a lot.

He'd been biding his time with reruns of *The Golden Girls.* The costume director on that show, a fellow lover of the foot, must've had an unlimited budget or he'd sweet-talked the big names in the industry to donate the shoes for free advertising. That guy knew how to dress his women, and Borkow wanted to meet him. Those old biddies on that show had some ugly feet, but their shoes... whoa mama.

He clicked down to the local station. The talking heads came on the news with the top story. The video feed looked to Borkow like he had missed a major earthquake while he'd been messing around with Lizzy. A restaurant in LA had been trashed. Through the window of a place called Mel's, the cameraman panned the decimated interior.

The screen cut to some earlier footage of a black man grimacing in pain while strapped to a gurney and being loaded into an ambulance.

Borkow sat forward in his chair, his naked skin peeling away from the cheap vinyl. He pointed for no one's benefit. "Hey! Hey! That's Little Genie. They got Little Genie. Son of a bitch, they got Little Genie!"

Lizzette rolled over onto her side. The satin sheet fell away from her bottom and the tattooed woman on her back stared at him. Odd as it seemed, that woman now resembled the face of Gloria Bleeker glaring at him.

Borkow closed his eyes and shook himself. He looked again. Bleeker disappeared and the resemblance to Twyla returned.

Lizzy muttered, "Huh?"

The TV screen cut away again, this time to a stand-up with a female reporter talking to an overly tanned guy dressed in a cheesy western-cut polyester suit.

Borkow jumped to his feet. "Hey, I know that dude." He was the guy with that asshole Bruno Johnson, the bailiff. The ones who raided the Grand Orchid. Borkow, his fingers shaking, hit the button on the remote to take off the mute.

The cowboy in the suit, the one who'd flipped off the SWAT team leader, spoke first.

"Members of The Los Angeles County Sheriff's elite violent crimes team tracked the notorious murderer Sammy Eugene Ray to this location. Ray had escaped from the county jail and was considered armed and extremely dangerous. After a gun battle two blocks south of here, members of the team chased Ray—known on the street as Little Genie—to this location, where he refused surrender. As you can see, he was extremely desperate."

"Lieutenant Wicks, isn't it true that one of your detectives shot Sammy Ray twice, once in each leg, and that Sammy Ray was unarmed?"

"I cannot comment on an ongoing investigation. But maybe you didn't hear me when I said that the man was wanted—listed as armed and extremely dangerous. He was in custody for the murders of four men and—"

"But he's still going to trial, so isn't he innocent until proven guilty? Doesn't that mean your detective shot an unarmed, innocent man in both of his legs?"

"You can spin it any way you want and you usually do. And you have your facts wrong—he's already been convicted and he got four life terms. But as far as I'm concerned, the proper amount of force was used to effect the arrest. He is back in custody where he belongs and will stand trial for these new killings over on Tenth. Thank you." He walked away.

*   *   *

"Payaso! Get your ass in here!" Borkow's demand echoed off the walls of the indoor pool area. Lizzy raised her head and looked around, her hair mussed and her eyes tented.

"Get dressed, babe, we have to roll."

"Huh?" she said. "Really? Can't I stay here and sleep?"

"I said get your ass dressed. I'm not going to tell you again."

Payaso silently appeared at his side, almost as if he'd come through the wall. Borkow jumped. "I wish you wouldn't keep doing that." He pointed to the TV. "Did you see this? They got Little Genie."

"Yes. I warned you it would happen."

"You warned me that they would get Little Genie so quickly? I don't remember you telling me anything of the sort."

Payaso shook his head. "No, I told you that Bruno Johnson doesn't play games. He's the real deal."

"The news just said that cowboy's team took him down, not Johnson."

Payaso shook his head again. "No, it was Johnson. He also shot down two of Genie's men, then chased Genie on foot to that restaurant."

"How do you know? Never mind. Johnson did all that?"

"The judge shot one of them. Johnson took the other two by himself. Genie was about to get away. Johnson shot him in both his legs to stop him. He'll be coming for us next. You won't be safe here much longer. We have to make a move. We need to do it right now."

"He shot him in both his legs?" Borkow hopped around putting on his pants without bothering with underwear—going commando.

He was real careful when he zipped up. "Don't just stand there, bring the RV around. We gotta make some moves, all right. We're going to put that big black bastard off his game. He shot Little Genie in both his legs, you believe that shit? He's not going to shoot me in both my legs, that's for damn sure. Make a call to that kid. Tell him we're coming to see him about his girlfriend, now. Right now."

CHAPTER FIFTY-FOUR

DAD DIDN'T SAY much on the ride from the hospital to Wilmington Boulevard where I'd left the Ford Ranger. The brooding silence meant he didn't approve of something that I had done. I'd left the hospital against doctor's orders. In Dad's world, why go to the doctor if you didn't follow what they recommended? But I sensed that was just the catalyst for a much larger issue.

"I'm sorry," I said. "I might've stayed if I didn't need to talk with Olivia. It's important."

"No, you would not have stayed, and with Olivia, it's nothing that couldn't wait until you got out of the hospital in a few days. They wanted you to stay. The doctor *strongly* recommended it."

I didn't tell him how Borkow used his granddaughter as a diversion so Borkow could escape from jail. He didn't need those kinds of worries, that kind of white-hot anger. If I told him, Dad might've been mad enough to go against his own edicts, pick up a ball bat and go looking for Borkow on his own. No one messed with Dad's granddaughter.

"I'm okay, Dad, really. But there is something that needs to be addressed with Olivia right now."

He nodded and pulled up behind my truck still parked in the same place where the judge had met us hours earlier, just before I made the wrong choice taking the judge and Nicky with me.

"She's at the house doing homework," Dad said. "She told me she wanted some time away from you so she could think this through. With all that's happened, I suggest that you respect her wishes, let things cool off just a little before you talk to her. She's more mature than you give her credit for. She's a bright young girl. You did a great job raising her, Bruno."

A lump rose in my throat, because I hadn't done a great job, not really, not if she was linked to the likes of Derek Sams and I'd allowed it to happen.

We sat there for a time, both looking out the windshield of his car.

I put my hand on the door latch to exit out of the uncomfortable situation. I didn't want to leave it like that and didn't know what else I could say to make him see how I felt about what needed to be done and when to do it.

"Hold it just a minute, would you, Son?"

I let go of the door latch and waited.

He said, "You remember what I always told you and Noble about what's most important? The one thing in life that makes all the difference, the one thing that means everything, and that tells the most about a man's character?"

I nodded but still couldn't look at him.

I felt his eyes on me. When he spoke next, his tone came out lower, more sincere than any time in the last few days, any time in the last six months. "Say it, Son, show me that you know what I'm talking about."

I swallowed hard. The words to his lesson came out of my mouth by rote. "No matter what the circumstances, always be nice. More important than that, be generous. If you always do those two things, you can never go wrong in life."

"That's exactly right. In your job you always followed your heart, you did what you most desired, what you wanted to do, and you were—*you are*—very good at it. You might even be the best there is. That's very commendable. But in doing it, you've missed out on a lot. I thought that when you transferred to work in the court, you'd finally made the change and had gotten back on the right path."

I had no idea this was really the way he thought. His words hurt worse than the buckshot cut from my flesh. "Now you're saying I'm right back to where I was, back in the hunt, a job that lacks all generosity and the ability to be nice to my fellow humans. Is that what you're saying?"

"What do you think? All those people you chased down, you never had the opportunity to be nice, not once. It's not your fault. It just wasn't in the nature of the job. That meant you never had the opportunity to be generous either. Did you? Not that you could. Don't get me wrong. I understand you did what you had to do and that you were left with no choice. I love you for it. You did accomplish a great deal by taking those bad people off the street. They would have surely hurt others had you not stopped them."

I didn't have to reply. We both knew the way all of those events turned out, all the blood and bone. He was right. It was the exact opposite of nice and generous. How could that kind of life not change a person?

"I know," I said. "I realize that now, being on the hunt all the time, I wasted my chance to live. That's what you're really trying to say. I understand that now. I do."

Sitting there in the car with my dad, reviewing the past events in my life in a flurry of memory, all those images of violence, the smell of gun smoke, the rictus of pain on the faces of the crumpled and captured, pain I'd inflicted on those who'd asked for it, I realized I'd been running hard without letup. That in doing so, I'd been living in a false world, one I'd created in my own mind and at the same time forsaking all else.

In comparison, Dad was a stalwart pillar of the community, a stellar example of what it is to live a healthy and upright life. I had to look at the raw truth about myself. I was beat to hell, shot, and stabbed; my relationship with my daughter in shambles; my daughter, my reputation, and integrity impugned over a relationship, and for what? His words never meant more to me than in that moment. I now understood the magnitude of my error in my life's chosen path.

Dad was a postman. He was never called upon to move heaven and earth and never would be. He never saved anyone's life, but what he did do was live a clean and untarnished life, free from moral turpitude. He did it to the best of his ability. At the same time, he did his best to raise two boys in a difficult environment. He did a damn good job with what he had to work with.

He'd always been proud of me for each one of my accomplishments: first becoming a deputy sheriff, passing the strenuous and difficult sheriff's academy, going to work in the jail, then working patrol on the same streets where I grew up. For all of those things he literally beamed with pride. He told everyone who would listen, and even a few of those who wouldn't, how proud he was of me.

Then I transferred to the violent crimes team, where I chased violence. I chased death. Things changed. I changed. From that point on, I'd missed my chance at living a life like his. I'd deviated from the path. The job had changed me. The job had changed everything. The worst part about it, the absolute horrible thing about it, was that I couldn't take any of it back. I had to live with all that I had done, all that I had screwed up. Olivia was the biggest casualty of that error in judgment. Leaving the violent crimes team and taking the job in the courts hadn't been enough. No matter what, I had to fix my life even if it meant quitting the sheriff's department.

I was going to quit.

That decision stood out blatant and obvious, a choice without rival. I had tried to leave the life and at the same time keep one foot in by working in the courts. But that hadn't worked. My past and my ability to run down the violent and morally bankrupt had pulled me back in. If I went back to the courts, it would just happen again. The only way to truly escape that life was to leave it altogether. Maybe I'd apply at the post office.

I definitely would not continue working for Robby Wicks or chasing that morally demented Louis Borkow. Law enforcement would catch up to him soon enough. I needed to let go of my anger. I needed to get back on the right path and retake control of my life.

I would quit the sheriff's department.

"I really need to talk with her tonight," I said. "Do you think she'd talk to me on the phone?"

Dad reached over and put his warm hand on my arm. "I can only promise you that I'll do my best when I ask her."

"Thanks, Dad. I'll go back to the apartment and wait by the phone."

"Good boy. Please, Son, I really want you to rest for the next three days just like the doctor said. Stay in bed. If I can't get Olivia to talk to you on the phone tonight, I promise I'll talk her into coming to see you tomorrow."

"I'll call Wicks as soon as I get home and tell him I'm out for good."

"I know how difficult that's going to be for you. You won't regret it, Bruno."

I got out and closed the car door. The Smith and Wesson automatic hung heavy in the back of my waistband. From leaning back against the seat, the steel frame made an imprint in my flesh. I'd never been so aware of a gun before, the instrumentality of my chosen vocation that had led me astray.

Dad drove off down the street. I watched him go. I had no desire to go back to an empty apartment. I wanted to see my daughter, hug her, and make sure she was okay emotionally over what I had done to Derek. Only I couldn't, and my subconscious mind had a difficult time trying to understand why I couldn't.

I got into my truck, pulled an illegal U-turn, and headed for a hot, empty apartment. To wait there alone.

CHAPTER FIFTY-FIVE

I DROVE UP and down the street twice looking for a parking spot close to our apartment and didn't find one. It was too late. Everyone, all the neighbors, were home from work and inside for the night, getting ready for bed, watching prime-time TV.

I parked around the corner, two blocks down at the edge of a manufacturing district, and hoped my truck would still be there in the morning. My body creaked and ached with every step, the pain still not enough to pull me out of the deep depression that stifled and smothered. Olivia needed me, needed my entire focus.

I'd made the decision to leave the sheriff's department, a job I loved, a job where my fellow deputies, every single one of them, were like family, like brothers.

But who was I trying to kid? It was the job that I'd miss. What scared me the most, though, was that I might be more like Wicks than I wanted to believe, that I'd miss it for the wrong reasons. There isn't any other job in the world that offers such excitement, such pure emotion.

I was halfway up the walk before I noticed someone sitting on the concrete step at our front door. My hand immediately went to the small of my back and gripped the Smith 9mm.

The person slowly stood, rising out of the shadow and into the haloed streetlight.

Nicky.

With one arm in a sling, I pulled her into a hug and held her there. I whispered, "Thank you."

"For what, big guy?"

"For being here."

Even in the warm summer evening, her body heat transferred to mine, a comfort I needed at that moment.

"You going to ask a girl in or are we just going to stand out here all night?"

"Oh, sorry." I tried to get my left hand into my right pocket to get my keys and fumbled the job. Nicky moved my hand out of the way, stuck her hand in, and pulled the keys out. She sorted through the keys until she found the one she thought would work. As she stuck it in the lock and twisted the knob, she stopped and said, "You know you're supposed to still be in the hospital so tonight I'm only going to help you to bed and maybe make you some chicken soup."

"Huh? I never heard it called chicken soup before."

"What? Oh, my God, Bruno."

Her reaction made me smile. "You going to open the door?"

She opened it and stepped aside. I turned on the lights. She closed the door and ducked under my good arm into another hug, my chin on top of her head.

She whispered, "Bruno, you scared the hell out of me today. I thought that—"

"Sssh. That's all ancient history now." Her words brought back the awful decision I'd made to quit the department, a decision that, if I didn't act on soon, I'd gradually try and talk myself out of. And, in all likelihood, I'd succeed.

"You going to show me to the bedroom?"

"I need to make one phone call first, okay?"

"Work?"

"Yeah, and it's okay if you want to listen."

I let her go and went to the phone. My body cooled without her touching me. I wanted that warm feeling back. I dialed Wicks' desk phone. He picked up on the first ring. "Wicks."

I said, "You're not going to catch Borkow sitting in the office eating apple fritters."

"Bruno? Where are you? You home? How you doing, buddy boy?"

"I feel like ten pounds of ground round. You have any leads on Borkow?" I was stalling. I didn't need to know about Borkow or anyone else, not with what I had to tell him.

"We're dead in the water, pal. We've run down every possible lead. Borkow just isn't moving around. He's gone to ground somewhere, and we're just waiting for something to break, someone to spot him and call it in. You have an address for me, an address on that broad, Lizzette, so we can put up a tap? That anonymous informant of yours call you yet?"

I squirmed a little out of guilt for what I was about to tell him. "You have to promise not to hit the place."

"No shit, you have an address? Come on, give."

"I doubt there's going to be a phone there, but there might be, you never know. And it's not Lizzette, it's Twyla."

"I don't give a crap, give it to me."

"16357 Atlantic Drive, right off Atlantic Boulevard."

"Excellent. I'll get the tap up and call you. Then you can go talk to her and tickle the wire."

You tickled the wire by telling the target something that will spook them, in order to get them to call the real target. We'd used the ploy many times and it worked well.

"I'm not going to be able do it this time."

"Ah, you're fine. Don't start whining like some kind of baby. You were hurt worse when you jumped up on the sideboard of that truck and that asshole—what was his name, Jack something?"

"Boles."

"That's right, Boles. I didn't have the shot because you had to play John Wayne and jump on that truck. Boles took the first corner so fast you got flung off at thirty, forty miles an hour right into those rose bushes. Remember that one, partner? You were cut to shit."

"Yeah, I remember."

"Hell, I'll drive you over there myself. All you have to do is go to the door and scare the shit out of this Twyla broad so she'll call Borkow."

"She won't be calling Borkow. She'll be calling Lizzette, but it will have the same results."

"Whatever."

"I'm out." I swallowed hard and looked at Nicky, locked onto her eyes. In saying those simple words, I felt like a coward running away from life, from what I'd been built to do.

"What do you mean *you're out*?" Wicks asked.

"I'm out. I'm quitting the department."

"The hell you say. You're just banged up a little. You took a couple hard knocks to the coconut and you're not thinking straight. Don't do anything stupid for a couple of days, you hear me?"

Nicky didn't move. Her expression didn't change. She didn't seem to have an opinion on my work status one way or another.

"I'm stone-cold serious. There is nothing that's going to change my mind. I'm out. I'm going to submit my letter of resignation tomorrow morning."

"Don't do it, buddy boy. I'm telling you, it's a big mistake, one you will regret the rest of your life. Besides, you can't leave me hanging like this, not with Borkow still out there. Let's take down Borkow; a little blood and bone will clear your head. It always does for me."

Had he already forgotten what happened at 10th and Slauson? Then at the restaurant called Mel's? There had been enough *blood and bone* at those two locations to last me a good long while, maybe even a lifetime.

"I'm out, Robby, I mean it."

"Wait, wait. Just do me one favor, one last favor for an old friend? I'll get that wire up and running. Then you can go and talk to this Twyla broad, okay? Spook her good. Then you take two or three weeks off before you make that kind of decision about quitting, okay? What do you say?"

"If she's still there, and if you can get a warrant for the wire, I'll go talk to her."

"Thanks, buddy. I'll get back to you in a few hours, okay? You take it easy."

When I hung up, Nicky came toward me, slowly unbuttoning her blouse. I eased my arm out of the sling and let it hang at my side. She made it over to me in time for me to help her with the last button. With my good hand I eased her blouse off one shoulder and moved to do it to the other side.

When someone knocked at the door.

CHAPTER FIFTY-SIX

NICKY PULLED HER blouse back up onto her shoulders and held the two unbuttoned sides together with one hand, her breasts still exposed at the top. "Who's that?"

I shrugged. "Can't be good news, not at this hour." I reached to the counter, picked up the Smith 9mm, and went to the door. "Who is it?"

No answer.

"Who is it?"

The knock came again, more forceful this time. I opened the door.

John Lau barged in, his eyes going wide with anger when he spotted Nicky in her state of semi-dress.

Oh, this wasn't good.

She let go of her blouse. It parted, exposing black lace and tanned, uplifted breasts. Her hands turned to fists she held down at her sides. "What are you doing here?"

"I knew it," he said. "I knew it when they told me my gun was involved in that shooting. I knew you were banging this smoke."

"Hey, watch your mouth," Nicky said.

Nicky took a step toward him. "You followed me here? What the hell are you doing following me? We're legally separated, John, as of this morning. You were served the court papers."

He pointed a finger at me. "I couldn't find you, so I followed him, and look what I found, a slut spreading her legs for the likes of this son of a bitch."

"Now, *I'm* telling you watch your mouth, keep it civil." I pulled the magazine out of the Smith, ejected the round in the chamber, and set the gun back on the counter. I'd been present at enough domestics to know loaded guns were a recipe for heartache and grief when emotions ran hot. This little squabble was right on the edge of going nuclear.

Domestics were the most dangerous call a deputy could go on, and guns only made them worse.

Something else on the counter caught my attention, but with all that was going on, I let it slide.

John still wore his uniform pants and shoes. He'd taken off his uniform shirt and only had on his tee shirt, one size too small; form-fitting muscles rippled as he moved. He smelled of beer, lots of it, something that also reflected in his demeanor—his slow speech, his impaired motor skills, and bloodshot eyes.

Nicky pointed. "Get out. Get out right now before I call the police."

He pounded his chest with his fist. "Go ahead. I *am* the police, baby cheeks. I'm a lieutenant with the Los Angeles County Sheriff's Department."

"You won't be much longer if you don't leave right now. I'll get you busted back to patrol deputy. You'll be driving a patrol car in Compton on graveyard."

His mouth opened into an O. He knew she spoke the truth. If he took this issue one step further and committed even a simple assault he would get busted back and have to start all over again from the bottom of the pile.

"Is that right? If I'm going down, then so is he." He took a step toward me ready to fight, ready to get revenge.

I held up my hand. "Whoa, there. You won't be hurting me, my friend. I'm resigning in the morning. You'll be going down in flames all by yourself."

That stopped him.

"John, if you don't leave right now, I'm going to take out a temporary restraining order. With one of those pinned to your tail, you can't carry a gun. They'll put you on the rubber-gun squad for ninety days. How's that going to play with your commander at SEB? A lieutenant on a SWAT team who can't carry a gun?"

Her words worked the same as a slow leak in a balloon. His shoulders sagged along with his expression. "Why, Nicky? Why are you doing this? I thought we had this all worked out. What happened?"

"Don't you dare give me that 'Oh, poor me' act. You know exactly what you did."

"I don't, really I don't. Whatever it is, I'm sorry." He looked genuinely confused. "Tell me what I did wrong."

He almost had me convinced there'd been a terrible mistake somewhere along the way. Nicky hadn't told him what she knew about how she'd tailed him to the hotel. She'd blindsided him that morning by serving him with papers.

"We've been sleeping in separate rooms for the last six months, and you're telling me you didn't think there was something wrong? When I asked you to move out, you said you wanted the house. What exactly did you think was happening?"

"I just thought we were going through a rough patch and that you'd change your mind. That's why I didn't want to move out. I love you."

"*A rough patch?* Are you kidding me? *Change my mind?* After what you did?"

He held his hands out. "What'd I do?"

"Really?" Nicky said, raising her voice. "Why don't you tell me about your little tryst that started with a dinner at the North Woods Inn and ended across the street at the hotel?"

His mouth dropped open again. "How did you—"

"What, no denial? You just want to know how I found out? That's classic John Lau." Her chin started to quiver and her eyes filled with tears.

I saw it in her expression—she still loved him. She'd inadvertently been using me as a salve to mask her emotional pain, using me for nothing more than a vehicle to move on. I'd lost her. With all that was happening, I didn't know how I felt about it. Maybe after some sleep, I'd suffer a deeper sense of loss.

"I am so sorry, baby," he said. "That was a long time ago. I was a fool. I know that now. She meant nothing to me. You're all I want. Please, please forgive me. I love you. I'll do anything to get you back."

I no longer wanted to be standing there. It was my apartment, and I had nowhere to go. I felt a little ashamed and embarrassed for him. He'd turned from an angry brute to a weepy, vulnerable lump of clay begging for her to come back to him.

"This is all my fault," he said, tears brimming his eyes and rolling down his cheeks. "I was working hard for one goal. I was doing it for you, for us." He reached into his pocket.

"Don't," I said. I took a step toward him.

He slowly pulled his hand from his pocket clutching something. He stepped closer to her, not taking his eyes off of hers. "I did it all for this. It'll mean nothing if you're not with me." He turned his hand over and opened it.

A sheriff captain's badge.

"They promoted me today. I'm sorry, baby. Please forgive me? I promise, it will be different. I won't work as hard anymore. I'll pay more attention to you. Please?"

He stepped toward her, and she flung herself into his arms.

"On your way out, could you please close and lock the door?" I turned and headed out of the room.

Good for her. She deserved to be happy.

CHAPTER FIFTY-SEVEN

I WALKED DOWN the hall into the bathroom and closed the door. I filled the sink with hot water and used a washcloth with soap to wipe the sweat and grime off my body. With the sutures in the knife wound and the shotgun pellets the doc had removed, I wasn't supposed to take a shower for three days. I did the best I could using one arm. The bandages on my hands got wet and I unwrapped them. My palms were pink and sore to the touch. That had been foolish, picking up a hot toaster, but in the heat of the moment, logical thought took a back seat to survival. After I finished, I felt much better.

Before I opened the bathroom door, I put my ear to it. I didn't want to walk back out if they still stood in my living room kissing or doing something worse on my couch. It hurt bad enough to have lost Nicky so abruptly. I didn't need to compound the loss with unwanted images.

I hadn't seen their reconciliation coming and should have. She'd been using our relationship as an emotional crutch to get over her husband. Only she couldn't; she still loved him. Good for her.

I peeked out. The living room was empty. In only my underwear, I walked through the apartment and made sure the door was locked. It wasn't. I locked it and headed for my room for some well-deserved sleep, if I could sleep at all with Olivia so heavy on my mind. I picked up the Smith 9mm on the way, shoved the magazine in, and charged the chamber. I eased the hammer down and set it on the nightstand next to the bed. I stretched out and tried to relax.

My body, now given the chance to catch up with all that had happened, began to complain in earnest. Everything ached or throbbed. The doctor had prescribed pain pills. I had the bottle in my pants pocket, the pants in a pile on the bathroom floor. I had never liked pain pills, the way they clogged the brain with cotton and smothered all logical thought. I tried to focus on the dark ceiling above and on my breathing. My mind began to relax and wander in and out, going over all that had happened that day, scene by scene, until I got to the garage at 16357 Atlantic Drive in Compton and the mock-up of the jail's visiting windows. The way it looked exactly like the windows in the jail. The way the—

I sat bolt upright in the bed. "No. No, no, no."

I sprang up on weak and shaky legs and opened the bedroom door. I walked down the hall to the counter that separated the kitchen from the living room, and where the phone hung on the wall beside it.

Earlier, during the argument between Nicky and her husband, John, I'd dropped the magazine from the gun. I ejected the round from the chamber and set the gun down. At the same time, I'd seen something—an item on the counter. Now I stared at it, an innocuous and unassuming little tool, more *a piece* of a tool really. I picked up the ¾-inch socket.

I grabbed for the phone and dialed. It rang and rang. I fought the urge to grab my clothes and run out, make the drive like a madman breaking all vehicle code laws. Finally, Dad picked up, his voice thick with sleep. "Johnson residence, this is Xander Johnson."

"Dad, it's me. Is Olivia there?"

"What? Come on, Son, we had this discussion. I'll have her call you in the morning. Now go to bed and get some sleep." He started to hang up.

I yelled. "Dad! Dad! Wait. Listen to me."

"What is it?" His tone took on an edge that I rarely heard.

"Please, just go peek in the room and see if she's there. Please?"

"She's there. I checked on her before I went to bed. Now go on and get some sleep."

"Just check for me right now. I promise I won't bother you again until tomorrow."

"I suppose if I don't, you're just gonna drive on over here in the middle of the night and wake up God and who knows who else with your overheated paranoia. Just a minute, I'll check." He set the phone down.

I closed my eyes tight and prayed. Seconds ticked by.

He came back on the line. "I'm sorry, Son, I don't know how she got by me. You know I'm a light sleeper. Don't worry though, she'll be back. She's done this before. You know you used to—"

"Stay there. I'm coming over."

I hung up and ran for my clothes. I took off my sling and tossed it. The sutures in my shoulder from the knife wound tugged and pulled as I dressed fast and headed for the door. I stopped and went back for the Smith and Wesson on my nightstand.

Outside, I stood on the sidewalk, confused for a second. Where was my truck? Then I remembered. I'd parked it a few blocks away. I ran full out, my lungs burning. When I made it to the truck, I bent over and took two deep breaths to push away the light-headedness. That wasn't enough. Didn't matter. I got in and started up.

I drove on the near-empty streets as fast as I dared. My right arm hurt each time I shifted the stick. I could only hope that she'd snuck out with Derek, that she'd gone with him to Lucy's to sit on the picnic bench and talk like they did the last time, talk about what I'd done to poor Derek. It was a sad world when that scenario was better than the alternative. I hoped that I would pull up to Lucy's and find them both safe sitting on the picnic bench.

But I knew better. The cop instinct that had served me well through the years whispered in my ear that I had better be prepared for the worst, and that the worst was about to gut-punch me.

We didn't keep any tools in the apartment; there just wasn't enough room. To have a socket on the counter in the kitchen, a socket the size that matched the mock-up of the visiting window taken out in the jail escape, was too big of a coincidence. I should've recognized it right off, but I'd been too distracted with Nicky, and then with John Lau suddenly appearing to wreak further havoc of a different kind.

Borkow was sending me a message. One that said he could get to me through my family. Just like he had used Olivia to get his trial delayed in order for him to escape.

I could only hope that it was just a message, that he hadn't taken the next drastic step and done something to Olivia.

A slice of yellow light illuminated the front yard of the house on Nord where I'd grown up. Dad stood on the stoop just outside the open door waiting for me. He wore a tattered maroon robe I'd given him for Christmas at least two decades ago. I hurried over to him. He looked tired and older than I ever remembered, another reminder that I'd let life slip through my fingers while I had been out playing cops and robbers, all those years on the violent crimes team.

"What's the matter, Son? What's all the hubbub about? Olivia's snuck out before. She'll come back. She'll be back safe and sound, you'll see."

I didn't answer and checked the doorknob and the jam for tampering. I didn't want to believe what I knew to be true.

No one had forced entry or picked the lock.

I hurried into the house looking around for anything out of place, any evidence at all.

Dad followed along. "What's going on? Bruno, stop and talk to me."

I froze.

On the floor, by the couch where she always left it, sat Olivia's purse. My knees turned weak and the floor wobbled under my feet. Olivia never left the house without her purse.

Never.

I slowly moved over to it and went down on my knees. I picked it up.

Behind me, Dad said, "Bruno, why would she leave her purse? What's going on?"

I opened it and gently dumped the contents on the floor. The heaviest item tumbled out first among the other normal things a young girl might keep. It lay there on the carpet. I sat back on my butt, my worst fears realized.

"What is it? Tell me, Bruno."

I took the socket from my pocket. I picked up the wrench that had fallen out of Olivia's purse. I fit the socket in place. My voice came out in a hoarse whisper. "He's got her, Dad."

"Who's got her? Derek? You mean Derek took Olivia against her will?"

"No, Louis Borkow took her."

"Oh, my dear Lord."

CHAPTER FIFTY-EIGHT

"YOU'RE GOING TO get her back, aren't you, Son? You can get her back, I know you can." He wrung his hands, his eyes filled with the same fear as mine.

"I'm going to get her back."

"You're sure?"

"I'm sure."

I looked at him, my rising anger needing a place to vent.

After what he'd just said to me, not a handful of hours earlier, about getting out of the life. Now he'd forgotten all about that and wanted me to use that same skill.

I took a deep breath and put my hand on his leg. "Yeah, I'm going to get her back." I gave him my hand. He helped me up from the floor. My body hurt all over, and when I stood up too fast, dizziness spun the room a little, the end result of the kicks to my head administered by Little Genie.

"Every cop in California is looking for this guy," Dad said. "You think you can find him?" He had never questioned my ability before. But this was Olivia we were talking about. A fear as pure as that could shake lose any solid belief system.

Even Dad's.

I walked over to the phone. "I'll find her. I promise you that."

Behind me, Dad said, "If he's really got Olivia, if he really took Olivia, you be sure to give him what he's got coming. You hear me, Bruno?"

His words shocked me. Where had *nice* and *generous* gotten off to? I shook it off, picked up the phone, and dialed. Wicks answered on the first ring.

I said, "Come pick me up."

"What? What's going on?"

"I need your help."

He paused. "What's happened?"

"Borkow took Olivia."

"*He what*? Where are you? I'll bring the entire team."

"No, just you. *You're my first phone call.*"

He'd understand. I didn't want any witnesses. Not for what we had to do.

He paused again, thinking about it, absorbing the full meaning of what I'd said. "I understand. You need anything else?"

"Bring me a shotgun and a box of double-ought buck. I'm at my dad's. You're not here in twenty minutes, I'm gonna start without you."

"*You wait for me, buddy boy*. You understand? You wait. I'm coming." He hung up.

This was the second time in two days that I'd called on him for help. He didn't hesitate.

I headed down the hall with Dad close at my heels. He said, "Let me change, I'm coming with you."

I stopped, turned. The emotional pain in his eyes made me want to lie down, curl up, and cry. "No, you don't have any training. I'm sorry, you'll just get in the way."

He nodded as his eyes filled with tears. "You think she's okay?"

"He took her because he doesn't want me chasing him. He hurts her, he loses that hammer. He won't hurt her."

But he will once he doesn't need her anymore. I couldn't tell him that. The words wouldn't form.

"But you *are* going to chase him. What if—"

"Dad, trust me, this is what I do."

He was right. I had to find Borkow without him finding out I was on his trail. Which meant I had to be right with each decision with no room for error, act quickly, and get real lucky.

I opened the door to my old room, now the room where Olivia stayed when she visited Dad. I kicked the doorframe down at the base.

"What the heck are you doin', Son? Have you gone crazy?"

Kicked it again and again until the section of doorjamb came loose from the wall, where I'd cut and sectioned it off years before. I went down on one knee and wiggled the section of the jamb until it came away from the wall. I reached in between the drywall where I'd removed the 2 x 4 brace and found what I was looking for. I brought it out into the light. A Charter Arms Bulldog .44 revolver, wrapped in an oilcloth, the same make and model The Son of Sam had used in New York to kill all those people. A gun I'd taken off a crook and never turned in as evidence. I never thought I'd need it.

Never say never.

Dad didn't say a word about having a gun hidden in the wall in his house. He understood that with Olivia involved, nothing else mattered, that all bets were off.

The gun still had rubber bands around the grip to avoid fingerprints being left behind. The serial number was filed off so it couldn't be traced. I opened the cylinder, checked the rounds, spun it, and closed it. The gun had a 2½-inch barrel and was designed for close-in work. A bellygun, one that worked best if you shoved it into your victim's belly and pulled the trigger. I stood and stuck it in my waistband.

Dad said, "How long do you think it'll take to find her?"

"It'll take as long as it takes, Dad. But I better find her in the next twenty-four hours."

"Can you call me with updates?"

"I don't know. I'll try." One part of my brain said the words; the other part automatically moved off to the more important issue, going over everything that had happened in the last few days, looking for anything that had been missed. I leaned against the wall, closed my eyes, and tried to concentrate.

The phone rang.

I bumped past Dad and headed into the kitchen to the phone on the wall. High anxiety buzzed in my ears. I picked up on the third ring and listened.

The person on the other end said nothing.

"Who is it, Son?" Dad stood close, his eyes pleading for relief.

I said into the phone, "You hurt her, there won't be any place you can hide."

"Now, I don't think that's any way to start a conversation with someone who's sitting in the catbird seat, do you?"

I recognized the voice, Borkow. "What do you want?"

"Honestly, I can't say that I want a thing. I'm good here."

If he didn't want anything, there wasn't any reason to keep Olivia safe. It might already be too late and he'd just called to gloat.

"You have to want something." If he wanted to just send a message, he wouldn't have taken her; he'd have just done her harm and moved on.

"Nope. Like I said, I'm good here."

"Where's here?"

He chuckled. "Not a chance. But, Mr. Bailiff, maybe there is one thing you can do for me. You can quit chasing me. That's what I really want."

"Done. Now give me my daughter back."

"Not just yet. There's one last thing I need to do before I get out of town before sundown, as the saying goes."

"How long is that going to take?"

"Depends."

"Maybe I can help you with this one last thing so we can get this over and done with."

"Don't know how that would work. No, no, wait, maybe . . . yeah, sure. I think I can risk it. You see, the thing is, I'm in dire need of talking to someone whom I need to . . . Well, let's just say I need to talk to this person very sternly. You find that person and bring her to me, you can have your daughter back. Then I'll be out of your hair. I'll be gone. Goodbye, bon voyage, adios."

"Who?"

"A cute little thing who goes by the name of Twyla."

CHAPTER FIFTY-NINE

I CLOSED MY eyes and put my head against the wall. I had never betrayed an informant. How could I trade Twyla for Olivia and live with myself afterward? If Borkow wanted Twyla, it wasn't for a friendly reunion and could only be for dark designs.

I said to Borkow, "Where do you want me to bring her?"

"Just like that? You know you can find her? You know where to lay your hands on her?"

"I said, where do you want me to bring her?"

"You get her in hand. I'll call this number back in eight hours. But I'll only stay on line long enough to give you instructions, you understand? Sixty seconds max."

"Make it four hours, call back in four hours. Now let me talk to my daughter."

"I don't—"

"Put her on the phone, now."

Borkow paused. I might've pushed too hard.

"Fair is fair," he said. "She has no idea where she is, so don't waste your time trying to get her to give you some cutsie little clue. We're constantly on the move, so it doesn't matter anyway."

Constantly on the move? Did he mean from house to house, or motel to motel?

Borkow put the phone down. A scuffling came across the line. Borkow said, "Here, talk."

"Hello, Popi?" Sobs filled her words

"Hey, baby, it's me. Are you okay? Did he hurt you?"

"I'm okay. Really, I'm okay."

"Everything is going to be all right, you understand? I'm coming for you."

"I'm sorry I was mad at you, Popi."

"I am too, baby. It was all my fault."

"Now I wish I woke you up when you were sitting by the door and gave you a big hug instead of making fun of you. I made you breakfast though, your favorite."

"What?" What she said didn't make sense.

"I'm so sorry I made fun of you and put that sign on you. I shouldn't have done it. It was a mean and an ugly thing to do. I'm sorry."

"What? No, that's okay."

"That's enough," Borkow said. He grabbed the phone from her. "You got four hours, Bailiff." He clicked off.

I hung up and slid down the wall to the floor. My hands shook. My mind wouldn't function, not under that kind of stress. I was emotionally drained and more scared than I'd ever been before.

Dad knelt beside me. "Well, come on, tell me, what's going on? She's okay, right?"

"Yeah, Dad, she sounded good. As good as can be expected. He hasn't hurt her."

"What does he want?"

"He wants me to find a woman named Twyla and bring her to him."

"Can you find her?"

I opened my eyes and looked at him. "I think I can, yes. But what's going to happen to her when I make the trade for Olivia?"

"Oh, yeah. I'm sorry, I hadn't thought of that. I'm not thinking right, not with Olivia involved. What are you going to do?"

"I have to find Twyla and somehow, during the trade, keep them both safe."

Dad shook his head. He put his back to the wall and slid down sitting next to me. "How are you ever going to do that?"

"Please, Dad, just give me a minute to think. Olivia was trying to tell me something."

"What? What'd she say? Let me help you."

"Dad."

"Okay, okay, go ahead and think. I'll be quiet."

The puppy rounded the corner into the kitchen, losing traction on the linoleum, his feet skittering under him, his pink tongue hanging out. He regained control and jumped up in my lap. He licked my face. How had I forgotten all about Junior Mint?

"Here, give him to me. I don't know how he got out." Dad took him, struggled to his feet with the energetic ball of fur, and disappeared, his footfalls moving down the hall.

I had a hard time focusing. What exactly had she said, her exact words? She said that she was sorry and that she'd been mean to me. She wasn't mean. She was being funny. It *was* funny. That was obvious. She'd put the sign in my hand that said, "*Save a dolphin, don't eat tuna.*"

Dolphin and tuna? What had she meant by that?

If she truly didn't know where she was, and Borkow wasn't lying about being constantly on the move, that meant she couldn't have been giving me a clue about her location. Then what? If it wasn't the where, and it wasn't the how or the why, it had to be a who.

The other sign, the one hanging around my neck, had said, "*Hi. I'm Bruno the Clown. Don't Clown me.*"

I snapped my fingers and stood. I dialed the phone, an old number from memory, Mike Moore from OSS, Operation Safe Streets, the gang unit at Lynwood Station. Mike worked swing shift. He picked up. I told him I needed a big favor. I needed him to run the gang moniker "Clown" through the gang system and to call me right back. I told him it was life or death.

I stood by the phone waiting for it to ring. Willing it to ring.

Then started pacing.

Dad came back and sat at the kitchen table. From the time on the wall clock, ten long minutes passed. I went to the phone ready to pick it up and dial Mike Moore and stopped myself. I again paced the kitchen floor. "Come on. Come on."

Dad said, "You want me to make you something to eat? You might not have a chance later. You need to keep up your strength."

He needed something constructive to do just like I did. I wasn't hungry and wouldn't be able to keep anything down. "Sure."

He stood. "How about some bacon and scrambled eggs? Maybe some wheat toast?"

"That's sounds great." I looked at the pinkness in my palms, insignificant and foolish in the big scheme of things.

The phone rang. I leaped at it. "Yeah, talk to me."

"I found seventy-six Clowns in Los Angeles County."

"That's too many. That won't work."

"I checked to see how many are in the can that narrows it down to forty-five."

"Still no good."

"Out of that forty-five, seventeen are deceased, leaving twenty-eight. Fifteen of those are over the age of forty and have gone quiet. They're not active in the life anymore. Does that help?"

"That's not going to work. Under normal circumstances, it wouldn't be a problem, but we're on a clock here. If there was more time, thirteen would be a workable number. Not tonight, Mike, thanks for the effort, I owe you."

"Sorry, man,"

I started to hang the phone up then stopped and yelled into it, "Mike!"

"Yeah, Bruno?"

"How many of those left are male blacks?"

Borkow had aligned himself with the blacks during his escape, and his girlfriend, the woman he'd killed, the one he was on trial for killing, had been black.

"I thought that's all you wanted. They're all male blacks, Bruno."

"Damn. That's it then, thanks." I hung up.

I went back to trying to remember exactly what Olivia had said word for word. She couldn't say too much, so she would have tried to bury the information using as few words as possible.

My lips moved as I restated the conversation.

Cops interviewed hundreds if not thousands of victims, witnesses, reporting parties, and suspects, then they transferred that information to paper. They got used to memorizing things people said and could easily play back entire conversations verbatim.

"What is it, Son? Tell me. Let me help."

"Sssh, just a minute. She said she made me my favorite breakfast."

Dad nodded. "Your favorite breakfast is huevos rancheros."

"That's right. Yeah, that's right." I grabbed up the phone and dialed. Mike picked up.

I said, "What's the Hispanic word for clown?"

"Payaso. Ah, shit, sure, sure, I'm with you. I'm checking now. Wait, Bruno. Is this about the Borkow thing?"

"That's right."

"Borkow ran a string of massage parlors, right?"

"Yes. Whatta ya got?"

"The Feds came in a few months back. They're working a human trafficking ring and their target's a guy named Payaso, a Phillip

Cortez, male Hispanic thirty-eight years. A no-account kinda thug without any violence on his record. At least none that's he's been tagged with."

"That's gotta be him. That's the guy. I need everything you got on him. His last known address."

"Sorry, that's a no-go. We didn't have anything recent. The Feds wanted all of our info. We gave them all our old intel, mostly associates, and Field Interrogation cards."

"What did they have? What did the Feds tell you?"

"They're the Feds; they want the world, but wouldn't share anything they had. You know the routine. It was need to know, and, of course, according to them, we didn't need to know."

"So we're talking about the FBI then?"

"Yep."

"But I know you, Mike, you did a workup on this guy anyway, didn't you?"

"Yeah, I did, but I didn't know he was linked to Borkow until now when you made the connection. Cortez is off parole. When I went to check on his last known, he'd moved months ago. He's off the radar. No one's had a line on a good address for the last three years."

"Okay, listen, I need a deep background on this guy tonight. Wake people up if you have to. I can have Lieutenant Wicks call you. He has the full authority of the deputy chief to order this and approve any overtime."

"You got it, I'll take care of it. But, Bruno, I wanna be in on the takedown. I want a piece of Borkow."

"You dig this Phillip Cortez out of his hole and you're in. Page me as soon as you get something. I mean it, the second you have something."

"I'm on it. Give me three hours."

"You can have two. Page me."

CHAPTER SIXTY

BORKOW PUT HIS hand over Olivia's mouth, his face close to hers as they sat side by side in the dinette in the motor home. "Ssssh. Don't make a sound or I'll fix it so you can never make a sound again." He moved in even closer. His lips touched her ear. "I'll cut out your squeaker box, you understand?" He kissed her ear. Her body shivered and caused a scintillating effect that made him shiver with arousal, almost as if that shiver had transferred from her to him.

Her sun-kissed skin accented her green eyes, which, though scared, also carried a hint of challenge. She smelled of... of what was it? Cherry blossom. Must've been her shampoo; little girls didn't naturally smell of cherries.

She nodded. He leaned past her and peeked out the curtains of the RV that was now parked amongst cars in the strip center in between Muscle Max and the Grand Orchid massage parlor.

Borkow told Payaso to park in the strip center because he could no longer take the shimmy and shake of the RV moving in and out of the never-changing landscape, the same streets, the same shabby, broken-down houses, over and over again. He couldn't take any more of it. He also thought there might be a muffler leak venting to the inside of the RV. Why else would his headache be so severe?

They had only been parked a couple of minutes—his body still vibrated from the constant movement of the drive—when Payaso said, "Nobody move. Nobody make a sound." He came from behind the driver's wheel and into the living compartment by the dinette. He reached, took the sledgehammer from the table, and stepped quietly to the back door. He eased the curtain aside. In his other hand he held the hammer cocked back at the ready.

Borkow slid out of the dinette and peeked out the curtain over the sink next to it. In a harsh whisper, he said, "I don't see anything. What's wrong? What do you see?"

Payaso said nothing.

"Tell me, what did you see?" *You little shitweasel.*

"It's that big mayate from the jail, the one that is angry with you."

Stanky Frank? "What? Where?"

"He's at the corner of the building by the street. He's looking around."

The street was behind them, which meant Payaso had seen Frank in the side mirror skulking about. "Just what we need right now."

"What do you want me to do?"

"I don't know, let me think. Just gimme a second to think."

"There are cops out on the street, a block down, watching the driveway to this place—you saw them when we drove in. I pointed them out to you. They see Frank and recognize him, they're going to swoop him. That'll bring the whole world down on our heads."

"I know that."

Frank left the corner of the building and lumbered along in front of the other offices, his attention focused on the Grand Orchid, or so it seemed. He moved in and out of the halos from the parking lot lights.

"He's mad. He's looking for you, boss."

"I know that."

The bailiff's kid asked, "What did you do to him?"

Borkow quick-stepped over and grabbed her face in one hand, pinching both sides of her cheeks. "I told you once, I'm not going to tell you again—shut your piehole. You say one more word, you'll not live to regret it, you understand?"

She nodded, but her eyes remained defiant. He'd fix that later, when he had the time, when he wasn't so vulnerable. He'd make her understand exactly whom she was dealing with. He didn't care if she was just a teenybopper, either. He wasn't ever going back to prison, so he didn't have to worry about a kiddy raper tag.

No one gave him that look and got away with it, especially not a woman, a girl.

Payaso said, "He's coming this way." He closed the curtains and stood to the side, cocking the hammer back even farther, ready to bash in Frank's head if he chose to stick it someplace where it didn't belong.

Borkow stuck a finger in the girl's face. "Remember, not a peep. Now lie down on that couch and curl up your legs." She did as he asked. Borkow leaned over the kitchenette's sink and peeked out the curtains of the small window, trying to see.

Frank cut across the parking lot, making a beeline right for the RV. He came up to the back-door, put his hands to each side of his face, and tried to peer in through the back-door window. He moved around to the driver's door to do the same. Borkow stood in the deep shadow. It was darker inside the RV than outside, and if nobody moved, it would be difficult to see objects, let alone the occupants.

Frank didn't look good under the sodium vapor light. He had dark half-moons under his eyes, his complexion was pale for a black man, and sweat beaded all over his face. His baby-blue shirt was soaked in a wide band down the center of his chest and back. A darker splotch on his huge girth stained the shirt. He'd not received proper medical attention for his gut injury. The one he got when they shoved him through the jail's Visiting window. It must be infected and hurt like hell.

Borkow tried to push away the image he'd conjured up of what it must look like; pus-filled, swollen, and bloated with purples and reds, a giant boil about to burst. Ol' Stanky Frank wouldn't be walking around much longer.

Frank moved off, headed toward the glass doors of Muscle Max.

Payaso whispered, "You want me to take care of him?"

"Of course not. Not if we don't have to. What kind of freak do you think I am? He was an integral part of the escape. He shoved that window out, or I wouldn't be standing here right now. I owe him. Doesn't matter anyway; he's going to collapse all on his own. It's not going to be long now. I just hope it's far away from here."

Frank shook the door to Muscle Max, tried to peer in, and then moved on. How had he known to look in Muscle Max? He shouldn't have known anything about the place. Why didn't he try to get into the Grand Orchid instead? Or any of the other offices for that matter? Only three people knew about Muscle Max: Lizzette, Harold, and Payaso. Somebody had ratted.

Frank finally moved off down the front of the buildings and disappeared around the corner out by the street.

"Stay here. I need to go in and talk with Harold."

"What about the girl?" Payaso asked.

"Put her in the bathroom."

He shook his head. "I don't mess with children."

"Then what good are you? What exactly? Tell me."

Borkow grabbed the girl, yanked her up and out of the dinette couch. She let out a little yelp, caught herself, and cut it off, a lot like that puppy had at that place on Bronson.

He tugged her along to the bathroom door. He ripped off a piece of duct tape from the roll and put it across her mouth. He spun her around and taped her hands together behind her back. Maybe a little too tight, but she was a smart-mouth and deserved it. He opened the accordion door, leaned close to her ear, and whispered, "Now I don't want you two girls gossiping and telling secrets about me, you hear?" He chuckled at his little joke. When he peeked in, he saw that Lizzette sat on the floor with one shoulder to the wall and the other to the toilet bowl. Her eyes were frozen wide and had a milky film over them. Her mouth sagged open and her tongue was purple and dried out. He shoved the girl in on top of Lizzette and closed the accordion door.

From inside came an attempt at a scream muffled by the tape. He said to Payaso, "If that goes on too long, you're going to have to shut it down. You understand? I'm going inside to talk with Harold. I'll be right back."

CHAPTER SIXTY-ONE

WICKS PULLED UP and parked on Atlantic Boulevard with a full moon high in the night sky. I got out of his car and headed for the back of the Mexican market, a carniceria. I kept my flashlight off for fear of giving away the tactical advantage, or worse, ruining my night vision.

"Hey, wait up," he said sorting his keys to unlock the trunk. "Let me get the shotgun out."

"Come on, we don't need it for this."

He hurried to catch up. "What are we doing here, then? You haven't said two words since we left your dad's place. I need to know what's going down."

"We need to lay our hands on Twyla to trade for Olivia."

"Borkow wants this Twyla and is willing to trade for Olivia? That's a new twist you don't see too often. That's the name of the broad we were going to tickle the wire with, right?"

"That's right. Did you get the wiretap up?"

"No, the place doesn't have a phone, just like you thought. Why does Borkow want this Twyla?"

"He didn't say."

I came to the chain link in back of the small strip center. Someone had cut a downward slash through to the adjoining big backyard, which was overgrown with weeds and shrubs and trees that made it jungle-like. Wicks followed along without having a full explanation of what we were doing. We both knew the odds for a favorable outcome were not good, especially with a freak like Borkow involved.

We walked along the side of the house and popped out on Atlantic Drive.

"Hey," Wicks said, "I didn't know you could get to this street from Atlantic Boulevard, not like this. Slow down, or we're going to trip and break an ankle." He hadn't turned on his flashlight either.

I kept going, hurrying now to 16357. I followed the long driveway to the house, keeping my shoulder close to the overgrown oleanders. Something wasn't right about the house. It felt empty. Or maybe it was something else.

At the back wooden porch, I hesitated long enough to pull the Smith 9mm. Wicks pulled his Colt .45 and took up a backing position on my right flank covering the back door. "What's the matter?"

I shook my head and took the steps. "The place doesn't feel right." I turned on my flashlight and peered inside.

The house was in shambles, trashed, overturned and broken furniture, curtains shredded, dishes broken; anything that could be damaged was ruined. Borkow had released a lot of rage; it must have taken him at least twenty minutes.

And he had Olivia while under the influence of that anger.

We checked the whole house.

Wicks came down from upstairs. "It's clear up there, no sign of anyone. It's tore up, but not as bad. He's looking for something and he's one angry dude. Is this where Twyla was hiding out?"

"That's right. Come on, let's check the garage."

We followed the broken concrete walk to the side door of the garage. We entered following our guns in.

I froze.

Beside me, Wicks held his flashlight illuminating the garage interior. He said, "Son of a bitch. Those are mock-up windows from MCJ Visiting. This is where they practiced for the caper, isn't it?" He pointed. "Who's that?"

He'd noticed and commented on the windows first before saying anything about the dead woman.

In the eerie light, a thin, deflated woman sat on the round stainless-steel seat under the Visiting window. Her shoulders were slumped and her hands hung down close to the floor. Her eyes were tented and her lips purple. Her bottle-blond hair looked straw-like and too yellow, as if it came from a doll's wig. The top of her forehead above her eyes was caved in the same way we found Gloria Bleeker. Done with the same-sized blunt object.

"I don't know," I said. "She wasn't here before."

"You were here before and you didn't report this? You didn't drop a dime and at least tell me about these Visiting windows? That was a mistake, buddy boy, a big mistake. I don't know if we're going to be able to cover you on this."

"I'm not concerned about covering this up."

"The problem is, the bosses are going to think that if we knew about this place, we might've prevented this killing. We could've set up on it. If we had, we'd have Borkow right now."

"I don't think so. Not the way this whole thing went down. And right now, I really don't care what the bosses think."

"What do you mean you don't think so? What? I . . . Wait. Wait. Twyla was the one who gave you Little Genie, wasn't she? She was your unnamed confidential informant who told you where to look on Slauson, wasn't she?"

Twyla had fled before the cops arrived, and no one—not Nicky or the judge—gave up Twyla's name or that she'd even been present.

I ignored him and moved closer to the victim. "You recognize her?" I asked.

"You going to answer me?"

"Do you really want to know?"

"You're right. Maybe I don't. Yeah, it's better if I don't."

"You recognize her or not?"

"I think so," Wicks said. "We have photos of the women involved in the breakout at MCJ. She looks like one of them. Yeah, I'm almost sure."

"She wasn't killed here," I said. "She was moved and posed for a reason. Borkow wanted Twyla to see her like this. He must have a good reason. It has to be to intimidate Twyla."

I got down on one knee and took a closer look. People looked different in death. For some, their personality makes up so much of who they are, how they appear, that when they die, they leave behind someone entirely different, an unrecognizable shell, an abandoned husk.

I sat back on my heels. "Oh man," I said. "I think I know her. This is that girl I was telling you about with the nice shoes from the Willow Tree massage parlor in Hawthorne. This is Lizzette."

"Huh. Too bad. This is going to slow us down some. We can't leave. We have to secure this crime scene. We have to call Homicide and stand by until they get here. That's protocol. That's policy, buddy boy."

"You can. Not me. I'm going after my daughter."

"Bruno—"

I glared at him.

"All right." He held up his hand. "All right, then, let's get moving. What's next? You got some other lead to chase down? Do you know someplace else we can look for this Twyla broad that you haven't told me about?"

I turned and headed out.

"Hey, did you hear me? Don't walk away like that. Tell me what you're thinking. I'm in it now, up to my nose."

That was the problem, I didn't have anything else to chase, not unless Mike Moore from OSS came up with something. That was a long shot if the FBI was also looking for Cortez/Payaso. I had no idea where to look for Twyla, which made the rising anxiety to get Olivia back all the more difficult to suppress. I wanted to break something. I wanted to destroy something. I didn't need Wicks picking at me with his questions.

Wicks caught up out on the long driveway. He grabbed my shoulder and spun me around. "Come on, we're partners, talk to me. Where are we going to look for this Twyla broad? Right now, she seems to be the only path to Borkow." He waved his hand behind him. "It looks like Borkow's looking for her as well. So if we can get on her trail, we might even run into him."

"She's gone."

"What are you talking about? Gone? How do you know?"

"She said she was afraid of Borkow. She said she was going to run to San Francisco as soon as she fingered Genie. She's gone."

"Wait. She's living in a derelict house without power, no water, and no phone? Where the hell is she going to get enough money to get across town let alone all the way up to Frisco?"

I stopped and turned to him. "I gave her ten grand."

"You what? Where did you ... Oh, the judge. It was the judge, wasn't it? That's why he was out there with you. That's why he was rollin' with you."

"I didn't say that, you did."

"The judge gave her money? That's a huge conflict of interest."

"We got Little Genie, didn't we?"

"He shot and killed someone savin' your ass and you two got there with money paid to an informant involved up to her tits in this thing. Twyla's probably one of the other women in the escape. Worse than that, some crazy media outlet is going to claim the judge paid ten grand for a hunting tag."

"That's ridiculous."

"To you and me, but not to those blood mongers in the media."

"Just take it easy; it's not as bad as you're making it sound."

"Ah, man," Wicks said, "you can't give a coke whore ten thousand dollars. That's the same as handing her a hemp rope with the hangman's noose already tied in it. She'll buy a big hunk of rock and smoke herself to death. Come on, no more secrets, tell me what we're doing right now or I'm shutting you down. I'll cuff you to the bumper of the car for your own good. You know I'll do it."

I recognized that look. He was serious. I needed something to feed him, something to keep his mind busy. I grasped at anything that came to mind. "I think I recognized the guy on the tape."

"What tape?"

"The tape of the phone conversation between Borkow. The guy who set up my daughter as a hostage in that rock house on Pearl, in Compton, to get me outta court. You got the tape so I can listen to it again?"

"That's good. Yeah, that's good. I should've thought of that. Now you're talkin'. It's in the car, let's go." He hooked his thumb over his shoulder. "We'll call this in from the pay phone and screw 'em if they can't take a joke. Right, partner?"

I didn't answer and walked faster, trying hard not to break into a run.

CHAPTER SIXTY-TWO

WICKS STOPPED AT the pay phone attached to the wall of the car-niceria and called Homicide. I continued on and stood by his car waiting. Every second ticked by in my head and merged into an-other minute spinning faster at an unbelievable speed toward an hour. Soon it would be two, then three. I couldn't get out of my mind the images of Gloria and Lizzette, their caved-in foreheads. I closed my eyes tight and fought to keep those images from merging with Olivia. My beautiful Olivia.

Wicks hung up and came over. "I called a friend in Homicide who's going to handle it with kid gloves. But it's all going to come out when the CO reads the report and sees we didn't stick around. So we're good for now, but we're going to take it in the shorts down the road." He opened his trunk and went into his briefcase, bringing out a small tape recorder and a tape cassette. He closed the trunk and set the recorder on top.

Cars zipped by now and again, traffic light at that hour.

Three gangbangers walking on the other side of Atlantic Boulevard eyed us. I eyed them back so they knew we weren't afraid. If you showed weakness, the rules of the jungle gave them the go-ahead to menace and harass and even kill.

Wicks put in the tape and hit play.

"I want you to do what we talked about."

"Huh?"

"Do I need to spell it out for you?"

"Naw, I think I got it. You want me to get Olivia Johnson over ta this house on Pearl."

"That's right, nothing too difficult. I want you to put her in jeopardy so she calls her daddy for help. I need it done tomorrow at noon or just before, so I can get out of court and catch the early bus back. Can you do that?"

"I can do it, but it's going to cost you. You gotta wipe out what I owe dem boys on Pearl."

"That's not a problem. And if you do this right, you can be sure I'll take good care of you, ah . . . soon, if you know what I mean."

Wicks shut off the tape. "Well?"
"Play it again."
He did. I could, without reservation, recognize Borkow from my exposure to him in court. The other voice came off with small pings of recognition, but I still couldn't put a face to that voice. Not at that moment. He must've had something covering the receiver of the phone, a piece of cloth.

I knew how my mind worked, though. Tomorrow night, or the next, when I lay down to sleep, and I relaxed, the answer would bubble to the surface because I did know that voice from somewhere, and I'd regret it took so long for me to pull it up.

A day or two later would make it too late for Olivia.

The harder I tried to pull up the face, the further back in my memory it fled. I couldn't think about it directly. I needed to let it fester a little.

After the second time through, Wicks hit the stop button. "Talk to me, buddy boy."

"Yeah." I cringed at the lie about to flow past my lips. "It's the guy from the Pearl address in Compton."

"You sure?"

"Sixty percent."

"That's good enough for me. Let's roll." He opened the trunk and put the cassette player away, then pulled out an Ithaca 12 gauge. He handed it to me with a box of double-O shells.

I pointed. "Bring along that tape and recorder."

"Good idea." He put it in his suit coat pocket and closed the trunk.

Wicks started up the Dodge and headed south on Atlantic Boulevard. The big engine roared and I was shoved back in the seat from the acceleration. Wicks never did anything half-assed. He always put his head down and barreled through.

Ten minutes later, we parked perpendicular to Pearl on Compton Avenue. We got out and eased our doors closed. Wicks pulled his Colt and checked the round in the chamber, just like he always did on operations where a shooting might occur. I racked the shotgun and fed another round into the magazine. I put some extra shells in my left front pants pocket. "We're gonna have to go hill and dale on this one. They have lookouts on the street side."

"You sure? I'm getting kind of old for that kind of shit."

"Okay then, just wait here until you hear the first round go off. Then come running."

"You know, you've turned into a real asshole." He smiled. "I'll follow you."

We took our time going over the fences and across the backyards to keep the noise to a minimum. We crossed the last yard and approached the final fence without having made a sound. The house lights were off. Living next door to a rock house, the owners had to be lying low. If they were smart, they'd be sleeping in their bathtubs to stay safe from stray rounds.

We both crouched by the fence. I did a quick peek and came back down. I whispered, "The wrought-iron door is open and there's one OG and two poo-butts sitting on the back steps smoking weed and talking smack."

Wicks moved in close to my ear. "They're there for only one reason, to slam that door if they catch the slightest whiff of trouble. We can't get over the fence in time and get to that back door before they slam it shut. So what do you want to do?"

I looked around in the light from the moon high in the night sky and spotted a flower garden sectioned off from the grass with a border of decorative river rock. I pulled up a couple, hefting them for weight, until I found the one I liked, a little smaller than a softball. Maybe a little too heavy, but it would have to do. I came back to the fence.

Wicks took out a cigarette and put it in his lips. He wouldn't light it until we'd contained the scene, another routine christened with a lot of blood and bone.

He said, "What are you going to do with that, chunk one of them boys in the head? What's that going to get us? There are still two others."

I whispered back, "Just get ready and follow my lead."

I did another quick peek to check alongside the target house through to the front yard and spotted my objective—a tricked-out ghetto ride. A silver Lexus with two grand worth of wheels and an after-market, metal-flaked paint job worth thousands sat at the curb. I stepped back away from the fence trying to gauge the distance. I pulled back my good arm and wolfed that river rock as hard as I could. It still hurt my other shoulder.

We both held our breath.

A crash of metal and glass, then a car alarm went off.

Out front someone yelled, "What the fuck!"

I popped up to look over the fence. The three on the porch ran to the side of the house and stopped. They knew they weren't supposed to leave their post under the threat of the ass-kicking of a lifetime.

"Now," I whispered. I did a half pull-up putting most of the stress on my good arm and vaulted the fence. Wicks tossed me the gauge and came over a little slower. I was up the steps before the three gangbangers even knew we'd penetrated their domain.

Behind me, Wicks braced all three. "On the ground, now. Get on the ground."

I knew the layout of the house from before and went through the kitchen and into the living room with the shotgun in the lead. I caught two sitting on the couch and three others at the front door looking at the excitement in the front yard through the closed security gate.

"Hit the floor. Everyone on the floor, now. Do it right now."

Their heads whipped around. Their eyes went wide when they saw the shotgun held by an angry black man in a trucker's shirt. All five eased down to the floor, the 12-gauge a huge motivator.

"Keep your hands away from your body. Spread your legs. You know the routine."

From behind, Wicks yelled, "Coming in."

"Come ahead."

He came in escorting the three from outside all in a line, with their hands on their heads. I stepped aside to let them pass. "On the floor with your buddies. Now."

I covered them with the shotgun. Wicks searched. He came up with five handguns. He emptied them and tossed them on the couch. "Which one is he?" Wicks asked.

Someone from out front came to the wrought-iron security door and spoke through it. "What's going on?"

Wicks growled. "Sheriff's department. Get your skinny ass away from the door."

"Whoa, shit. It's Five-O. Dey in the house. How the hell dey get in the house?"

I stepped over the bangers on the floor and prodded them with the gauge. "Hey, look up at me."

I found one I recognized from the day we came in after Olivia. "You. Get your ass up and come with me. Come on, get your ass up."

He complied. I tossed Wicks the shotgun. I held out my hand. He flipped me the recorder.

I yanked the guy back into the kitchen. The place smelled of chemicals and rotting food. The only dishes in view sat on the stove: pots used to cook the cocaine hydrochloride down to base or rock. Next to the stove, baby-food jars with white residue littered the counter. Jars from which they'd knocked out the white "cookies" of rock. All that paraphernalia had not been there the first time I'd come through, days earlier.

Piled high on the opposite counters were fast-food wrappers and cardboard containers from Pizza Hut, the Waffle House, Popeye's Chicken, replete with piles and piles of gnawed chicken bones. These boys liked their spicy chicken wings.

The kid I held by the jersey looked to be about twenty, with brand-new clothes. Rock dealers rarely wash their clothes. They take them off, throw them in the pile, and put on new ones. This guy, like most all of them, went in for the Raiders and wore the black-and-white jersey over red denim pants the color of the Bloods street gang. They didn't follow football; they just thought the name Raiders was cool. He was handsome. If you put him in a nice suit, he could pass as an attorney or stockbroker anywhere in the U.S. Until he opened his mouth to speak.

I grabbed him by the throat, shoved him up against the counter, and squeezed. I got up in his face and whispered, "You remember me?"

His body trembled. He choked and sputtered. I let off a little. "Yeah, you that Bruno The Bad Boy Johnson. What do you want wit' me?" He tried for courageous, but fear burned through in his eyes.

"I'm only going to ask you once. You don't tell me, I'm going to do you dirty and leave you on the floor. Then I'll go to the next homeboy, and the next, until they tell me what I want to know. I'll pile all you assholes up right over there in the corner just like Popeye's chicken bones. You understand?"

He nodded.

"You ready for the question?"

He nodded again.

"I want to know who this is." I hit play on the recorder.

CHAPTER SIXTY-THREE

IN THE PEARL Street kitchen, I stood with my face close to the gang member's and played the tape. I watched his expression for the slightest reaction. My aches and pains took a back seat to the task at hand.

All through the short conversation on the tape, he remained expressionless. I hit stop.

"Okay, you get one shot, who is it?"

"Dat's not one of our boys."

I punched him in the stomach. He bent over and moaned. "I didn't ask you that, did I? I didn't ask you if it was one of your boys. Who is it?"

From the living room Wicks yelled, "You okay in there?"

"Yeah, I'm about to trade this one in for a fresh one. This one's gone stale on me."

"Okay, let me know. I'll send another one your way."

The gang member held up his hand. "Wait. Wait." He coughed and sputtered. "Dat white boy from the jail, dat's him on the tape. He sent his man, some Mex, over here and paid off the debt. Paid us in hunert dollar bills, no twenties or fitties, only hunerts."

"What's the Mex's name?"

"Dey call him Pay So or some shit like dat."

"What's he look like? Where does he live?"

"I doon know any of dat kinda shit."

"What kind of car does he drive?"

"A real clean Monte. A nice ride, kinda stock though, not fixed up any, no wheels or paint."

"What color?"

"Blue or black or dark gray, I don' know for sure. I wasn't lookin'. All I saw was his green when he took it out of his pocket."

"You know anyone who knows where to find this guy, Payaso?"

He shook his head and tried to stand upright. "Naw, I tolt ya true, he ain't from around this hood."

Damn. How was I gonna find him?

"You got his phone number?"

"Naw, he just come knock on the door, dat's all, man. I swear."

Cortez and Borkow had picked the Pearl house for its close proximity to the courthouse. So I could make it there quickly and wouldn't be tempted to call the cops in first.

"All right," I said loud enough for Wicks to hear. "I'm sending you this one. Pick out another victim for me to interrogate."

The gang member in front of me held up his hand. "Wait. Wait." He lowered his voice. "Why don' you ax dat poo-butt—he knows him good."

I grabbed onto his jersey. "Which poo-butt?"

"The one on the tape. Not the white boy, the other one."

"You know the other one?"

"Dat's what I was trying to tell ya. He ain't one of our boys but he come here to cop his dope. He owed us on some rock we fronted him."

"You what?" I took a step back, stunned. I should have put it together before. It'd been right there in front of me all along. I just didn't want it to be true. The face suddenly matched the voice for me. I caught myself almost saying the name out loud but I needed him to say it first. "Who? What's his name?"

"Man, that poo-butt, he got two first names. It's Derek, Derek Sams."

I grabbed him by the throat and shoved him up against the sink. "He was the other one on the phone? You're sure. You're sure it was him?"

"Ease up on it, man." His words came out choked off. He nodded vigorously. I let go.

"Yeah," he said. "Dat's him. I don't mind givin' him up. We don' need him around here no more. Not wit' all the trouble that follows his ass around."

I grit my teeth so hard my jaw ached. *Derek Sams*, Olivia's boyfriend. I had thought him only a pawn in this when in reality he had not only taken her to the rock house, he'd been the one to set it up ahead of time. He took a payout for it at the expense of Olivia's safety. Now he'd been the one to sell her out again to Borkow. No one else could've gotten into our apartment or Dad's house without forced entry or leaving some other form of evidence behind.

I'd had him in hand and lost my nerve when I put him on a bus to Barstow. I needed to crush something.

I grabbed the banger by the shoulder and shoved him into the living room.

"Well?" Wicks said.

"I got what we need, let's go."

"Excellent. See all you chumps later."

We exited the front door and out into the night. Five more gang members stood on the sidewalk by the street glaring at us. Angry that we'd gotten past all their security. Angry that we'd bashed in their cherried-out Lexus. Wicks made sure they saw the shotgun. He brought it down off his shoulder. He let it casually hang at waist level, the barrel pointed at them, finger poised on the trigger. We swung around to head north to Compton Avenue. As we passed, he turned and walked backward, the one large and hungry eye of the shotgun watching them, keeping them honest. We made it to the corner and walked fast to the car.

We got in.

"Tell me," he said.

I punched the dash again and again.

"Hey, take it easy, pal, this is county property."

"It's Olivia's boyfriend. He's the other one on the tape."

"Well, I'll be damned. That makes a lot of sense now. You know where he lives?"

"Yeah, I do. Head for the projects. Jordan Downs."

"Oh, this is really getting interesting." He started up, put it in gear, and smoked the back tires making a U-turn.

CHAPTER SIXTY-FOUR

THE BIG DODGE wove in and out of the light traffic, Wicks running red lights as soon as the intersection cleared. He knew the way and knew the fastest streets to get there. "So you know where this little shitass lives?"

"Yeah, I do. He lives with his auntie now. He used to live with his foster parents for years until he ran away a few months back. Or so the story goes. But if he's anywhere, he'll be at his auntie's right on the edge of the Downs on 101st."

Now I questioned all the things he'd told me while we sat in the bus station.

"So Sams has got a direct link to Borkow. That's really something, huh?"

I turned to look at him in the kaleidoscope illumination from the passing streetlights. "Sams set Olivia up to be menaced so I'd leave the court. Now he's gone and fed her to Borkow so I'd back off Borkow's trail."

"Whoa, buddy boy, I know you're a little pissed right now, and I've never said this before, but maybe you better let me handle this. You're gonna pinch his head off before we get the info we need on Borkow."

"I'm good."

"I don't think you are. When we come up on him, you let me handle it, you understand? I'm not kiddin' here, Bruno."

"Not a chance in hell."

"You're not going to do Olivia any good if you get your ass thrown in the can. Think about it."

He was right, but I'd let Sams off the hook once too often already. It wouldn't happen again. I was going to—

My head whipped around as we drove up Alameda and crossed Imperial Highway. "That's him! That's him at the light. Pull a U. Pull a U! He's at the red light, third car back in that piece of shit Volkswagen Rabbit."

Wicks pulled a U-turn and stopped behind the line of cars about six back from the Rabbit.

I grabbed the Ithaca shotgun and jumped out.

"Bruno, wait. Wait, Bruno, don't do this."

I hurried alongside the cars. Each driver turned scared as I passed. Who wouldn't be with a big angry black truck driver toting a gauge?

One car back, Sams saw me in his side mirror. His expression paled and his eyes went wide. He laid on the horn to get the car ahead of him to move. But nothing happened. Everyone froze, front and back, keeping his car pinned.

I shouldered the shotgun and yelled. "Get out of the car, now."

He hit the gas and rammed the car in front of him—bumped it, really. The Rabbit's engine was too small to do any real damage or to move it at all. There hadn't been room to get up enough speed.

He'd fed Olivia to that freak Borkow.

I aimed the shotgun at his left front tire and fired. The shotgun roared and kicked.

The tire disintegrated. The front end of the car dropped on that side.

People in the other cars screamed and ducked and hit their horns. Some pulled out of line and scattered.

The back tire of the Rabbit spun, smoking white. The two cars in front of him took off in a panic against the red signal. I racked the shotgun and blew out the back tire. The Rabbit gave a little shudder. The rim hit asphalt and spun, grinding a rooster tail of sparks.

I racked it again. "Last chance," I yelled. "Get out of the car."

With an open path, he took off at low speed on his two rims. I did a quick sidestep around to the other side and blew out the other back tire. He slewed sideways a little out of control, still trying to flee and moving away at seven or ten miles an hour.

A shadow and a breeze blew past. Wicks, in his big Dodge, came in from a wide arc and slammed into the side of the Rabbit. The small car slid sideways on three rims and one tire. It came to a stop, smoking and hissing.

I let the shotgun drop to the pavement. The driver's glass had shattered with the broadside from the Dodge. I reached in and yanked Derek Sams out through the window. He screeched like a little girl, then yelled, "Help! Someone please help me. Please help. Call the police."

"Where is she? Tell me where she is." I had him shoved over the hood of the crumpled Rabbit, pinned there.

An LAPD cruiser pulled up. Two uniforms jumped out, guns drawn. Wicks, out of the car now, held up his badge. "I'm a lieutenant with Los Angeles County Sheriff's Department. Stand down. Stand down. He's a wanted fugitive in an ongoing kidnap/ murder investigation."

I saw and heard it, but was focused only on Sams. I shook him again and lowered my voice. "You're gonna tell me or so help me this time *I will* feed you to the fish."

"Okay. Okay."

His quick capitulation stunned me. A small part of me didn't believe a seventeen-year-old kid could possess such evil. I didn't want it to be true. "Where is she? Tell me where she is."

One of the LAPD officers said, "That's not right, he's only a kid."

Wicks said, "You have no idea what's going on here. I'm taking full responsibility. Get back in your car and get the hell out of here."

"I'm calling my supervisor."

Wicks came closer and leaned in. "We don't have much time, my friend. We have to move."

I pulled a fist back slow to let Sams see what was coming.

"Hold it," he said. "I'll tell you. I'll tell you all of it. Jus' don't hit me."

"Then talk. Now."

"He's in one of dem houses on wheels. He's always movin' around. I don't know exactly where."

"Bruno," Wicks said, "grapple his ass up, put him in the car, and let's get outta here."

I pulled Sams off the Rabbit and onto his feet. I half dragged him to the Dodge. I opened the back door and shoved him in. I started to climb in on top of him. Wicks stopped me, his hand tugging on my shoulder. He handed me the shotgun. "You're driving, no argument, that's an order."

I froze, looked at him, still seeing red, my fists clenched. He shoved me hard. "Snap out of it."

That was all I needed. He was right. I took a step back. He got in. Up at the shoulder, the knife wound bled and wet my shirt. The pain still had not made an appearance—that's how powerful a drug adrenaline could be. I got in the driver's seat and hit the gas before my door had closed.

CHAPTER SIXTY-FIVE

IN THE CAR, Wicks sat next to Sams, his forearm across the kid's shoulder pressing him into the car door. I headed south on Alameda and took the first left to get us out of view of LAPD. Then took another quick right and another left. I kept stealing glimpses in the rearview.

"Talk to me," I said to Sams. "Tell me the rest of it."

"What do you want to know?"

Wicks leaned in harder. "You're going to tell us everything we want to know, right now."

"Okay. Okay. I tolt ya, it's one of those houses on wheels."

"You mean an RV?" Wicks asked.

"Yeah, one of them."

"Describe it."

I let Wicks take the lead on the interrogation. I tried to control my breathing and at the same time drive without piling up the car.

"It's ugly, man. I mean, like, it's fallin' apart. You'd never think to stop that thing. I mean never. It's a perfect hideout. I wish I woulda thought of it."

Only something a true street thug would say.

I wanted to ask him all the questions about how he'd betrayed Olivia for the second time. How he'd lured her out of Dad's house and into the RV. How he did Borkow's bidding, to send me a message by leaving the socket on the kitchen counter of our apartment. But if he told me those things, I knew I wouldn't be able to contain my rage. I would pull to the curb, yank the back door open, drag him out, and snap his arms off his body like twigs and beat him with them. Kid or no kid.

Wicks asked, "What does it look like? Describe it."

"It's got one of those van front ends and that big thing kinda built up on the back. Part of it goes over the top of the van's front. You know what I'm talkin' about?"

"What color is it?" Wicks asked.

"White and brown. It's more white with these shit-brown stripes."

"You get the plate?"

Wicks was barking at the moon with that one. Gang bangin' poo-butts didn't think to get plate numbers. Especially this one, who cared only about himself.

"Naw. But it's got this thing hooked on the very back."

"What kind of thing?" I asked.

"I think it's a tire or some shit. I couldn't really tell, but the cover is all shredded, you know, and it's real easy to spot."

"No, I don't know." Wicks elbowed him.

He yelped. "Come on, man, I'm tellin' it straight. You don't need to do that."

I watched in the rearview mirror. "Hey, take it easy, he's only a kid." I really didn't know where that had come from.

My pager went off. I checked it. Mike Moore from OSS. "I need to get to a phone, fast."

"Don't just talk about it," Wicks said. "Go."

He pulled away from Sams, took out his handcuffs, and cuffed one of the kid's hands to the headrest post behind my seat.

"How many are with Borkow?" Wicks asked.

"Jus' that crazy Mexican. He carries a hammer. A big one. You don't even know he has it until he pulls it out from under his shirt. He almost broke my head with it. He's mean as a snake."

I looked in the rearview and caught Wicks' eyes. Cortez had used a blunt object like a big hammer on Bleeker and Lizzette.

"Where does he park the RV?" Wicks asked.

"I tolt ya, I don't know that. He just pages me. I call him back, and he tells me where to meet him. That's all I know."

"The pager—we could page him," Wicks said.

"Nah, he uses pay phones, and he's given up on me. I've tried callin', and he won't call me back. He cut me loose."

I pulled up onto the sidewalk and drove on it along the front of a small strip center. A woman stood on the sidewalk talking at a phone booth, the kind with a single post and a blue half-dome shell. The headlights made her brighter as we closed in on her. I slowed down to a crawl but didn't stop. The woman started talking faster and faster as the car drew near. She finally got mad, flipped us the bird, dropped the phone, and hurried away. I moved the car so the booth came right up to my window. I rolled the window down, leaned out, and dialed Mike Moore at the OSS desk.

"It's me, Bruno."

"Sorry, man, it's a dead end. I got nothing."

The anxiety over finding Olivia quickly returned in force. "Come on, there's got to be something, anything. I'll even take the long shots."

"Okay, well, county tax records show that two years ago Cortez purchased a piece of property that had been abandoned for taxes. He got it for a song."

"And?"

"And what?"

"And nothing. It's right next to the Grand Orchid massage parlor. It's called Muscle Max. No way would he be hiding out in the hottest place in LA. Sorry, Bruno, I tried."

"Keep looking. Keep digging."

"I don't think—"

"Please?"

"You got it. I'll page you if I turn anything up."

"Mike?"

"Yeah?"

"He's driving around in a beat-up RV, white with brown stripes. It has a spare tire on the back and the cover is shredded. Put it out to everyone, you understand? I mean everyone."

"You got it, brother. I'm on it."

I hung up.

Wicks said, "That didn't sound too promising."

I shook my head.

"What did he say?"

"Cortez—this Payaso—bought a piece of property two years ago."

"Well, hell, let's go."

"It's in the same strip center as the Grand Orchid."

"Ah, shit. We checked the Orchid. He ain't there. I had a car parked down the street. Two guys from the team were watchin' in case Borkow thought the place cooled off enough to go back after we hit it. It was a long shot, but I had nothing else. I pulled them about four hours ago. Borkow's not going back there. He knows it's too hot. I'm sorry, Bruno. What's our next move?"

"I'm out of moves." The words came out in a half-whisper. They tasted too much like a death sentence.

Sams smartened up and had gone quiet to let the adults talk.

"Let's get this kid back to headquarters," Wicks said, "and really debrief him. He might know something he doesn't know he knows. We'll also put an emphasis on that BOLO for the RV. We'll have every cop in the tri-state area looking for it. It'll pop."

Not likely in four—no, now an hour and a half. We were out of time.

Wicks said, "We'll try and page this turd anyway. Something will work. We'll have Olivia back in a couple of hours. You wait and see if we don't. Come on, let's go."

I didn't share his enthusiasm and knew that if I asked him honestly what he really thought, he'd give long odds against it.

I put the car in gear, turned the wheel, and drove over the curb. We bounced into the street and headed into the empty night.

CHAPTER SIXTY-SIX

BORKOW SAT IN the chaise lounge with the young girl's feet in his lap about to rub them with aloe-infused lotion as he watched Harold working the weights, his bicep muscles slick and bulging.

Borkow found it difficult to suffer a fool. Harold fit that category and then some. But he stood six-foot-three and weighed in at two hundred and fifty pounds of muscle, the kind of muscle that thumped like hard rubber when you hit it with a ball bat. He'd been one of the muscle heads who practically lived at Muscle Max in its heyday, and when the joint closed, he was cast adrift in an unfamiliar world that lacked routine and discipline. Borkow had found him living inside the closed-down Muscle Max and let him stay on as a property manager of sorts. Though he'd not known Borkow long, Harold had an absolute loyalty toward Borkow, one that had recently been tested in blood. And that was good enough.

Borkow had told Harold that if he, without hesitation, did what he was told, Borkow would sign the gym over to him when Borkow was finished with it. With that news, Harold's eyes came alive, and Borkow knew he had Harold's undivided loyalty no matter what Borkow asked of him.

Borkow sat on the edge of the chaise lounge and wondered what would happen if he sicced Harold on Payaso. He tried to envision that battle. It would be a David vs. Goliath–type contest. Only this David would be armed with a six-pound sledge instead of a slingshot.

A slingshot—who believed that drivel? Give Borkow a shield and spear, he'd go up against a kid with a slingshot any day of the week. Who wouldn't? So if that legend didn't hold water, then Harold, when the time came, would have better than sixty-forty odds taking down Payaso. No, seventy-thirty, once you factored in all of that hard rubber muscle.

"Come on, stick your other foot over here."

The bailiff's daughter with the perfect feet lay on the chaise, her hands and her mouth still duct taped. She'd curled up, trying to stay away from him.

Borkow had wanted to spend more time rubbing more lotion into her feet, but the sickening reek of chlorine in the large room with the pool drove him into the weight room. Brown butcher paper covered all the windows that used to look out onto the front parking lot on one side and the delivery area in the back on the other.

He'd had Harold carry in the chaise and then the girl. In the back of his mind, he knew it wasn't the chlorine that had driven him out. It was the bloody splotch on the concrete deck by the pool's edge, a splotch that wouldn't come out and constantly drew his eyes back to it. The brownish red stain was the unfortunate residual from Lizzette's head splat. That's what really drove him out. It shouldn't have, but it did. He had to accept that he had a little thing for Lizzette and rued the day she disobeyed him for the last time. She forced him to punish her after repeated warnings. Well, not him, but Payaso with his hammer of Thor.

Over in the corner, Harold moved to a different weight station. He loaded the bar with four hundred pounds that bent at the ends as he did squats, making his quad muscles swell and reveal thick veins just under the skin. Borkow realized he had traded chlorine for body odor and pulsating muscle.

He squirted more Vaseline Intensive Care lotion in his hand and applied it to the girl's foot. She deserved a more gentle and expensive lotion, but such was the life on the lam. Amazing how a little emulsifying can transform a beautiful foot into a flat-out gorgeous one. Yes, he'd be keeping her around a while longer.

The girl watched his every move as if waiting for him to make the smallest mistake. Foolish little girl. What could she do if he did? It was that defiant gene again, the one she'd inherited from Daddy. He'd have to fix that or she'd end up going the way of Lizzette.

A loud crash shook the building. Borkow swung the girl's legs off his lap and jumped up. The window section facing the back side of Muscle Max came down with a clatter as a large boulder rolled in. The tiny cubes of safety glass entangled in the brown butcher paper folded over and rattled down to the floor.

Stanky Frank stepped through the opening. He held a tire iron in one hand and carried a hateful gleam in his expression.

Borkow pointed. "Harold!"

Harold stepped out from under the bar. As he did, he shoved it back. The weights fell to the ground and caused the building's concrete slab to quake, at least a 3.0 on the Richter Scale.

Frank roared and came at Borkow. Harold ran to cut him off. He picked up a forty-five-pound weight on his way, picked it up as if it were no heavier than a large dinner plate. Frank saw he wasn't going to make it to his goal. He turned to face Harold, who held up the weight chest high like a shield.

Frank feinted with the tire iron. Harold raised the weight to block. Frank clubbed him in the gut. Harold acted like the attack came from a child with a twig. He shoved the weight toward Frank and let go. It hit him in the chest, knocking him back against the unbroken window. The weight fell and crushed Frank's foot. He went down moaning, one hand holding his injured belly.

Harold looked to Borkow for direction, and Borkow put his finger to his neck and drew it across. Without a word spoken, Harold picked up the tire iron and finished off Frank with one sickening whack to the head.

A noise drew Borkow's attention. In all the hullabaloo, the girl had gotten up and silently made her way to the broken-out window. Her bare feet crunched the broken glass as she tried to pick her way through. She was ruining those lovely feet. They were going to be all cut to hell.

Once she realized Borkow was watching her, she took off running, her hands and mouth still duct taped. She was going to disappear out the broken window and into the night.

"Harold?"

Harold took off running full tilt.

Payaso appeared at Borkow's side and said, "For a muscle head, that dude can really run."

"Where were you?"

"Eating some chicken mole; it's my lunch break."

"What exactly are you good for, huh? Tell me."

"It's time to get back in the RV and start moving around. We've been here too long. You said just for an hour. It's been four."

"I say when it's time. Me. I do. Not you."

"Suit yourself, it's your life. You know that bailiff is closing in and every minute we stay in one—"

"All right, get everything we need gathered up, let's get moving. But we're not just going to drive around in circles anymore. We have a destination."

Harold stepped back through the window carrying the girl under one thick arm. She struggled and kicked against all that immovable muscle. The bottom of her feet flung tiny droplets of blood everywhere.

Payaso paused, using a wooden toothpick on his teeth working on a piece of chicken mole caught in an incisor. "Where we going?"

"Costa Rica, via Mexico. Let's get moving."

"Now you're talkin', *mi jefe*. So you're not going to wait on finding Twyla?"

Borkow glared at Payaso. Who was he to goad? Chasing Lizzette and Twyla may have been a fool's errand—with every cop in the state already looking for them—but Payaso just didn't understand loyalty vs. deceit. Borkow had wanted those two women to answer for both violations. It was the principle of the matter after he had treated them so well for so many years. He'd half-succeeded—he'd taken care of Lizzette. When it cooled down, he'd come back for Twyla. He promised himself that.

Soon as they crossed into Mexico, he'd sic his Goliath on Payaso and enjoy the show.

CHAPTER SIXTY-SEVEN

I MADE THE turn south on Wilmington from Imperial Highway with Sams in the back seat handcuffed to the headrest and Wicks sitting right next to him.

"Hey," Wicks said. "What gives? We're supposed to be going to HQ."

"I'm going to get my truck so I can drive around and look for that RV. That's the best bet right now, to catch it on the move." I checked the rearview. Wicks nodded. His expression looked like someone who watched a family member at a funeral, a family member who couldn't accept the painful reality fate had plopped down in his lap.

I pulled up and stopped in front of Dad's house. "Page me if you get anything at all and I mean anything."

Wicks got out, came around the front of the car, and offered his hand. "You got it, buddy boy. Good luck. Keep the faith. Trust me, that RV will pop. You'll get her back safe and sound." I shook his hand and he got in the driver's seat.

I watched them drive off. When I turned to get in my truck, Dad stood close. He'd moved up on me silent as a mouse like only he knew how to do.

"You didn't find her?"

"No. I'm sorry I didn't call you."

"Was that Derek in the car with your boss?"

"Yes, it was."

"What are you doing with him?"

"Not now, Dad, please?" He didn't need to know the part Derek had played. I started around the side of my truck. He followed along and stood at the passenger side, waiting.

I said over the top of the truck cab, "What are you doing?"

"I'm going with you. I won't sit around anymore. I'm all done with waiting. Not with that look on your face."

I nodded, got in, and unlocked his door. I started up and drove, not knowing where to go, where to look. Borkow and his RV could be anywhere. Derek had been right when he said it was the perfect hideout. At that very moment, it could be headed for the Mexican border. Borkow could disappear down south taking Olivia with him, never to return. The thought raised my blood pressure, and I fought the urge to head south.

Dad finally spoke. "Why did you have Derek in your car? It looked like he was handcuffed. What did he do?"

I looked over at him and knew that expression. He wouldn't stop asking until he got the truth.

I nodded. "You sure you want to hear this?"

He said nothing and stared.

"Okay." I pulled over and stopped to give him the bad news. "Derek owed those boys on Pearl money for some dope they fronted him and that he somehow pissed away. They were going to beat him bad for it. We talked about part of this before."

"You're sure about that? Olivia says different."

"Dad, there's a tape with Derek talking with Borkow setting it up. Borkow needed me out of that court so he could escape. Derek made it happen."

Dad's expression fell. "Oh, dear Lord."

"That's not the worst of it."

He looked out the side window. "Tell me."

"Derek is the one who turned Olivia over to Borkow. He also left two items so I'd know it was Borkow who took Olivia. Borkow was sending me a message."

Dad's voice came out in barely a whisper. "It was that wrench you found in her purse and the socket from your apartment?"

"Yes, that's right."

His eyes filled with tears. He shook his head in disbelief. I leaned over and took him into a hug. He positioned his head so he could speak closer to my ear. "Olivia, she came over to stay with me because she's scared. More scared than I have ever seen her."

I tried to pull away. He wouldn't let me and held on tight.

I said, "Yeah, she's scared of Derek as she should be. He's a—"

He shook his head and clamped down even tighter. "No. Son, she's afraid of you."

"What? No. I've given her no reason at all to be afraid of me."

He said nothing.

"Of me? No way, Dad. Why?" I tried to pull away to look into his eyes to see the truth. He was too strong and wouldn't let me. "Why, Dad? Tell me, please."

"She confided in me and made me promise not to tell you, not under any circumstances. But after what's happened, I think you have a right to know."

I went slack.

He spoke in a soft whisper. "Bruno, Olivia's pregnant."

The world stopped turning.

CHAPTER SIXTY-EIGHT

MY DEAR LITTLE Olivia was pregnant with Derek Sams' child.

Every muscle in my body went numb. I couldn't move. Breath wouldn't come without conscious effort.

I'd never been numbed by emotion before. Heard it talked about, read descriptions of it, and thought it nothing more than hyperbole.

Somebody please restart the world. More important, somebody tell me it wasn't so. Please, tell me it wasn't so.

Dad let me go. I sat back, my mouth sagging open. His eyes were filled with such pain for me, for Olivia.

Dad reached out, took my hand, and squeezed. "Listen, it's not your fault. She's a little misguided in love. That's all. She didn't know any better. What she felt for Derek, she believed to be the real thing. She made a mistake. One mistake."

Words wouldn't come. I nodded.

He spoke as if I'd be angry with Olivia. I wasn't, not at all. More than anything else, I took responsibility for what happened. I hadn't been there for her.

"I'm not mad, Dad, I'm not."

I needed to move. To kick-start the world moving again. I fired up the truck, clutched, shifted the gears, and headed off. I didn't know what else to do. My hands and feet and subconscious mind did the work while the rest of me lay off in the weeds trying to put right what had gone so severely off the tracks. But I knew where I was headed—to the only lead, no matter how far-fetched. It still needed to be checked out.

The truck moved in and out of streets.

"Son, maybe it would be better if we go home. We can sit on the couch and talk about this. Huh? Why don't we do that? Come on, let's go home."

"I've got to find Olivia."

I kept driving, my eyes not really seeing where we were going.

"Maybe you should call your boss and tell him not to charge Derek. You can do that, can't you, Son?"

The world suddenly kicked back into gear. My head whipped around to look at him. "Are you for real? He needs to be prosecuted to the fullest extent of the law. He needs to be put away for the rest of his pathetic little life. And you can damn sure know that's exactly what I'm going to recommend. Getting him off for ... for ..." I couldn't get those words out. *For getting my little Olivia pregnant.*

I slowed and pulled to the curb just down from the Grand Orchid massage parlor and Muscle Max.

My rage continued to do a slow burn that would need a vent soon or I'd burst into flame. I opened the truck door. I was angry with Dad, even though that didn't make any sense. I leaned in. "I need to check something. You wait right here. You understand? Don't you move from this truck. I'm not kidding, Dad. Don't step one foot out of this truck."

He nodded. His expression hurt. He was going through the same thing I was, only worse. He'd been keeping a secret that had to be gnawing on his soul, eating him from the inside out. I eased the door closed, took a step, and froze. I realized now why I had driven there.

Instinct. Experience.

I remembered the last time I'd been there, when we hit the Grand Orchid and found it empty. The feeling I had when standing in the parking lot after we'd searched the Orchid. The feeling that someone was watching, a feeling I couldn't shake. I pulled the Smith and Wesson 9mm and wished I had my two .357s back. But those two guns went with the crime scenes on Slauson and 10th and the one at Mel's. I'd get them back after the investigation was complete, after the DA had ruled the shooting justified. That would take a year or more. I'd have to buy two replacement guns in the meantime.

I adjusted the Bulldog .44 in my waistband and walked down the street in the gutter, headed toward the Muscle Max.

CHAPTER SIXTY-NINE

THE MOON HAD moved from high overhead to low in the night sky. It would be dawn in a few hours. I wasn't thinking clearly and had no right to be out chasing leads. My decision-making would be hindered, and in a violent confrontation, that could be catastrophic. But like Wicks said, the odds were that the Muscle Max would lead to a dead end. I trusted his opinion. I just needed to be doing something, anything. Why not rule it out as a lead and move on?

I played the game as if it were real and walked past the strip center not looking directly down the center between the two buildings with the parking area in between. I acted as if uninterested. Instead, I took several peeks at the parking lot checking for the RV as I continued to walk past.

It wasn't there.

I'd kept the 9mm down by my leg and put it back in my waistband under my shirt next to the Bulldog. I moved around to the back of the corner gas station and into the alley. I peeked over the fence to see into the rear of the strip center.

In the moonlight the hulk of an RV cast a giant shadow. At first, I couldn't believe what I saw. It couldn't be that easy. Relief washed over me.

Could it be just that easy?

Could it be a different RV? There were thousands of them in Southern California. Wouldn't that be too big of a coincidence for another one to be parked back here? I walked along the fence line to get a closer look. When I came to a spot I thought was parallel, I did another quick peek.

I froze when I saw the tire mounted on the back with the tattered cover. My heart jumped into my throat.

This was it. They were there in the Muscle Max. Olivia was there. For a fleeting moment, the right thing to do flitted across my thoughts. I should go back to the gas station and call it in. Get backup. Surround the place with forty or fifty cops all with long guns and then call them out of the building.

That thought lasted a microsecond. If I did that, it would turn the whole mess into a hostage situation, the hostage being Olivia. I nixed it and moved on to what any father would do under similar circumstances—bull my way in and rescue my daughter. I had the training. I had the experience.

I raised my Smith and Wesson and went over the fence as quietly as I could just as someone came out of the building. I crouched in the shadows next to the fence and held my breath.

A big dude—a huge dude about thirty years of age, wearing shorts and a tank top—carried an armload of shoeboxes out to the RV and climbed into the back. The RV canted one way then the other as the guy stepped inside. The suspension of the vehicle was shot. Derek had been right about one thing—no one would've looked twice at this rolling hideout. No wonder Borkow had successfully evaded the hundreds of cops looking for him.

After a few seconds, the muscle head came out of the RV, not bothering to look around, too intent on the task at hand. He disappeared into the building.

I moved up to the door he'd disappeared into and peeked inside. The lights were on and the place smelled of swimming pool chlorine. Quiet. No noise escaped outside. Farther down, along the outside of the building, it looked as if a large section of window had been knocked out.

I stopped suddenly and stood up straight. A random thought hit. My God, was that why Olivia kept saying she was sorry when Borkow put her on the phone? Was she apologizing for what she thought was her mistake of getting pregnant? My poor little girl; how blind I had been. I'd make it up to her. I had to make it up to her.

The sadness and grief of that thought quickly flashed to anger, an anger so pure and hot I wanted to tear down the entire building barehanded. I stuck my gun out and followed it inside through the open door, ready to gun Borkow as soon as he came into view.

Down at the end of the hall, the muscle head turned left and disappeared through an interior doorway. I hurried to the door, hesitated, and then peeked inside. It was a weight room with free weights and machines, lots of them everywhere. Off to the right against the wall sat a dead man, his head caved in. I recognized him. Frank Robbins, aka Stanky Frank. One of the escapees from the jailbreak.

Then I saw Olivia sitting on a chaise lounge, her mouth and hands taped with duct tape. Dried blood, some of it still wet, covered the bottoms of her naked feet.

My heart skipped. She was all right. She was safe. I wasn't too late.

Borkow stood close to her, his back turned, watching the huge man gather up another armload of shoeboxes from a tall stack along an interior wall.

I stepped in and moved toward Borkow, my sights lined up on his head. I needed to get close enough for a clean shot. I wasn't familiar with the gun, the accuracy of the sights.

I'd made it halfway. I still needed to be closer for an accurate pistol shot when a Hispanic male appeared through a doorway at the other end of the room. He didn't startle, he simply said, "Boss?"

Borkow looked at him and followed where he was pointing. Borkow turned and looked at me. I froze. He didn't look scared at all with a gun aimed at his forehead. Instead he smiled.

The man was a psycho.

A knife appeared in his hand from out of nowhere.

He moved quickly.

I fired, the sound loud and intrusive, a sound that banged around off the interior walls. White smoke billowed out.

I missed him. I couldn't try again; he'd moved too close to Olivia. If I'd had my other guns, the .357s, I wouldn't have missed.

He put the knife to Olivia's throat. "Nice try, Bailiff. You fire again and I guess I'll just have to fall on my sword, if you know what I mean? Don't take another step."

The muscled man dropped the shoeboxes and stood up.

Borkow said, "Careful with those, you idiot."

The Hispanic, who had to be Cortez, the one called Payaso, didn't move any farther into the room. He didn't pull a gun either. He just watched. He'd been the one to kill Lizzette and Bleeker with a hammer. Frank Robbins had died in the same manner, head trauma—brutal, and unconscionable murders.

Borkow chuckled. "Looks like it's a Mexican standoff."

Olivia's eyes pleaded with me.

"It's okay, baby, I'll get you out of this. Everything is going to be okay, I promise you."

"Oh, how sentimental. Don't make promises you can't keep, Bailiff. There are three of us and only one of you."

I looked up at Borkow. "You're right. I'll wait here if you want to go get two more of your cronies—that should make it a fair fight."

Borkow laughed. "You hearing this, Payaso, the balls on this guy? Get your ass in here."

"I'm good right here, boss. I wanna see how this plays out."

Borkow stopped laughing. He lowered his voice. "Chickenshit." Then at me, "Drop the gun, Bailiff, or I draw blood." He stuck the knifepoint to Olivia's scalp.

"Okay, just hold it, don't do anything you're going to regret."

CHAPTER SEVENTY

"I SAID DROP the gun, Bailiff. I won't ask again."

"Okay, take it easy." I slowly went into a squat and set the gun on the floor. "See, we're all cool here, just take it easy." I stood.

Borkow lost his grin. "Payaso, we need to get out of here fast. There will be others coming right behind him."

"I don't think so," Payaso said. "I told you this guy likes to hunt alone. If his backup isn't in here by now, they're not coming."

"Oh, really?" Borkow said, his grin returning. "You've caused me a great deal of heartache, Bailiff. I've had to spend hours of my life rumbling around in that rattle-trap, hours I'll never get back, mostly because of you. I think you need to pay for that. Harold?"

Harold came at me, walking fast. His quads were so big he was forced to waddle. Most muscle heads worked on their upper body more for show and they neglected their legs. Not this guy. He'd built his body from the floor up. An opponent with legs was the most dangerous kind. In a fight they stabilized his fighting plat-form, and up close, they turned into lethal weapons used to stomp, kick, and scissor. If I let him get a hold of me, I'd be through. I looked around for a weapon, anything to counter his overwhelming advantage. I needed to distract all of them long enough to get close where I could use the Bulldog .44. I had to figure a way to pull them together and away from Olivia. I had five rounds in the Bulldog.

Harold sped up. I dodged and ran around a multi-station weight machine. I grabbed up a discarded twenty-pound dumbbell and chucked it at him. It thumped off his chest with little effect. I stayed on the opposite side of the machine each time he tried to move around. In my peripheral vision, Payaso came closer and stopped ten feet from Borkow. That had to be close enough; I couldn't keep dodging Harold. He only had to get lucky once and I'd be through.

I took the risk—now or never. I ran toward Borkow and Payaso and knew Harold would cut me off. There was nothing for it. I had to get closer, draw them in.

Harold wasn't an experienced fighter. He should've used his legs to kick the bejesus out of me. Instead, he grabbed me in a bear hug, a move I'd hoped for. A second before impact, I stuck my hand under my shirt.

Harold pinned my arms to my sides and squeezed. Blood pressure immediately flushed my face and bulged my eyes. I wouldn't last but a few seconds before total collapse and game over.

Borkow giggled like a little girl. "You see, Payaso? Harold is my Goliath."

I couldn't move my arms, but I could still move my hand and wrist. Harold's face was inches from mine. His heated breath smelled of soured vanilla protein drink.

I pulled the Bulldog and stuck it in his gut. I forced out the words, "Say goodnight, Harold."

I pulled the trigger. The discharge was muffled by muscle and the closeness of our bodies.

Harold lost his idiot smile, traded it in for confusion. He should've dropped me, but he held on and renewed his squeeze. Stars appeared in my vision that turned into flickering bright lights. I pulled the trigger three more times trying to blow the monster off me.

The fourth round did it. Those .44 specials did their work and turned his organs to mush, shutting him down. His grip eased. I fell to the floor and almost lost the Bulldog. The Bulldog only held five. I'd used one too many. I still had Borkow and Payaso to take down with one round left.

My vision started to clear but not fast enough. My head lolled to the side, and I couldn't raise it up. I tried to shake off the near delirium.

Payaso pulled a short-handled sledge that had been under his shirt hooked in his belt. He came for me, expressionless. I raised the Bulldog and shot him center mass, six inches below his chin. He wilted straight to the floor.

I pointed the empty Bulldog at Borkow, who had turned and started to flee. "Don't. Stay right there or I'll shoot you in the back."

He froze and turned around, fear in his eyes.

I tried to roll to my feet and couldn't. Harold had broken something inside me, ribs, or herniated some disks, something. My legs wouldn't readily respond. I floundered like a fish.

Borkow said, "Wait. Why didn't you just shoot me like those two idiots? I think you're empty, Mr. Bailiff. Is that correct? Are you out of bullets, in your chickenshit little gun?" He turned with the knife in hand. "You've ruined things. Now I'll to have to drive that rattle-trap myself all the way down to Costa Rica. You're going to pay dearly for that." He pointed the knife at Olivia. "But her first." He walked toward her. "I have to get out of here. Someone had to have heard all those shots. Too bad, I would have liked to take my time with—"

Gunshots to the right came from the broken-out window. Loud explosions that made Borkow's body contort and jump. The heavy rounds slapped into his body and backed him up until he tripped over his feet and fell.

Twyla stepped through the broken window with one of my .357s smoking in her hands.

Silence ruled the day.

Twyla let the gun sag and hang from her hand. "I'm glad I killed him. I'm not sorry at all. I'm glad I did it. He killed Lizzette."

She must've picked up the gun I'd dropped in the street when I'd confronted those thugs on 10th, just before she fled.

Twyla looked over at me for moral support. "I didn't think I could. But I did. I'm not sorry for doing it, Detective Johnson. I'm not."

"Twyla, it's okay, it'll be okay. You did the right thing. Can you please cut my daughter loose?"

She looked over at Olivia. "Sure." She went to Olivia, still rambling. "Borkow, that asshole, he didn't have to kill my friend Lizzette. He killed Lizzette, Detective. He left her in my garage for me to see. He didn't have to do that. I told Frank where to find Borkow thinking he'd be strong enough to take care of him. When he didn't, I . . . I . . ." She was in shock from having killed someone and rambled on.

She got the tape off Olivia's mouth.

"Popi?"

"It's okay, baby. It's okay."

Twyla cut the tape off her hands and the one long piece strapped around her waist holding her to the chaise. Olivia hurried over to me. "Oh, Popi, I'm so sorry."

"I know; me, too," I said. "I've been a complete fool. It's me who should be sorry." I put my hands on her arms and face and head, not believing she could actually be unharmed. "Are you okay?" Tears burned my eyes. What did pregnancy matter? She was still alive.

"I'm fine, Popi, you saved me." Tears ran down her cheeks.

Twyla stood there with the gun in her hand.

"Help me up." Both women got me to my feet. The temporary paralysis had started to fade. Olivia stayed close with her arm around my waist. She wasn't scared of me anymore.

I took the gun from Twyla's hand.

"I am going to prison, aren't I?"

"No, not at all. This is my gun. I'm the one who shot him. You understand? I'm the one, not you. Now you better get out of here before the police arrive."

"Really? You're not kidding?"

"Really. Get going."

"Thank you, Detective Johnson." She started to run for the open hole she'd come through and detoured over to the wall of shoeboxes. She pulled the tops off, going through them quickly, picking out six boxes, almost too many to carry. She loaded them up in her arms and fled.

She exited out the hole. Seconds later, in came Dad. He shook his head in wonder at all the carnage and death. "Oh, my dear Lord."

He saw Olivia in my arms. A huge smile filled his face. He hurried over and joined in the hug.

AUTHOR'S NOTE

In August of 1995, San Bernardino County Sheriff's Department had the largest jailbreak in its history. The record still stands today. The conspiracy, the organization, and its execution was stunning. Suspects on trial for separate murders used accomplices armed with cordless drills to take out a window in the visiting area of the jail.

I had left the Violent Crimes Team and was working a major narcotics crew at the airport investigating smuggling cases. Two weeks into the massive manhunt, all six of the suspects were still at large. I was called back into service on the Violent Crimes Team to run them to ground. I convinced my captain at the time to offer a reward. When he hesitated, I asked him the cost of all the overtime for the fifty or sixty deputies involved in the manhunt. He agreed and it worked. It took another ten days to track down the first murder suspect. My partner and I caught up with him in a county section of Los Angeles. The suspect was death row eligible and had nothing to lose. He had been the one to behead a woman in front of her five-year-old daughter. A violent confrontation ensued in the parking lot of a popular family restaurant. There were four of us—two uniforms from another agency we'd called in to assist—trying our best to take him into custody. He wasn't a large man, but he had fear and desperation on his side. You would think four highly trained officers could subdue one suspect without too much of a problem.

He broke through every pain compliance hold, he resisted blunt-force trauma, and pepper spray had no effect. The fight turned so brutal, people driving by on the street started honking their horns. They didn't understand the situation and, of course, mistook the absolute need to take the suspect in hand to protect the public. With four officers on him, he wasn't losing and we were not gaining the upper hand. He continued to sock and kick and bite. We were taking a beating as well. At one point, my partner, near exhaustion, stepped back and drew his gun. He yelled to stand clear. He was going to shoot him. That was how desperate our plight had become. We couldn't take a chance that the suspect might get away.

We ultimately tackled him one last time and took him to the ground, where he ran out of steam. It was amazing, for the amount of force used, that he came away without any major injuries, no large bones broken. But the next day, he was hardly recognizable from the soft tissue injuries. One of the officers from the assisting agency was a probationer and he lost his job over the incident, a sacrificial lamb tossed out to placate a ruthless media. It was grossly unfair, the loss of a career over something that had to be done. The murderer had given us no option.

When I went to the department to secure the reward for the informant who'd led us to the suspect, like in any bureaucracy, the deputy chief balked. I was angry—it was my promise they were going back on. The informant threatened to go to the press. The words the informant used almost sounded as if he'd been coached. The informant was later paid in full.

The other five were eventually taken into custody. One of the captures will forever be memorialized on video. One of the popular reality cop shows on TV rode with the team. The suspect was in the attic when the relatives swore he wasn't in the house. He had a gun—a very dangerous situation. The attic was filled with pepper spray. The suspect moved around and fell off the support beam and through the dry wall ceiling. He hung down in the hallway, his legs dangling. He surrendered.

AND ABOUT THE OTHER THING

During one segment of my career, I had the opportunity to work with a detective who told me about a boyfriend she once dated. This man had a sexual proclivity involving women's feet—a real fetish. He loved the shoes women wore almost more—maybe even more—than the women. A woman's shoe catalog did the same for him as a soft porn magazine. To add a little color to Louis Borkow, I gave him a bit of that same shoe fetish.